Blue Becomes You

Blue Becomes You

To Jan,
Greetings from Manitoba.

Bettina von Kampen

Bettina von Kampen

GREAT PLAINS PUBLICATIONS

Great Plains Publications
420 – 70 Arthur Street
Winnipeg, MB R3B 1G7
www.greatplains.mb.ca

Great Plains Publications gratefully acknowledges the financial support
provided for its publishing program by the Government of Canada through the
Book Publishing Industry Development Program (BPIDP); the Canada Council
for the Arts; the Manitoba Department of Culture, Heritage and Tourism; and
the Manitoba Arts Council.

Design & Typography by Gallant Design Ltd.
Printed in Canada by Kromar Printing

CANADIAN CATALOGUING IN PUBLICATION DATA

Main entry under title:

Von Kampen, Bettina, 1964-
  Blue becomes you / Bettina von Kampen.

  ISBN 1-894283-37-6

  I. Title
PS8593.O556B58 2003   C813'.6   C2003-910139-8
PR9199.4.V66B58 2003

This book is for all my friends and family and, for a million reasons, is especially dedicated to my mom.

chapter one

Charlotte woke up at two-twenty. She reached for her clock to shut off the alarm and then remembered. She wasn't going to work today. She had taken the day off so that she and her sister could drive into the city for Charlotte's test. Her heart skipped a beat when she thought about it. The hands on the alarm clock glowed pale green in the dark. It was set to go off at seven-thirty. Five more hours of sleep, if she could. Charlotte lay back down and stared hard at the ceiling as though, through sheer mental effort, her eyes would bore holes into the ceiling to reveal the stars above. Her stomach gurgled. She sighed and rolled over and stared at the opposite wall the rest of the night.

In the morning, Charlotte fiddled with her hair awhile. There was so much grey now. Too bad hair wasn't like the leaves on the trees and could regain its original luster each spring. She decided she looked younger if she pulled it back and left a few strays to give her an air of reckless abandon. She slipped on a pair of jeans and laced up her red runners and figured she could pass for at least fifty-five.

The trip from Norman to Winnipeg took eighty minutes. Charlotte and June set out after breakfast. June drove while Charlotte gazed out the window at the land rolling by. Norman was surrounded by long, uninterrupted stretches of wheat and canola. It was not unusual to have to poke along behind a combine or a tractor on the highway. City people got impatient and their hearts sped up at the very sight of them. They zoomed up fast, then crawled along, wondering if they would ever be able to pass. The locals took it in stride. It gave them a chance to wave hello to a neighbour – that hand-on-the-wheel wave country people give each other. The one that says, you have been sighted. A wave that meant you'd probably come up in conversation later on. Yeah, I saw Hank Curmudgeon out on his combine this morning. Holding up a line of traffic, as usual.

Some people liked that familiarity and some hated it. Those who hated it tended to move to the city, where anonymity gave them security and more control over whose lives intersected with theirs. In Norman, your life intersected with everybody else, one way or another. It was a matter of probability. Simple math. Six thousand might sound like a lot of people, but when there are three banks, one movie theatre, eight restaurants, half a dozen churches and a sprinkling of other services and sundries, you will find yourself again and again in line with the same people.

About twenty minutes away from the city, the traffic began to thicken. June adjusted her grip on the steering wheel and leaned forward. She peered over the dashboard through the windshield as other drivers sped past her. People in the city always drove so fast. She approached an amber light and pressed on the brake. The car lurched to a stop.

"Can't you go through on yellow?" Charlotte said from the passenger side, steadying herself on the dashboard.

June's eyes were on her rear-view mirror. "That guy nearly hit us."

"Just get me there. Good thing we still have about two hours."

"Oh, go on. If we had listened to you, we would be sprinting down the hospital corridors even before your test.

8

I'm the one who's driving. I know how long it takes. Now, don't stress your heart before your test."

Charlotte sighed. "I don't know what Dr. Wilson thinks they're going to find out from a stress test. What kind of a medical system puts a sixty-three-year old woman on a treadmill and tells her to run until she's ready to drop? You'd think it would have become more sophisticated by now."

"They have to see how your heart reacts to stress."

"Well if that's the case, they should hook me up and let me drive around with you all day. Then they'll really see something. What are you all dressed up for anyway?"

"I always dress up when I come to the city." June's dress was scattered with palm trees and coconuts. Two giant palms sprouted from her armpits. There was some essence of perfume around her too, though it smelled a little stale. And on her feet she wore her sturdy driving shoes, the ones that didn't slip on the pedals.

The parkade of the Health Sciences Centre came into view and their car crept towards it.

"I hate these machines," June said as she got out of the car to retrieve her ticket. The arm swung up and June threw the ticket onto Charlotte's lap, then plunged back into the car and gunned the engine to make it under the arm before it pinned them. The tires squealed just like the cruisers in a police drama.

"How come they make it so dark in these parkades? I can't see a thing," June complained. The car inched into the darkness and slowly June's eyes adjusted to the orange lights. Round and round they drove until they reached the top level and drove into daylight once again to park the car.

Waiting rooms in hospitals are the same as waiting rooms in banks, Charlotte thought as they settled in. A row of chairs with just enough padding not to get you agitated, facing a wall with no clock. Instead of the clock, you can look at posters. In the bank the posters are of nicely groomed bankers showing anxious clients how their money can grow, and in the hospital the posters showed you Ten Steps to a Healthy Heart. There are magazines too, except at the bank, the magazines are all about money and in the hospital they have *People* and *Glamour* with healthy people in them. People who didn't need to take Ten Steps to a Healthy Heart or learn the Warning Signs of Diabetes.

Carts of linen and autoclaved instruments rattled past while June and Charlotte sat breathing the antiseptic air and remaining calm under the cold white lights.

"I hate that smell," said Charlotte.

"What smell?" June raised her chin and sniffed the air.

"That hospital smell. You know. I don't know what it is. It's just the air in hospitals. Death and cafeteria food."

"Oh Charlotte. Shush." June flipped open her magazine.

The nurses wore soothing pastel uniforms and wrote on clipboards with pens that hung from strings around their necks. They moved all the time, in and out of the swinging doors, behind the desk, to the shelf of files, to the computer and then to the waiting patients. A red-haired nurse came over to where Charlotte and June sat.

"Ms. Weiss?"

Both June and Charlotte turned towards her.

"Charlotte Weiss?"

"Yes, that's me."

Nurse Audrey led Charlotte through the swinging doors leading to the "Unauthorized Persons Prohibited" area. She pulled the curtain across the cubicle so Charlotte could change into her shorts. A vent blew cold hospital air onto her head and her knees turned purple and splotchy.

Audrey scrubbed the skin over Charlotte's heart with an alcohol swab, quite vigorously, Charlotte thought.

"We need to make a good connection." Audrey explained.

The electrodes snapped onto her chest, the same as button snaps. Charlotte climbed on the treadmill. It started slowly. So slowly. Charlotte figured they already knew something she didn't. Every two minutes Audrey asked Charlotte, "How're you doing up there? Do you feel faint? Dizzy?" And when Charlotte shook her head Audrey increased the speed of the belt. Then, the nurse smiled and inflated the blood pressure cuff. It tightened around Charlotte's arm and made her fingers tingle. Wasn't that a warning sign of a heart attack? Tingling fingers? Should she say something to Nurse Audrey? Maybe that was part of the test. To see if Charlotte even knew what a heart attack would feel like. Her feet tripped along with the belt not particularly wanting to co-operate. The walk from the parkade had been enough. Charlotte began to feel uncomfortable and slightly winded. Maybe they wanted her to go into cardiac arrest, just for their own satisfaction. They could nod their heads knowingly, as though they knew all along Ms. Weiss would succumb once the treadmill test was administered.

Charlotte first noticed the fatigue and the heaviness in her arms last month. She had to sit down a lot more to catch her breath. Things she had always done with ease, lifting the trays, measuring her dough, rolling the pastry, had become arduous. Real labour. The heat from the oven became stifling and made it hard for her to breathe. Perspiration sprang up on her brow for no reason. Charlotte knew the work and her routine at the bakery so well, she could tell something was wrong as soon as it started to happen. Sometimes she felt palpitations in her chest and had to step out back and sit down until the fresh air diluted them. Fresh air and a glass of water worked for just about everything. At least it used to.

"How're you doing there, Ms. Weiss?" Charlotte could no longer talk. And her legs wouldn't move as they should. They felt so full and heavy. She walked to work everyday, but it was nothing like this. Not only was the treadmill churning away beneath her but, at the push of a button, Audrey could make Charlotte walk uphill. When Charlotte didn't answer, Audrey chirped, "You're doing just fine. We're going to go up one more. Ready?"

Charlotte's hands gripped the sides and she puffed her way up a steeper hill. Some people had these things in their homes, or gave them as gifts. They talked about 'the burn' and 'the high', which then turned into a craving; some even said, an addiction. Everyday they got on their treadmills to get high. They bought stretchy clothes and bouncing shoes. What kind of person develops an addiction to this feeling? She made a mental note never to go to the doctor again. So what if something was wrong with her heart? How much proof did they need?

A thick jelly filled Charlotte's legs and her face glowed with an unnatural sheen. The moisture under her arms made her cold. The electrodes pulled at her skin, impervious to the sweat beading in Charlotte's cleavage. Nurse Audrey watched, but didn't seem to register the distress on Charlotte's face.

Charlotte focused on a wall chart. A human form with arteries and veins squirting like silly string from the squeezeable heart. Its transparent body came to life. First twitching a little, then quivering all over and then it moved towards her as she walked towards it. She focused her eyes on the heart and envisioned her own, a flabby piece of blubber which had somehow come loose and was now lodged in her head, pounding as though it was on a mission to split her skull and break free. All at once the veins and arteries on the wall became balled up and twisted like a knot of yarn and Charlotte became transfixed. Everything went black except for the heart at the centre of her vision. She no longer felt her legs or her lungs. The wall-heart turned into a bright star and soon there were more and Charlotte was no longer on the treadmill but lying in a meadow, looking up at the brilliant night sky, amazed at the expanse of space before her. But, before she had a chance to ponder her insignificance, her eyes opened and gazed upon the ceiling and the lights shimmering overhead.

Charlotte lay on a narrow examination table covered with a heavy green blanket. Audrey smiled over her clipboard and reached for Charlotte's wrist. At first, Charlotte thought she wanted to hold her hand, the comfort of a caring, compassionate nurse. But, Audrey pressed her fingers hard onto Charlotte's wrist and looked at her watch.

"What happened?"

Audrey scribbled onto her clipboard. "It happens sometimes, quite a lot actually. You fainted."

"Is it supposed to happen?" Nobody else was in the room. Audrey looked at the door and back at Charlotte.

"I've called the doctor to come and examine you Ms. Weiss. You're going to be fine."

On cue, the doctor came and huddled in the corner with Audrey. They both looked at the clipboard. Charlotte couldn't hear them over the buzz of the lights.

"How are you feeling, Miss Weiss?" The doctor placed his stethoscope on Charlotte's chest. The cold made her jump and she saw Audrey jump a little too.

"Is it normal to see a tunnel of light?"

"Heh, heh." He patted her arm. "We'll send the results to Dr. Wilson and he'll go over them with you in his office."

"So I can go now? That's it? How do you know I'll make it back to the waiting room?"

"You can go, Miss Weiss."

Behind the curtain, Charlotte sat on the bench to change. After each sock and shoe she had to stop and sit up to let some air into her lungs. Her fingers fumbled with the buttons and they couldn't grip the zipper so, she untucked her shirt and let it hang over her open pants. She left her laces untied, picked up her backpack and went to meet June. Her legs could barely support her, her hands were still numb, her lips were dry and her mouth parched. If this was what it felt like to come back from the dead, she'd take death any day. So much for trying to appear youthful. Despite Charlotte's protests, June requested a wheelchair and had Charlotte wait until she brought the car around.

"So, how was it?"

"I think I had an out-of-body experience. I fainted and my lips turned blue, but Nurse Audrey didn't seem too concerned."

"You weren't in there very long."

"Dr. Wilson will get the results in a few days. Then we'll see."

"Why don't you just quit. Right now. You never know what could happen if you keep working, with your heart."

Charlotte frowned. "I told Vi I'd give her until next week. Next Friday I'm done. I'll make it until then and if I don't, then I won't have to go to my big retirement party, will I?"

"Since you sound no worse for wear I'd like to stop in at the Magic Hair Solutions and say hello. See who's working at my station."

"It hasn't been your station for ten years." Charlotte was too exhausted to argue. As long as June drove and all Charlotte had to do was sit in the car, she didn't really care if it took all week for them to get home.

"You should be happy we care enough to give you a party." June paused. "I always stop in when I'm in town. They look up to me, those girls. I used to train some of them. I did good work there. Brought a lot of clients in."

"Sure and they all got the same perm and blue rinse." The same way June wore her hair now. A blue-grey bob. She had it done every two weeks.

"I am happy. Hopefully my heart can take it."

14

"If you can work one more week, then I'm sure you'll make it through the party."

They drove along Academy Road. Snell's Drug Store, Bob's Tomboy and Gurvey's, where kids used to line up with their allowance for candy were all long gone. Now the things that could be bought on Academy Road were expensive shoes, gourmet dog biscuits and over-priced artifacts for the home. Nothing practical, but then medicine, candy and fine cuts of meat could all be bought at Supervalu, leaving lots of time to browse in front of the ceramic wall tiles fired in Italy and placemats woven in Nepal.

"It's harder than it looks, working with grey hair," June was saying. "Only a professional can tell the difference between greys. You wouldn't expect others to be able to tell."

Charlotte waited in the car while June went inside the salon. Her skin itched where they had stuck the electrodes. Her shirt was damp from perspiration and her legs burned inside. It was their fault she fainted in public. It was like a bad dream, except when she woke up, it had really happened. Happened quite a lot, Nurse Audrey had said. Did this not concern them? Dr. Wilson would have his suspicions confirmed and tell her, "See, I was right. There is something wrong with your heart."

As if she didn't know that already. The fluttering pitter-patter kicking up in her chest over the past month wasn't puppy love. The catch at the back of her throat when she tried to even out her breathing was in no way related to giddy exuberance of any kind. She was sixty-three years old. What should she expect by this point? To be able to run the fifty-yard dash with no effort? How long could she expect her heart to keep drumming along and maintain a steady beat? Things wore out.

She turned the car radio off. Music on the radio put her on edge. Thin, bubbly soda pop dripping through the car speakers, spraying sugar into the air and covering everything with a sticky film. It gave Charlotte gas.

June came back sooner than Charlotte expected. "Nobody I knew was on today," she said as she wiggled back into her seat and pulled at the seatbelt. "It's like I walked into the wrong shop."

* * * * *

Dr. Wilson was the only doctor left in Norman. The other doctors had grown tired of the limited scope of practice a small town offered and moved on to set up practice in Selkirk. He had a hobby farm just outside of town where he grew pumpkins in the fields and lillies in the greenhouse. He thought the ostrich farm next to his would be gone within a year, but, to everyone's surprise they had been there five years now and continued to peddle their ostrich steak and eggs to pricey restaurants in the city.

The stickers on the magazines in Dr. Wilson's office were addressed to Shirl, his nurse and receptionist. Shirl was a stout woman with carefully applied lipstick and yellow home permed hair. A cardboard nursing cap perched nattily on top of the perm, secured with long bobby pins. Rolls of flesh bulged and creased beneath her uniform and threatened to launch the buttons holding everything together into the waiting area. When Charlotte looked at Shirl's legs, stuffed into white nylons, all she could think was sausage casing. Charlotte had never seen Shirl without her uniform and cap. She did not look like the nurses at the hospital. She looked like the nurses who cared for soldiers during the war, efficient and strict. The kind who looked at the thermometer and then shook it down with one quick snap of the wrist, while the other hand took your pulse. Professional, competent, no-nonsense nursing. She rarely smiled and greeted Charlotte in a gruff voice, "He's running a bit behind."

Which was why Charlotte found the glossy magazines so curious. They were fashion and beauty magazines, with fresh, young faces on the cover and articles on the inside about right and wrong ways to wear a scarf, or apply eyeliner; workouts for your flabby thighs and sagging cheeks. The magazine on Charlotte's lap fell open to an article prescribing tips on the proper way to shave your bikini line. Number one: always use a new blade. Number two: use a moisturizing soap and warm, not hot, water. Number three: always shave in the direction the hair grows. Shaving opposite to the direction of growth can stress the follicle and result in a rash-like appearance or an infected hair follicle. Lastly, shave your bikini line a few times before beach season to toughen and ensure a natural look to you skin. And if you're not going to bother with the workout on page forty, then never mind, you're not fit to be seen at the beach this season.

Which parts of the magazines did Shirl read? Did she read the advice columns hoping someone else had sent in a question she needed an answer to? And then carefully read the answer and think it over? Did she go on diets of blended yogurt drinks and wheat germ? Did she get on the floor every night and do five sets of twenty leg lifts? What about her bikini line? *Number one, have a family pack of new blades ready.*

"He's ready for you, Miss Weiss."

Shirl rose from her seat to show Charlotte in. On the desk behind the counter, Charlotte spied a bag of Cheesies, open and waiting for Shirl's return. Charlotte wanted to remember to look at Shirl's orange Cheesie fingers on her way out.

Dear Beauty Advisor, Do you have a way of getting Cheesie stained fingers clean in a hurry? Please advise.

Those magazines served a different purpose for people like Shirl. How could someone like Shirl look at those pictures, those absurd standards of beauty and not eat

Cheesies? It was her only recourse. Twist her heel in the face of glamour, jam five Cheesies in her mouth. Sure, she read the beauty columns, every word, but not for the advice, not to learn how to become beautiful. But to stockpile ammunition for her battle, to provide her with armour to shield her from the arrows of the thin army. The more she read, the more pictures she looked at, the more she convinced herself of how impossible it would be for her to join their ranks. Unattainable. Thin people fought to stay thin and fat people fought a lonely battle against them. Shirl fought with Cheesies. How could she go on a watermelon diet? How could she get abs of steel? She could not. Ever. And none of the hundreds of thousands of women like her could. They didn't want anyone telling them it was okay to be fat. They didn't want to be empowered and feel good about being huge. They were mad as hell and the stacks of grease stained beauty magazines littering the waiting rooms across the country proved it.

Charlotte's file lay open on the desk with her ECG results taped in rows across the page. Her stress test was in there too and Dr. Wilson bent over the file, whistling air through the hair in his nose as he studied it. Charlotte waited for him to say something. She sat up on the examination table. Her dangling feet had turned mottled and blue. A draft from somewhere got at the opening in her gown and her spine contracted from the cold. The calendar on the wall and the doctor's gothic university certificates did not provide much of a distraction. Finally, Dr. Wilson looked up from his desk.

"You have an arrhythmia, an irregular heart beat and your blood pressure is a bit high. The stress test showed quite a few irregular beats. Charlotte, you're doing the right thing by giving up your work. The work you do at the bakery definitely puts your heart at risk."

Charlotte's hands turned clammy. She brushed them against the paper gown. Why was she reacting this way?

She already knew everything he was saying. They had had a long discussion the last time she was here. Maybe she thought the tests would prove him wrong, that her heart was strong as steel and would last and last. She could go to Vi and say there had been a mistake, her heart was fine and she didn't have to quit. Now, there were no more tests for her to take. No more chances. The investigation was over and the results were in.

"It's not serious, just something you have to watch. You have to take it easy. I'm giving you a prescription as well. For your blood pressure."

"I'm getting a bit cold," Charlotte said. "I'd like to get back into my clothes."

Dr. Wilson left so Charlotte could dress. A heart at risk. At risk for what? Would the irregular beat turn into some kind of jazzy syncopated rhythm her body couldn't follow? Would she wake in the night to her be-bopping heart pounding inside her trying to get out?

Such a milestone in her life determined in such a sterile place. This was how she would slide into old age, dressed in a paper gown with a bespectacled old man telling her she, too, was now old. How come he got to keep his job? He had been old for ages. The stethoscope lay on the desk where Dr. Wilson had left it. Charlotte picked it up and stuck the ends in her ears. She placed it over her heart and listened. Very still, so that she could hear. At first there was a lot of whooshing and rustling. When she held her breath she could hear it perfectly. It sounded like someone gently knocking on the inside the wall of her chest; her heart trying to get her attention. It made her feel a bit better just to listen, to know her heart really was in there and beating the way it should. So what if it skipped a beat here and there? Wasn't it enough that it beat at all?

On her way home, Charlotte walked down Main Street. A scene so familiar, she could sense where she was, just by the shape of the buildings around her, the slope of the sidewalk beneath her feet, where the light fell to the street from between the buildings. It went beyond familiar, like the way people could find their way through their homes in the pitch dark of night. The way they roamed through the patterns of their thoughts, laid down over the years in the mind, always finding the same thoughts right next to each other. When Charlotte walked past the bakery she always thought of her mother, on her way home with packages of food for her party. Maybe humming *White Christmas*, like she did at home while she set the table for Christmas dinner. Then Charlotte imagined the tires, the brakes, the shower of glass. Even though she hadn't seen the accident, she knew the exact spot. For weeks blood had stained the sidewalk under the bakery window. Charlotte was sure she could still see a slight discolouration in the cement.

The bakery was situated along a row of two-storey brick buildings on Main Street. Some of these buildings had been among the first built in Norman and still had the original stone facades. The top stories had apartments for rent, but most of them were empty or had been converted to accountant or lawyer offices. Norman had been a different place when these buildings were built. Back then the town had everything to offer because trips to the city weren't as easy to execute as they were now. People weren't so anxious to shop and compare. Merchants were able to rely a steady business from within Norman and not worry about what was happening in the city.

Through the window Charlotte saw Doris wiping down the showcase glass, her movements quick and precise. One squirt of the Windex and four swipes with the paper towel and onto the next. The display cases were empty. All the cookies and squares would be in the freezer until tomorrow, the bread transferred to the reduced shelves, fifty percent off. Vi was probably in the back with the cash drawer and her adding machine. In the window stood a three-tiered wedding cake Charlotte had let Doris decorate. Poor Doris hadn't realized the top two tiers were fake. Only the bottom layer was real. The top layers were formed from cardboard and then decorated. The plastic groom and bride were two of hundreds Charlotte had posed at the summit of wedding cakes past.

"It makes me think twice about getting married," Doris had said as she secured the couple at the top of the cardboard cake. "I always thought the cake was real. How can people go on and on about honesty when they serve fake cake?"

"Well, you can just have one layer for your wedding cake. Then nobody gets fooled."

"That's a good idea."

She thought maybe Doris would have come up with something other than the usual, but white icing and plastic couples would always be the people's choice. It was best not to take too many chances when it came to weddings. The couple had started to lean a bit to the right and it looked as though at any moment the groom would be on top of the bride in the frosting, like they couldn't wait until the cake was cut and the guests gone home.

Doris saw Charlotte outside as she turned the sign from *Open* to *Closed*. She wiped her brow and shook her fingers as though to snap off the sweat. They smiled at each other through the glass.

* * * * *

At home, Charlotte sat for a long time in the old armchair, staring out the picture window, listening to the creaks and groans of the house. Her father Charles had sat like this most of the day. The birch tree outside had an hypnotic effect. Her eyes followed the branches, back and forth, like a slow metronome, sweeping across the horizon, allowing the sun to peek through here and there. Maybe her father had seen the same thing when he looked outside. Maybe the tree had calmed him too, the way it did Charlotte right now. Helped him relax the rock hard muscles, which pulled at his body and didn't let him move. She imagined him trying to rock his body in unison with the tree and lull himself into a serene quiet where his mind left his body for a moment and let it rest.

She paid close attention to the beating of her heart. When she breathed out, the beat slowed down and when she breathed in it sped up. It beat seventy-three times in one minute. What did it matter if it missed a beat or if an extra one got thrown in? The most interesting rhythms were those with the unpredictable element, the steady beat shaken loose by a stray, unexpected beat. Maybe she had had this rhythmic anomaly her whole life and it just was more noticeable now that she was getting older. There had to be some explanation for what set the rhythm section apart from the rest of the band.

chapter two

C harlotte's big acoustic bass lay on its side in the study. Once again, she had forgotten how beautiful it was. How long had she left it this time? She picked up the bow and applied a few strokes of rosin. Charlotte sat on her stool and let the bass rest against her. It would take some coaxing to get the natural intimacy back, but it would come. Like a lover who had been neglected for too long, her bass made her work before it gave in and relaxed. She tuned the instrument, bowing across the strings, two at a time and turning the pegs until the fifth sounded perfect in her ear. When Charlotte pulled the bow across the strings she felt the vibration right through her chest. It stirred her heart. To play an instrument you have to hold it close and dance as you play. There can be no awkward shyness, no fear of contact. You have to hold it confidently and with affection.

Her father helped her decide on the bass. He said, "Would you rather people notice when you're playing or have them notice when you stop? Do you want to be front and centre, blaring away on a showy instrument or do you want to be lurking in the shadows, in control, but hard to detect? More noticeable when you stop playing, because the music can't fly without you?"

At first she wanted to play the drums, those sneaky rhythms, the sexy swishes and coy pops and patter of the sticks. Such a multitude of sounds and beats, all coming from one person. But Charles said, "Your mother will never forgive me. How about the bass? That's part of the rhythm section."

They drove to Croft's Music in Winnipeg. In the car they listened to a Glenn Miller broadcast on the radio: *String of Pearls, Little Brown Jug, Moonlight Serenade.* Past fields of corn and potatoes, canola and flax with the windows open, the perfumed wind rushed through their hair. The forever sky, wide open blue. All the way there, Charles tapped the steering wheel in time to the music while Charlotte *doom doom doomed* the bass line. The time passed quickly and soon Charles was navigating the Saturday traffic down Portage Avenue. They parked behind the store and went in the back door like privileged customers.

The stringed instruments were in the basement. There was a workbench in the middle of the room where a violin lay in pieces and all around were instruments waiting to be repaired. There were violins and violas and cellos hanging in rows like expensive suits. The room had an air of efficiency and craftsmanship. All around was clutter, bits and pieces of instruments which soon would once again be whole and producing exquisite sounds. Charlotte found the place enchanting, the smell of wood shavings and glue and Mozart on the radio. Old Mr. Croft peering intently through his black glasses at the seam he was gluing back together and without taking his eyes off his work said, "I'll be with you in just a minute."

Both Charles and Charlotte watched him work in silence. To disturb him would be to interfere with a divine task. They waited until he finished and turned his attention to them.

There were two double basses for Charlotte to choose from. She hadn't been up close to a bass yet and felt nervous about touching them. They were taller than she was. She wasn't expecting that. One had been varnished a dark black-brown and had a sinister gleam which intimidated her. There was something threatening about it, like a coming storm. It was daring Charlotte, the school-yard bully, putting up a tough front so that nobody would come close. It would require a seasoned professional's touch to bring the sound out of it, Charlotte thought. Amateurs, stay away.

The other one had an auburn finish, rich and warm. Much more inviting and a bit smaller. Charlotte wanted that one.

"You better try them both," her father said. "You can't tell what it will sound like by looking at it."

Mr. Croft got Charlotte a bow and rosined it for her. "You never touch the hair on the bow with anything but the rosin," he said. "The oil on your fingers will affect the sound the bow makes."

Charlotte stopped plucking at the strings. Mr. Croft placed the bow in her hand and showed her how to hold it, kind of cupped in her hand "You'll get used to it. It feels funny because you don't hold anything else that way."

She pulled the bow across the strings of the dark bass. The sound bellowed from the depths of the instrument. Her father raised an eyebrow and she crossed to the lower strings. The sound filled the room and when she stopped the bow, all the other instruments in the room were resonating.

"You're a natural," said Mr. Croft.

The second instrument sounded the same as the first to Charlotte.

"You have to go a little by feel. It has to feel right when you hold it. It should feel like your most comfortable pair of shoes. I'll play them both for you so you get an idea how they sound."

Mr. Croft took the instrument. All he played were simple scales and arpeggios and a few double stops, but to Charlotte's ears, the sound was so raw, so elegant, that she stood mesmerized, wanting to hear more. She couldn't decide. Both basses had lush, smooth tones. The dark one gave more depth, had more guts, but the auburn one was so gorgeous, its tone silky and golden. Its demeanor stately yet graceful.

She chose the auburn one. They drove home with the bass lying in the back of their station wagon across the back seat and extending almost to the front like a Christmas tree. "Stately yet graceful...inert yet fluid, static yet dynamic."

Charlotte laughed. "Stream of consciousness yet comprehensible."

"You're going to be a fine player," he told her. "You're observant. You notice things."

Then he fell silent and watched the road disappear under the car. Charlotte wasn't sure what he meant by that. Had he meant it as a compliment or as advice? They didn't listen to the radio on the way home which made it easier for Charlotte to daydream about her life as a bass player.

She joined the high school orchestra. Basketball didn't interest her much, but her height advantage still benefited her in the orchestra. Not everyone could play double bass. There were physical requirements. Her view of the orchestra was worth it. She could stand, or sit on her stool while the others had to sit and scrape their chairs around until they had Mr. Klassen in a clear line of sight. Charlotte watched from her stool as players faked their way through *Wildwood Flower* and made faces at their friends. It was easiest for the people in the flute section to fake. There were so many of them, one dropping out wouldn't be missed. It was impossible to tell if they were playing or not with just their lips and fingers moving.

Outside, the track and field team practised while the orchestra sawed through *Hoe-Down*, Aaron Copeland style. Charlotte watched them as they warmed up with their A's and B's. Stretching their sinewy muscles. The track members watched one another too. Charlotte got pretty good at playing while paying attention to something else, an all too common practice among bass players. After three years in the orchestra she knew how the get through *Pizzicato Polka* three different ways. The main thing for a bass player is to know how to count. Some pieces had rests that went on for seventy bars. Sometimes, Mr. Klassen didn't cue them for their entry to see if they had been counting. He pretended to be busy taming the nine flutes whose part overpowered the entire woodwind and string sections in what was meant to be a particularly delicate passage.

* * * * *

Charlotte didn't play as much as she used to, but about four or five times a year she unzipped the case and carefully slid the canvas over the body of the instrument. Each time she did this, she feared she would find the bridge collapsed, the strings broken and the sound-post rolling around inside like Jonah in the whale. Then the ghost of Mr. Croft leapt into her mind and admonished her for neglecting her instrument. When she discovered everything intact, she was so relieved she would keep the bass out for a few weeks and play almost every day, making her fingers red and swollen. But, the practices inevitably became shorter and dust would gather on the exposed wood so Charlotte would zip the instrument back into the case and lay it back on the floor for another few months. Were it a person, it would have been the love of Charlotte's life. The one steady presence in her life which brought her joy, which never disappointed her, which she could forget about for months and then turn to on a whim and demand attention.

The D string had unravelled from the peg. Charlotte tightened the strings and tuned to the A on the piano. She really should be playing more than four times a year. The bass or any instrument needed to be played or the wood stiffed and wouldn't resonate. The first notes from the instrument sounded like she was playing a cardboard box, lifeless and flat. It took a few practices to get the sound back. Those smooth rich tones brought the instrument to life.

It used to be she had to practice everyday so she wouldn't make mistakes at rehearsal or during a performance. Being unprepared slowed everyone down. Now, with nothing to prepare for, her bass wasn't a priority. She no longer spent hours working at a particular line of melody or rhythm. As soon as she got discouraged, she stopped playing. The bass nagged at her from its place in the study and sometimes she even avoided going in there to avoid feeling guilty. It wasn't the same anymore, playing all by herself. An instrument needs company. All it takes is one other instrument to join its spirit and together the sound soars and anyone listening won't be able to tell how many instruments are creating the music.

No matter how well it's played, one instrument never sounds as good as two or three. Music is harmony and in harmony lies all human emotion. Any two notes, sung softly and held for a moment, can bring on every possible kind of tear.

The piano and bass took up one corner of the room. Then, her practice stool and music stand, though she rarely played from music. A framed reproduction of Delacroix's *Liberty Leading the People* hung above the roll top desk where Charles used to mark exams. Along the inside wall was the record collection Charles had accumulated and his beloved RCA HiFi. There must have been at least five hundred records, often the same recording three or four times with different artists. Charlotte had inherited her father's ear and mostly played along to the records, pretending she was in Chicago in the thirties in some dingy smoke-filled bar, late at night with musicians who had not yet made history.

A window looked out onto the back yard and across the lane to Kuldip's house. In the summer, Charlotte played with the window open because the music and the summer heat went together and she liked to work up a sweat while she played. It brought her closer to the real thing.

Charlotte pulled a Louis Armstrong record from the cabinet. While Louis launched into the first track with that ground gravel declaration, *I Can't Give You Anything But Love*, Charlotte took the bass and leaned it up against her. Jazz legend had it that Louis Armstrong was the first performer to scat. He supposedly dropped the lyric sheet from which he was singing and started *shoo-bee-doo-waa-ing* with his voice in the same way he improvised on his coronet. Charlotte sat on her stool and plucked at the strings, softly at first to avoid the horrible buzz that erupted from the instrument's belly when she hadn't played in a long time. She carried the beat while Louis bleated away on his horn.

"We've still got it," she said into the scroll. One song and her fingers ached. Charlotte sat down and listened to the rest of the side, shaking out and rubbing her hands. She couldn't get discouraged. It always took a few days of practice before she could play for longer than a few minutes. Across the lane in his backyard, Kuldip tended his tomatoes and listened to Charlotte's music float from her house to his. He never mentioned anything for fear she may close the window and keep the music all to herself.

The bass needed some polish. Charlotte shook the bottle of linseed oil she used to revive the glow of the finish. The smell reminded her of the shop in the basement of Croft's Music: seasoned wood, pots of glue and varnish and a hint of something metal. All those instruments – she would never forget it. The worktable, covered with chisels of all sorts and mallets, loops of wire, Bunsen burners heating the glue. The repairmen who worked slowly, with careful tapping on the mallets and short strokes when they brushed on the glue. Some of the instruments had been taken apart and looked as though some terrible illness had smote them. Charlotte couldn't imagine having to see her bass slit at the seams, the innards exposed. She thought it would be like seeing your dog hit by a car.

Her bass had been made in Markneukirchen, a town somewhere in Germany. The sticker inside was hand written with turquoise ink. A drop of water had smudged the name of the maker. Josef K—, Markneukirchen, 1896. A player with the Leipzig Philharmonic had brought it in to sell. Other than that, she knew little about her bass. She imagined Josef in his workshop in a quaint German town where the horses clomped past the window on the cobblestones while he worked on her bass. Hunched over his worktable with the glue pot bubbling beside him and pieces of unfinished instruments in every corner and hanging from the rafters. Maybe apprentices, young men who aspired to learn Josef's craft, made parts of her bass. She peered inside her bass and saw the sound post, so carefully and precisely placed, and the seams, flawlessly glued together without so much as a single drop which got away, and the scroll, a work of art on its own. The entire instrument, all held together by dynamic tension and a little glue. A work of pure brilliance in her hands.

The world today would be unrecognizable to Josef. Did it ever occur to him that his bass would end up in a small town on the Canadian prairies? Or up on a stage playing jazz? Charlotte liked to believe she was the first person to play jazz on her bass. The metronomic rhythms the bass was used to became unhinged when she plucked along with Benny Goodman, slapping her fingers against the fingerboard and freeing sounds which never before escaped the f-holes.

She shook the bottle and dabbed some oil onto the cloth. She always started on the back of the instrument. Her shoulder began to ache as she worked the cloth in circles from the centre seam to the sides, top to bottom. The flat of her hand pressed into the cloth and Charlotte could see the varnish shine as the wood soaked up the moisture. Once she could make out her blurry face she started on the sides. With her fingernail up against the seam, Charlotte pressed on the cloth and felt the oil soak into her finger. This was where the instrument could dry out and crack most easily. The glue could become brittle and the seam could open. She checked for cracks in the seam by knocking on the back all along the edges and listening for differences in the sound. These ministrations were carried out with a sense of both guilt and affection. Her bass deserved better and as she carefully checked it over she felt the need to prove her loyalty with some pampering.

Charlotte did the front last. She shook the bottle again and tipped it onto the cloth. She held the bass, supporting it with a hand behind the neck. Rays from the low sun beamed hot through the window. Golden, syrupy light poured in over the sill as Charlotte wiped the whole instrument with a clean cloth. From her easy chair, Charlotte admired her work and watched the evening sun burn into the amber finish. She imagined the heat melting the varnish and leaving a puddle on the floor. The glare left fireworks in her eyes. Bathed in the golden red eye of the slowly setting sun, Charlotte watched the light slip away. Darkness fell over the bass and crept into the room. She sat for a long while in the dark, feeling the breeze on her face and the warmth the sun left behind.

chapter three

A sign had been taped to the wall next to the cash register with an old, creased photograph of Charlotte taped to it: *Look Who's Retiring*. The letters formed an arc over the photo and underneath was space for people to sign their names if they wanted to come to the party. A couple of balloons were taped there too, to give people the idea there would be no end to the fun. Her boss Vi must have made the sign on her computer. She did everything on her computer. Even the calligraphy signs for the display case that Doris had made had been replaced by Vi's signs done in computer calligraphy.

Find a funny picture, Vi probably had said to June, and we'll put it up with the sign. There was no turning back now. People's efforts for Charlotte's happy retirement had begun. Charlotte had one week to get through and it would be over. One week of June and Vi asking her what she wanted served for dinner. Should they have snacks at the end of the night? Did she want music? Before, during or after? What about dancing? The staff at the Driftwood would have to be notified. She promised to think about everything. What did people expect at these kind of things? Charlotte couldn't even remember the last time she had been at a party. When Vi paid off her bank loan they closed up fifteen minutes early and celebrated with lemonade and sugar cookies. There was the Christmas lunch they had every year, where Vi invited them all to the Chinese buffet. Everybody heaped their plates with breaded sweet and sour food and read their fortunes aloud after they were done. When Charlotte thought about that, she realized Vi was going all out for her retirement. The Driftwood wouldn't be cheap. But what would it be? Once June and Vi had their minds made up, the gleam in their eyes told Charlotte to back off. They had party fever and Charlotte would be safest to let them do their thing until the dust settled.

In the old photo, Charlotte's eyes squinted into the camera. It was June 14 and by noon the sun was high. June posed her in front of the bakery, under the Olafson's sign.

"It's your eighteenth birthday. We have to have a picture."

"Do you have to take it here?"

"Well, you're going to want to remember what you were doing when you turned eighteen, won't you?"

Charlotte searched her own eyes in the photograph to gain some sense of what she felt that day. It had been a year since she graduated. A year and a half after her mother had died. Most of her friends had left after high school for Winnipeg or Toronto. She was living at home with her father, still waiting for him to get well enough for her to leave. At that point Charlotte still thought she would be leaving Norman. She would take all her savings and get on a bus and go and catch up with Ray, wherever he was. That was when he was still writing every month or so. The last she heard from him, he was in New Orleans. Music and food that make you sweat, he said.

Charlotte remembered making her own birthday cake that day. Spice cake, layered with butter frosting an inch thick. She even wrote the inscription herself: *Happy 18th Birthday,* with smiley faces in the loops of the eight. She carried it home where June lit the candles and she and Charles sang *Happy Birthday*. June took another photo, but when they were developed, both Charles and Charlotte had red eyes from the flash. First the sun and then the flash. It was hard to see anything clearly that day. Charles ate only two bites of his cake. Then, his eyes became teary and he went to lie down.

How would she have looked on that day, had she known then she would be working at the bakery her whole life? Nobody thinks the present will last forever. The present is something to be endured until the future takes hold. The future; that dangling carrot you tread towards as the weeks and months fly by. You get a nibble here and there and before you know it, you've eaten the whole thing.

If Charlotte stepped outside right now, the exact photo could be recreated; apron, hairnet, the same impatient squint. The circle would be complete. If life progresses in cycles, Charlotte's so far had been one giant loop. Life stories have a finite number of themes: love, loss, hope, despair, faith, doubt, toil, reward and an infinity of variations. Even though Charlotte's life lacked variety, the themes were all well represented. Themes in need of variations, such was her life.

Inside, the bakery looked more or less the same today as it did on Charlotte's eighteenth birthday. The cash register was new, a reflection of Vi's priorities. Most of the equipment was the same equipment Charlotte learned on when Mr. Olafson first trained her. Things had been repaired and only when a part could no longer be found, did Vi give in and buy something new. The scales and the little round weights, most of the pans and tins and cookie sheets which had been used so often over the years, rarely needed to be replaced. Charlotte convinced Vi to buy some new rolling pins, nice shiny aluminum ones, with ball bearings inside so Charlotte could roll the dough with almost no effort.

Vi took over after Mr. Olafson retired and then all kinds of things changed. The old hand- painted sign taken down and hung inside and a new pink and green neon one was hung outside. Having the old sign inside showed that they were a business with integrity, Vi explained. Then they started accepting credit cards and stopped allowing people to shop on credit. Vi said you never could really tell who would be good for it and who wouldn't; they all talked a sweet line. Vi also wanted some of the products pre-packaged, the top sellers. Things like Charlotte's orange-buttermilk muffins and the cinnamon buns. People didn't like it at first. They couldn't properly see through the plastic and poked and sniffed at the packages and looked suspicious and then bought from the day old shelf for less, since everything looked the same once it was wrapped in plastic. There was a black board that Doris wrote on with fluorescent pens, all the specials, which weren't really specials at all, just a rotation of different things Charlotte baked all the time anyway. "It's because they're not available everyday," Vi said. "That's what makes them specials. It has nothing to do with the price."

The things people bought at the bakery changed over time too. When Charlotte first started, she and Mr. Olafson would make close to three hundred loaves of bread a day, dozens of rolls and buns and only a few sweets. Housewives – there were more of them then – baked their own sweets. They bought their bread from the bakery, but their cookies and cakes they made themselves. Only one of the three display cases was needed for all the sweets and meat pies. Now, Charlotte only baked a hundred loaves for each day and more and more people bought sweets. Women didn't have time to bake cakes anymore. They worked at full time jobs, shuttled their children around to hundreds of activities, volunteered for committees, signed up to bring snacks for meetings and then bought them at the bakery. They bought their bread at the grocery store and stopped by the bakery to pick up meat pies for dinner. Charlotte had to spend some of her free time at home watching children's television programs so she could recreate some of the popular characters on cookies with bright, garish icing. All three display cases were filled with cookies, graham cracker squares filled with chocolate and jam, muffins and puff pastries overflowing with whipped butter-cream while the bread lay on shelves on the back wall and the rolls, once dry, were grated into bread crumbs.

Once the IGA built their supermarket down the street, Olafson's had to find a way to stay competitive. A sign appeared in the window: *Now making specialty cakes.* Nobody knew exactly to what this referred because the bakery had always made special cakes for birthdays and weddings. Vi must have spread the word herself because how else could they advertise penis-shaped cakes? Apparently it was becoming quite popular in the city. Women ordered them for bridal showers and placed them in the centre of the table flanked by rows of knives and forks.

"Those are going to be pretty small cakes," Charlotte had said, puzzling over where she would find cupcake trays shaped like that.

"No, no," Vi said. "They're big. Full sized cakes, a foot long. Usually a white cake and frosting. It wouldn't be funny if we made them too real."

She already had one order to be picked up Saturday. Charlotte would have to come up with something by then. Just how big of a cake should she make? Size was important. People wanted their money's worth. Vi would have to find out where to buy the molds and in the meantime Charlotte was to use her expertise and improvise. After some thought, Charlotte used one of the long loaf pans and two bowls. She mixed up five times the white cake recipe and poured it in the pans. Once they had cooled, she placed the two round cakes and the one loaf in the appropriate configuration on a flat of cardboard. She frosted the entire cake with white frosting. It resembled the communion cakes they made in the shape of crosses, only those had red icing roses to adorn them. The penis cake was bigger, more bulbous and unadorned. Mavis Davis paid ten dollars for it.

"What a riot! The girls will love this." Mavis Davis had ordered the first penis cake in Norman. After that there was a steady stream of orders. It lasted about five years. The specialty cakes were still advertised in the window, but only a few were ordered each year and they were being ordered by high school girls for sweet sixteen parties rather than for blushing brides-to-be. Things did change with every generation. There was no such thing as innocence any longer. It was sneered upon by young people, who replaced it with fearless swagger and a boast. Only they understood what the world was becoming while everyone else stood by scratching their heads.

* * * * *

Maybe it was Wade Pancratz who deterred women from ordering the cakes. He had started at the bakery part-time a year ago and was the first male baker in town since the penis cakes became popular. The women were used to Charlotte being in on the joke and that was okay because it was a joke between women. Somehow the joke didn't seem as funny when a man was doing the baking. They didn't want him in on the joke. He wouldn't get it. He might get vindictive and bake some nasty poison into the cake to spite them. Then the ladies at their parties would only nibble gingerly from the end of their forks, rather than cram significant mouthfuls of soft white cake into their mouths and risk gagging on the crumbs.

Charlotte turned from the sign-up list. So far only Vi and June had signed up. The two of them had launched into the task of organizing everything like two girls on a shopping spree. Vi was constantly on the phone to June or to the people at the hotel. She chewed on the end of her pencil and checked things down on her list and twirled her hair as though the fate of the entire bakery rested upon the details of Charlotte's party. Charlotte could hardly bear to watch her. It made her more and more anxious about what to expect. How could she get excited about a mediocre dinner with all the bakery customers?

And at the Driftwood? Fifty-cents a draft Tuesday night, free baskets of pretzels, all you can eat, and the promise of a good, dirty fight in the parking lot every Saturday night. Were it not for the sale of beer, both cold from the vendor in the back and warm inside in the lounge, the Driftwood would have long since been boarded up. Beer sales, and the gatherings in the banquet room, where Normans hosted all the events which heralded the defining moments in their family histories, were the only things keeping the Driftwood afloat. Charlotte's dinner on Saturday would be no different from all the dismal, generic dinners and gatherings which preceded it. Countless pictures had appeared in the *Norman Herald* of guests of honour at the head table. Now Charlotte was up. The hall was booked, the tickets on sale and Charlotte would be retired next Saturday with a celebration at the Driftwood Inn. A moment she would have avoided with all her heart, had it not decided to conk out. A betrayal of her body against her spirit and there was not a thing she could do about it. Her body decided all on its own, after forty years working, it wanted to quit. All she could do was follow.

chapter four

That evening Charlotte stood on a footstool in the kitchen while June took measurements to call in to the girls at Rosa's Boutique. Charlotte didn't like having June so close to her, almost hugging her with the tape measure to get her bust size, tickling under her arm for the sleeve length. It wasn't saving her any time. She still would have to go into the store for the fittings.

"I think I'm two sizes smaller than I was for your wedding."

"What wedding?"

"Well, I still had to be measured for a dress. Thank God I never had to wear it."

"What are you bringing all that up for?"

"It just reminded me. Getting my boobs measured."

Charlotte dropped her arms and reached for her mug of coffee. Whatever went on between June and Lionel, Charlotte knew June was better off without him. He was a boorish man with no finesse and treated June like a new car. Years ago, while they were planning the wedding, June had invited Charlotte to dinner at Hy's Steak Loft.

The wine disappeared into Lionel at an alarming rate and his finger snapping at the waitress to bring more mortified Charlotte. Across the table, June focused on cutting her iceberg lettuce and dragging it through pools of

Thousand Island dressing. As he drank, Lionel's face turned beet red and he mopped sweat from the creases beside his nose with his napkin. Horrified, Charlotte stared at June who let Lionel touch her with his ham hands and breathe into her ear, his puckered lips almost touching her lobe.

"So, have you booked a church?" Charlotte ventured.

"It's going to be at our church, St. George's." Their church? The man went to church? She reconsidered Lionel as he sopped up the drippings on his plate with a piece of bread.

"We're going to have the reception in the basement of the church."

"Oh, I saw that in a magazine once."

"Cheaper," Lionel managed to spray across the table.

"The church ladies are going to serve. We're spending the weekend before making meatballs and buns. I hope you can come."

"Meatballs and buns? I think in the magazine they had bologna sandwiches and ripple chips. Come on June, you want a nicer wedding than that. How about a nice hotel? Or in the park?"

"It will be fine. Besides, everybody we want to invite belongs to St. George's. The choir is going to sing and for the last hymn, I'm going to join them."

"It's less than a month away. We had to find something quick and easy. Right, doll?" Lionel leaned over and kissed June's neck in a vulgar fashion, slurping at it with his tongue. June dabbed her napkin to her lips and once, quickly over the wet spot on her neck.

What bothered Charlotte most at the end of the evening was that Lionel had not once looked at her, only the waitress. She didn't care for Lionel at all. Acting like a teenager getting drunk for the first time, showing off to whomever was watching that he had a girl, who let him maul her anywhere. June was pregnant for Pete's sake.

Why didn't she say something? All evening Charlotte got
more and more furious with him. June had landed an
idiot. Charlotte knew June was anxious to be married, but
surely she could do better than this oaf. Why did she let
him get close enough to get her pregnant? Now she was
stuck with him.

Charlotte felt stuck with him too. How could June
inflict this blight on their family? Thank goodness Charles
had been spared meeting Lionel. It was supposed to
happen after June got up the nerve to tell him she was
pregnant, but things fell apart before she had a chance. It
should have given June pause, when she was pregnant and
planning her wedding, that she had not yet told her father.
It should have been a warning to her, the fear that Charles
would not approve. What she failed to realize was that the
apprehension she felt was hers alone and it had not so
much to do with Charles as it did with the man she wanted
to marry. The alarms were sounding, but in the wrong part
of her brain. The part of her brain that wanted to get
married and have a baby overpowered all the other, lesser
parts. She forged ahead, determined to be happy.

Lionel drove June and Charlotte back to June's
apartment. The wine was catching up with him and he
fixed a stuporous gaze on the road. He drove so slowly,
Charlotte thought he was going to cause an accident. The
lotion in his hair was starting to smell and Charlotte grew
queasy when he ran his hand through his hair and then
rested the same hand on June's leg. The man was a pig.

Back at June's apartment, Charlotte asked her if she
loved Lionel.

"I know you think he's horrible. He had a bit too much
to drink tonight. You know, he never used to act that way,
all physical, his hands all over. He was a gentleman before
this all happened."

"Before you let him screw you?"

June recoiled.

It was too late, so Charlotte continued. "How can you marry this man? He's utterly horrid to you. He thinks he owns you like a farmer owns a cow. How could you let this happen?"

June looked away, out the window into the street. Tears sprung to her eyes. "How can you say that? I finally get what I've always wanted and you have to try to convince me I'm making some awful mistake. We're having a baby and we're going to get married. I can't help it if he's not perfect, but he's more than you'll ever have."

It was such a feeble attack, Charlotte had to laugh. "Right. Really, June, I think my life is rich enough without someone like Lionel to slobber all over me. Are you sure this is what you want? He just doesn't seem your type."

"He's just scared right now. That's why he's acting like that. All men are scared to get married. Estelle told me. He has a lot to deal with both a baby and a wedding. It's hard on him. As soon as the wedding is over everything will be back to normal."

"Sure, whatever that is."

June was not going to give in. Her defence of Lionel endowed her with the belief that her love for him ran deep and in time he would be accepted by her family and they would all have to admit she was right and they were wrong. This would be her fight, her cause. They didn't talk about it again and two weeks later it was over and a month later June's life did return to normal.

* * * * *

June waited for Charlotte to drink her coffee so she could get the measurements. There was no point in discussing a would-be memory. Some things were better forgotten. Except those were often the things which haunted most. Not that Lionel haunted June. It was her own stupidity that gnawed at her. Thirty-five years gone by and still it made her temper rise, her face flush, her hands sweat. It was almost worse now than at the time, because when the thoughts surfaced they took her by surprise, Lionel's face springing from behind a fold in the mesh of her memories. Just when she thought she had forgotten, he flashed through her consciousness and all the uncomfortable fluttery feelings in her stomach and whirring in her head returned, strong as ever. She crammed the image away and turned her attention back to Charlotte's bust.

"Come on now Charlotte, how are the girls at Rosa's ever going to fit you for a dress if you can't even stand still and let me measure?"

"I can't believe I even let you talk me into buying a new dress. When am I ever going to wear it again? To your carpet bowling wind-up?"

"Bowling takes a bit of skill you know. The balls are weighted. You have to throw them a certain way. And age doesn't mean anything. Mrs. Beverage is almost ninety and has to be helped to the line, but boy, she never misses."

"Well, I'm thrilled to know she's still good for something."

"It wouldn't kill you to try it sometime Charlotte. What are you going to do after this week?"

"Dr. Wilson says I need rest. I'm not going to do anything for the rest of my life. That dinner next Saturday is the last time anyone will ever see me."

Charlotte sunk into the couch. "You wouldn't want me to go bowling with you anyway. I might be better than you."

"Hmmph, I doubt it." June went to put away her measuring tape.

Had June married Lionel, Charlotte mused, they would be old now and the baby would have been almost marrying age too. How different their lives would have been. Charlotte would have been an aunt. There would have been a child in their lives, to raise and teach and make parties for. Whenever she thought about Lionel, an image of a homeless person always sprang to Charlotte's mind.

She imagined him drinking to numb the regret burning inside him, despondent and destroying himself over his loss and lack of judgment.

Charlotte got off the couch and padded up the stairs to the bathroom and left June to the evening news. As the water filled the sink she pulled at the loose strands of grey-brown hair behind her ears. She put her face close to the mirror and marvelled at the thousands of lines etched into her skin. Like dough that had been rolled out with too much flour and wouldn't hold together. Most of them started at the corners of her eyes. Others above her upper lip. After that her most wrinkly part was her neck and apart from all that she was still relatively smooth. Her hands especially, because she rubbed them with butter everyday at work.

Steam rose from the sink and the mirror misted over. Charlotte's face became distorted and cloudy, an apparition about to fade from view. Let it, she thought. She could only look at herself so long. Through the hot wash cloth over her face, Charlotte let the moisture seep into her skin. Repeatedly, she dipped the cloth into the scalding water and held it over her face, inhaling deeply. Hot wet air filled her lungs and she felt cleansed. She held the corner of the cloth to her mouth and sucked the hot water out of it. The warmth on the back of her throat soothed her. The cloth hung from her mouth, gripped in her front teeth. She looked like a wild dog with its kill. Hair flung in all directions after the chase. She bared her teeth and growled. Shook her head back and forth and the cloth slapped at her face. The death-shake. Water splattered against the mirror and onto the walls. The wildness left her eyes and the limp cloth hung from her mouth down to her chest. Take that.

chapter five

The alarm woke Charlotte on Tuesday morning at two-thirty. Work started at three-thirty. She had been getting up at this hour for so long, her body knew nothing else. Even on vacation she rarely slept past five or six. The lamp on her dresser cast long shadows onto the floor. The breeze from outside, though cool, still carried with it the heat from the day. When she pulled up the blind she saw Kuldip had his kitchen light on. Charlotte was never sure if he stayed up this late, or if he went to bed and then got up. From her bedroom window she could see down into his kitchen. His enormous orange cat, Scarlet, cleaned herself on the window ledge, waiting for her share of whatever sweet, spicy dish he was preparing. Plates licked clean by Scarlet littered his back steps. He stood in front of the stove stirring something in a kettle pot. He was a sprightly little man, darting around his kitchen in his white cotton shirt and baggy drawstring pants, sandals on his bare feet. Even in winter he wore sandals. Through his open window and then through hers, Charlotte could hear the tinny, lament of the music which accompanied his stirring. Lovely, exotic smells drifted up towards Charlotte's window, where she stood, winter or summer, leaning out and breathing it in. She only watched for a few moments. Even though he couldn't see her, she felt as though she disturbed him. Let the serenity be his alone.

When he arrived in Norman with his wife and two daughters, Kuldip Channa was a young man, thirty-one-years old. During the drive from the airport, the endless fields of bright yellow canola waved them on towards Norman. Their silence in the car defined their disbelief. They had started their journey in a hot taxi careering through the mad, cramped streets of Delhi and then into the oppressive heat of the airport amongst the throngs of sweaty travellers. The frenzy with which their journey had begun, ill-prepared them for the fright they all experienced as the car pulled away from Winnipeg and the vast expanse of the Canadian prairies rolled towards them from out of nowhere. Where had he brought his family? What had he done?

Never had Kuldip imagined so much space. His wife had to lay back on the seat and shut her eyes fifty kilometres from Norman. The girls sat sideways in the car, their faces pressed against the side windows. As far as the eye could see, nothing but blue sky and shimmering wheat. Kuldip had to blink to keep his perspective in check. He was the boy who was taken from a tribe in the dense rain forest and brought to the plains of Africa. His brain never learned to see farther than it needed to amongst the thick growth of the forest. As a herd of elephants approached from afar, the boy grew wild with fright because he thought bugs were growing before his very eyes into animals of monstrous proportions.

The Anglican Church sponsored the Channa's into Canada. The members of the congregation had been bombarded with images of poverty; people wearing rags for clothes, living in dingy, stone rooms with only holes for windows and empty bowls for food on the floor; dirty children begging in the streets; babies so emaciated each tiny rib could be seen. Could the good people of St. Joseph's not see it in their hearts to save one deserving family from such a fate? A committee was struck and donations collected and today, here at last, after many forms had been filled out and letters and pictures exchanged, was the Channa family. A visible sign of Norman's Christian goodwill, all the way from India.

The car pulled up to the house, the front doors flung open and fifty people dressed in the clothes they normally saved for Sunday, spilled onto the front lawn and applauded as Kuldip and his family stepped onto the boulevard and stared back at the crowd and the mansion behind them. The girls were afraid to come out of the car and had to be coaxed with promises of sweets. The Channa family stood facing the expectant congregation. Though he wanted to somehow express his boundless gratitude to these people, he was distracted by the strength with which his youngest daughter, Pamela, gripped his hand. The people parted and guided he and his family towards the front door of their new home. Women reached out and fingered Meagha's *sari* as she walked by and patted the girls on the head. Men clapped Kuldip on the back and earnestly took his hand and clasped it in theirs.

The vast house fanned out before them as they came through the front door. In Delhi, they had lived in one room and here, each of them could have a room of their own.

"Kuldip, we welcome you to Canada." A gentleman in a grey suit stepped forward to greet them.

"Thank you very much," Kuldip stammered, unused to the Canadian predeliction to use first names, even with strangers. "Yes, my wife, Meagha, and daughters, Pamela and Sara." The man in the suit looked as though he had understood nothing of Kuldip's carefully rehearsed presentation, which made Kuldip feel stranger than ever.

The ladies auxiliary had brought platters of food. Buns, meats, pickles, devilled eggs. Most of it was eaten by the parishioners who were used to these coffee and sandwich parties. It all tasted too strange for the Channa's to enjoy. Meagha bit into at a salty pink sandwich.

"How do you like that?" A woman in ivory asked, seeing the look of concentration on Meagha's face as she chewed. "It's ham," the woman said, as though revealing a titillating secret.

Pig-flesh sandwiches! Meagha was almost sick. She didn't know whether to cry or throw up. She didn't know what was right anymore. Everything in the house was so lavish. The church had provided all the furniture, dishes, linens and had even bought the girls some crayons and stuffed animals. In return, the Channa's were expected to attend church every Sunday and the girls enrolled in Sunday school. Their Christian education was included in the church's charity.

The girls sat on the back steps in matching delicate yellow dresses during the party. One day ago they had been in India. They had travelled around the world in one day and now sat in their first backyard. They sat very close to one another and looked over the back yard with worried eyes.

"Everybody looks so strange," Pamela said.

"That's because they're missionaries. It's a whole country of missionaries."

"They dress funny."

"They only dress that way when they are working. It's the missionary uniform."

A lady brought them a plate of cookies. "How're you sweet girls doing? Everything okay? Have a cookie. They're peanut-butter."

Sara and Pamela hunched closer together and tried to smile at the missionary lady, but were too frightened. The lady set the plate down beside them and said, "I'll leave them right here. I'm sure you must be hungry. Coming all the way from India and all. My goodness."

Sara took a bite and spat peanut-butter cookie into the bushes.

"I don't like missionary food."

By mid-afternoon, they had found the courage to venture from the steps to the swing-set and took turns on the slide and pushed imaginary friends on the empty swings.

None of the Channas could sleep that night. The girls in their room, each tucked into their own bed, stared at each other across the gulf between the beds. When their father turned out the light, a clown with a rather malevolent smile lit up the room from a wall socket. Their parents, so far away in the large master bedroom down the carpeted hallway, lay very still and listened to every noise until silence fell over the house. Not even their breath could be heard, which made it difficult for everyone to sleep.

* * * * *

Charlotte waved to Kuldip Channa whenever she saw him and made a point of buying a few things each week at the Radio Shack where he worked. Reuben Gregory, the head of the church council had agreed to hire Kuldip after their sponsorship had been approved.

The door chimed when it opened and Kuldip popped out from behind display as though he was wired in with the door chime.

"Oh, hello Miss Charlotte," he said. "What do you need today?"

"I need a new needle for my record player." She showed him the old one and Kuldip scuttled off to find it for her down one of the pegboard aisles.

"How are things going for you here?"

"Oh, very nice. Very good, nice people." He didn't look at her when he said this and Charlotte wasn't sure if it was the truth or the only reply his limited English could articulate.

"If ever you need anything, I'm across the lane. Neighbours." She pointed at him and then at herself a few times.

"Yes, neighbours. Very good. Thank you."

Charlotte usually met him in the back lane, both of them carrying green bags of garbage. "Hello Miss Charlotte," he would say in his high-pitched voice. "What a beautiful day, no?" And he would take her garbage bag and put it in the bin for her. "Oh, I like to help you, Miss Charlotte. Thank you very much."

He would bow a little and go back to his house. The church people gradually dropped away, as though the Channa's were pets with which they had become bored, and re-directed their attention to raising money for a new organ.

One day, Kuldip arrived at the store and found some kids had spray painted *Paki go home*, in green paint, all across the front door. At first, Kuldip couldn't make out what it said because the paint had dripped so much. He prepared a bucket of soapy water in the employee bathroom and went to wash off the paint. This time, he read what the letters said and his heart stopped. They could only mean him. Who else? The soapy water didn't do much to get the paint off. Kuldip scrubbed at it for nearly an hour and then he had to open the store. Thankfully, it was summer and he was able to prop the door open for the day.

When he thought about it later, Kuldip found it quite harmless, really, compared to the horrible crimes committed in Dehli everyday. The streets of Norman were much safer; nobody had been hurt by the prank. Kuldip was not even Pakistani. But, to have any slight, no matter how small, aimed right at him and his family, he found unsettling. The intention somebody had to deliberately hurt or scare him made him shudder. What had he done to even draw such attention to himself? Most of the people in town didn't seem to notice him on his way to work, or at the grocery store. Why would they want him to go home, when nobody noticed he was here in the first place?

The paper printed a photo of Mr. Gregory and Kuldip in front of the half-scrubbed graffiti. The whole town saw what someone among them thought of the Channas and that they weren't afraid to violate private property to get their message across. Mr. Gregory was quoted as saying, "We sponsored the Channas into the country as an act of Christian kindness and goodwill. Something we thought abounded in our small community. Sadly, there are those among us who feel the Channas don't belong here. Well, it's you. You who committed this heinous act who do not belong here. There is no room for hate in Norman."

Righteous words from a man who didn't pay Kuldip minimum wage until the person helping Kuldip with his taxes noticed and pointed the discrepancy out to Mr. Gregory.

chapter six

The walk to work in the dark never bothered Charlotte. Tonight it was quiet with a single car passing by. They were probably more suspicious of her than she of them. The quiet felt like a thick blanket into which her feet sank with every step. A chill rose from the dewy grass in the park and Charlotte pulled her sweater around her. It used to be a lot darker, years ago, when she walked to work. The last ten years saw Norman try to revitalize itself by opening a string of fast food franchises – Pizza Hut, McDonalds, Kentucky Fried Chicken. These places stayed open late, their neon signs beckoning, even when the doors were locked. It gave the young people somewhere to go, was the argument at the town hall meeting. And if young people had a place to go right here in town, then maybe fewer of them would leave. And they could work there. The restaurants provided jobs, so people could stay in Norman and raise their families on french fries and minimum wage.

Main Street became a block party. Night after night the restaurants filled with teenagers and smoke. Tires squealed well into the night and sometimes Charlotte, on her way to work, had to be careful when she crossed the street that she didn't get in the way of a drag race. Garbage blew in the wind scattering logos everywhere. The young people still left Norman for the city. They should have been wise enough to know that fast food was only part of the equation. The fuel for the fire. The allure of the city was more than convenience and bright signs. Having a McDonalds did not change the fact that opportunities in Norman were scarce, that there was nothing to do. But, there they were and there they would stay. To get rid of them now would be anti-progress. They were a testament to Normans keeping up with the times, being hip, being cool. There was even talk of opening a second Pizza Hut next to the Driftwood Inn. Two of the same franchises in one town. How cosmopolitan.

The walk took Charlotte ten minutes. Down Elm Street to the corner and then up past the Anglican Church and the tiny cemetery with rows of moss-covered, blackened headstones which marked the graves of people long since forgotten. The wrought iron fence and imposing gates kept the irreverent and impious out. And no dogs allowed. A stray mutt got in there once in a while and darted around the headstones, trying to pick up a scent, and where he couldn't find one, left his. Charlotte cheered him on. The way he darted across the graves, not caring who he offended. He tore apart flowers and dug up newly planted cedar shrubs and never got caught. The fresh flowers that appeared at Christmas and Remembrance Day were placed there at the risk of annihilation. Once, Charlotte saw the dog tearing away from the cemetery with a single rose in its teeth, like those greeting cards for which only a certain breed of dog lover has a sensibility. Perhaps Charlotte would make an anonymous suggestion to the women from the legion to leave treats for the dog instead of wreaths of white and blue carnations. Were it her grave, she would rather the occasional visit from an appreciative dog, than somebody whose feeling of obligation led them to the cellophane-wrapped bouquets at the IGA.

When Charlotte unlocked the back door to the bakery, she found a chair and sat in the semi-darkness. The light from the alley shone through the window and bathed the stainless steel counters and cupboards in a silvery light. The lights exposed the permanent grease which no amount of scrubbing would remove, the stains on the floor which would not come clean, the old butcher block with years of use worn into a shallow depression in the middle. All these old, familiar things. She supposed one day she could walk in here and find everything changed. Vi did have aspirations for the bakery and she loved the phrase 'state of the art.' Nothing here was state of the art right now but, soon enough there would be something flashy that would catch Vi's eye and she wouldn't be able to resist.

Nothing new was about to happen in the next week, so Charlotte didn't worry too much about it. She heard of people dropping dead the first week of their retirement because of the sudden change in routine, especially men. Why wasn't it their wives, clutching their hearts and gasping for breath the first day of their husband's retirement? Suddenly having their husbands home all day, looking for amusement. Following them around in mismatched clothes, chattering about the birds at the feeder they built twenty years ago, digging through their old hockey equipment and actually considering joining an old-timers league. Asking what was for lunch an hour after breakfast, wanting to come along to do the shopping and banking. Watching their wives dust and clean and make dinner, having always wondered how the food got on the table and is that how you make meatballs?

Charlotte set to work determined not to become mired in sentiment in this, her final week. As long as Vi was paying her, she would do her job as expected. She weighed the ingredients for all the dough. The bread went into the mixer for about fifteen minutes. If Charlotte got distracted and it went a bit longer it didn't matter. The longer the better, when it came to bread. Then the dough sat for thirty minutes. Once she had divided it up into the pans, she loaded the wheeled cart and rolled the whole thing into the proofer for thirty minutes. That's where the bread rose, in the warm, moist air of the proofer. The baking took the least amount of time. Only about twelve minutes.

People thought there was some magic to making bread, that it required delicate handling and precise skill. Bread liked to be beaten up. The more kneading and mixing, the lighter and airier the loaf. The secret, if there was one, was in the proportions. Once everything had been properly measured, there was little that could go wrong. But, you could not rush bread. That's where people made their mistakes. They stopped kneading too soon, didn't let it rise long enough. Hurry, hurry and before you know it there will be hot fresh bread. When their dense loaves clunked onto the counter they scratched their heads and decided it wasn't worth the bother.

At four o'clock, she set the kettle to boil and measured out a teaspoon of instant coffee into her mug. Outside, the sun hinted at the horizon. Charlotte slipped on her sweater and stepped outside. She was perhaps the only person in Norman who heard the robins rustling and calling to each other as they woke. She sipped the bitter coffee and felt its familiar kick. As the light filled the sky and the first cars could be heard in the streets, Charlotte rose and went back into the bakery. The world was awake now and the period of tranquillity she enjoyed each morning had now passed. What she feared was one day losing the magic. The dawn would rise, pale and fragile and gain strength and brilliance until the earth was hot and vital, and Charlotte wouldn't be there to see it, or wouldn't get it or would rather stay inside. An unbearable thought.

All the yeast doughs, the bread, the rolls, the cinnamon buns were in the proofer to rise. Charlotte started on the pastry and checked the list for special orders. Two birthday layer cakes for Thursday: 'Happy Fortieth Keith,' white cake, green frosting; a chocolate cake, space ships and the number ten in silver balls; and a white pan cake, large, blue frosting, no roses, 'We'll miss you Charlotte,' for Friday. Was it a joke? Probably not, but Charlotte would let Wade make that one. She'll tell him to write, "I'll Miss You Too," instead. She didn't even want to go to her own party and she certainly wasn't going to make her own cake.

Charlotte could make out each loaf under the covering cloth when she peered into the proofer. Whenever Mr. Olafson pulled the rack out and proclaimed, "The loaves have risen." Charlotte would reply, "Hallelujah," and she still said it to herself each time the rack was pulled out with the dough soft and springy and three times its original size. The utensils twinkled, hanging from the rack over the centre-island. She ran her hand over the smooth, cool surface of the wood table. The oven, nothing more than a hole in the wall, like the mouth of an insatiable beast into which she and Wade fed tray after tray of sweets.

Her work seemed like a test of her endurance at times. Kind of like that dreadful stress test at the hospital, but longer, the increments less perceptible. Sometimes to get through the week, Charlotte imagined herself an athlete, pushing through to the end of a race. Weary, weakening in the middle stretch, her body straining to plod ahead, one task at a time. Thinking of nothing but the end of the week, her finish line, when she would be able to look back and put one more week behind her. Maybe she had been anticipating or looking forward to her retirement. What else could have crossed her mind on those days she did nothing but grumble all the way through? Everybody looked forward to the day they no longer had to work, no longer had a schedule. But then, when faced with their gift of unlimited time, what did people do? Make schedules. They get involved in a million things, which must be carefully planned so as not to interfere or conflict with something else. They are busier than ever, driving to university courses and watercolour classes. Yoga, tai chi, aquasize. They volunteer everywhere. They work harder than they did at work and wonder if they retired too soon. Maybe they could have squeezed out a few more years.

Charlotte dusted the long table with flour. Her cool, dry palm caressed the surface until a thin layer of flour covered it. She rolled out the pastry for the pies. Most bakeries bought everything frozen, their pastry, their bread, croissants. Everything was available pre-made. Bakers just had to unwrap it and bake it in the oven. Nothing was done by hand anymore and in the big commercial bakeries, not one hand touched the bread until it came out of the oven. The ingredients were measured and then the entire process was automated, right to the slicing and packaging. Charlotte might as well retire. It seemed she had become obsolete.

Wade Pancratz rushed through the door filling the air with the smell of his wetnap cologne.

"Good morning Charlotte."

"Sleep in this morning?"

"Damn rush hour traffic. I should know by now how crazy it gets out there." It was an old Norman joke. Wade pulled the apron around him and tied it in front. "How many special orders?"

"Vi ordered my party cake. She wants me to write on it that she'll miss me."

"Aw, that's sweet. What kind of cake did she say you wanted?"

"White, blue icing, no roses."

"No roses? How cold."

Wade had been hired after completing his course at Red River Community College. Vi thought the work was getting too heavy for Charlotte and hired him to help part-time. Then, when Charlotte's heart started acting up, he went full-time. Charlotte didn't know at the time what the heavy feeling in her chest was, or the dampness across her brow. She thought it must be her age. At sixty-three to still be carrying those trays of bread and rolls, to be getting up so early in the day and working a full week. Wasn't it natural to show signs of strain? She could still do everything, just more slowly and with less ease. She watched how Doris moved, smoothly and with no effort, her body still efficient and fluid in motion. It didn't creak and groan at every turn. Those years are so few in number, the years when you don't feel your body quaking at the thought of getting up to retrieve a pencil that's rolled onto the floor or to answer the phone. Now, Charlotte's arms and legs felt so heavy, almost dead, and she had to drag them everywhere with her.

It didn't happen gradually either. One day she slept late and woke to the radio alarm rather than on her own. A cello piece by Schubert with a simple piano part crept into her dream. "I don't know what you want." She was screaming at her father, in her dream, with tears of rage springing into her eyes, while he sat in his easy chair, knitting. He had taken the yarn in between his teeth and was smiling and baring his teeth while she screamed. She took the yarn and started pulling it from between his teeth, but he hung on and his lips and gums started to bleed from the yarn. But Charlotte kept pulling and screaming until that Schubert piece on the radio broke the thread and the dream stopped making sense and woke her up. That's when her heart started leaping about in directions she couldn't follow.

Dread hung over her all that day at work. She felt clumsy and dropped things onto the floor only to be startled seconds later by the clatter. Vi came into the kitchen and found Charlotte asleep, slumped in a chair with the oven timer ringing and she insisted Charlotte go straight home and see Dr. Wilson in the morning. Regardless of the outcome, Vi had decided to hire someone to help out. Sooner or later she would need to find Charlotte's replacement and it may as well be sooner.

58

Wade had felt hopeless, his first day. He stood at the back door, shifting his weight from one foot to the other like a big kid who had to pee. He wore a black leather jacket, a package of Cameo cigarettes visible in the pocket. His glasses immediately started to slide in the heat of the kitchen, revealing a welt-like pimple on the bridge of his nose.

"It's Wade, Wade Pancratz. I've been hired as assistant baker. I'm here for my orientation. Vi told me to come in the back."

He wrinkled up his nose to stop the descent of the glasses. His eyes behind the lenses darted over the kitchen, seeking out one implement, one familiar thing he could recognize from the classes he had just finished. All the equipment here was much older than he was used to from school. The scales weren't digital. They had the counter weights and balances. Maybe he should have looked for work in Winnipeg instead of running away. But when his mother called to say the job was open, it was two days after his life caved in and walking away from the rubble rather than trying to fix it seemed a natural thing to do.

"What happened to Miss Weiss?" Wade had asked his mother.

"I think she's slowing down. She's been there an awfully long time. I think she may be having some health problems. I'm not sure."

Wade tried to imagine waking up every day and walking to work, trudging through the same streets he used to take to get to school. His heart leapt to his chest at every corner in anticipation of an attack by those bastards on the football team. *Hey Princess Wade. Kiss any toads lately? Maybe you should do some wrist exercises. They're looking a little limp, or maybe you can't help it. Queer. Faggot.* And whatever else they could think of. Lame insults hurled at him as he walked as fast as possible to school. He should never have taken anything they said

59

personally. Anyone not on the football team was automatically a fag to those guys. They probably didn't even know what they were saying. He never turned around to confront them. They weren't afraid of anything and a threat from him would just goad them into action. Like the time Larry Pennyfather tried to take them on. The picked him up and tied him to the flag pole and sung *Oh Canada* while they pelted him with snowballs. There he remained until one of the janitors found him. Those were the kind of guys who never left Norman. Somewhere in their pea-sized brains, they knew the real world would expect them to grow up. So, they stayed in Norman where their brutish behaviour was excused, got married and passed it on to their kids. By now a new set of dim-witted thugs would be starting kindergarten and the poor kids like him would have their eyes opened with a slap.

It had taken less than a day to pack his things into boxes. Everything fit into his car and he drove home with an uneasy feeling growing in him the closer he got to Norman. He ate dinner with his mom, turkey soup and buns, before he made his way to his new apartment. There he sat long into the night on a couch which had been in the rec-room of his old house all his life, watching a television which his mother gave to him after she salvaged it from the church rummage sale pile. He felt displaced, disjointed in his new place. As long as he was inside the walls of his apartment, things felt fine. As soon as he walked over to the window and viewed the street below, a pang of regret shot from under his sternum. Something felt wrong. He had convinced himself that coming here would be like hitting the re-set button on his life. If he returned to where he started and set out again maybe things would turn out better for him. But, somehow this didn't feel like a new beginning. He felt like he had dragged all his garbage back here with him. The hollow in his chest rang with emptiness. His eggs were back in the same basket from where they once came, except this time they wouldn't hatch. They would be splattered all over the pavement and would harden into an insoluble mess.

"They might have to cancel the parade this year," his mother told him. She was standing at his window. "And you've got this great view."

What a depressing thought, to watch the Norman May Day parade from his one bedroom apartment window. A flood of memories came back to him, the reasons he had left in the first place. That damn parade, the small town community event he couldn't stand, with the farmers revving up the old tractors and threshers out in McAllister's field. Square dances and talent contests. Every year the same people participated and the rest of them stayed away. It was people from the city who liked all that country stuff. They loved to come and see how the simple country folk amused themselves with their corn on the cob and blueberry pie eating contests. Did they think we did that every day? Sure, every weekend the ladies bake dozens of pies so we menfolk can impress them by gorging ourselves. Then we square dance until we puke and ride the thresher all the way home and fornicate under a bale of hay and wake up with the cows. It's the country way of life.

It wasn't the people who came from the city who bothered Wade, but the people from Norman who acted as though things did happen that way all the time. They loved putting on a show and making fools of the visitors. They were snobs about their life in Norman. People who left for the city were derided. What, we're not good enough for you? It's not exciting enough here? He could hear them already. So, you decided to come back. The city's not as great as you thought it would be, eh? I could have told you that and saved you a whole lot of heartache.

* * * * *

61

Charlotte and Wade stood within reach of each other. Between Vi and Dr. Wilson, Charlotte was left with little choice but to accept an assistant.

"I think you used to deliver the paper to my house. Did you have a route on Elm Street?" Wade looked familiar. She remembered him, a careful boy who always folded the paper and put it in the mailbox and never cut across the lawn. "You were an excellent paper-boy."

Wade rubbed his palms on the skirt of his apron. He and his mother used to come here to buy bread, probably from Charlotte. He remembered her too.

"You gave my grade two class a tour back here once. You made a batch of cookies and told us to learn our fractions or we'd never learn to bake anything."

"Well, you've got the certificate. Was I wrong?"

They gave out certificates for everything these days. That's what she found ridiculous, not Wade. Certificates for baby-sitting, selling Tupperware, even retail sales. The sales people who lurk behind every *Sale Sale Sale* rack, have taken classes where they've learned this technique as an effective way to sell things. And here was the person likely to replace her when she left, fresh from a course in the big city and he probably hadn't set foot in a real bakery since grade two. How could they teach in a year what took Charlotte years to perfect? And what bakery could afford the state of the art convection ovens and mixers he probably learned on?

"You can get started on the whole-wheat. The recipes for white, whole-wheat and rye are up there. All the tins are marked. Ask me anything you like. We're going to have a busy week." Then she added, "You can take over the lemon meringue pies too. I usually make two a day."

"Um, sure."

"Good. But, start with the bread. I think there's still one pie left over from yesterday anyway."

Wade took a deep breath. Bread. Basic, elemental, just a matter of getting the consistency right and he would be home-free. He didn't want his first batch to turn out like the rubber bricks his swimming teacher used to make him dive for at the bottom of the pool. The recipes were clear enough and by the week's end he would have the required weights memorized. He poured the flour onto the scale. At school they had been taught everything in metric and here all the scales and recipes referred to pounds. Back to the good old days, he thought with some reservation. He lowered the mixing hook into the mound of ingredients and flipped the switch. The machine did all the work. All he had to do was watch as the hook ground the ingredients against the sides and bottom of the metal bowl. It took about twenty or thirty minutes. Charlotte was pulling tray after tray out of the oven and Wade wondered what kind of health problems she could be having. Whatever it was, it didn't seem to be slowing her down. She moved around the kitchen the way people danced with partners they've had their whole lives. Each step falling in time exactly where it should.

Charlotte watched Wade settle into the kitchen. When she first started at the bakery, she watched Mr. Olafson for a full week before she dared try any of the recipes herself. Even then, her first attempt was a tray of puffed-wheat cake and that didn't even have to go into the oven. By the end of the day they had sold three pieces and the rest of the pan had gone hard and had to be broken up for the birds. She had to admit, she couldn't have come in and made a batch of whole-wheat bread, with no direction and certainly not without watching first. And he was standing over the Hobart, watching the dough, not taking for granted the work of the machine. Maybe he would turn out to be as conscientious as she.

Wade cradled each ball of dough as he lowered it into a pan, like tucking an infant into bed, and covered them with a clean tea-towel. He set the timer, wiped off the counter and slid his glasses back up his nose with the back of his wrist. He saw Charlotte watching. "How'd I do?"

"Pretty good, I'd say."

"What's this thing for?" Wade held up the mold for the penis cake.

"It's a mold for one of the specialty cakes."

"What is it? A submarine?"

"Not exactly." Charlotte imagined Wade to be the type of permanently red-faced boy she remembered from high school. The type who asked her to slow dance and then pressed their persistent peckers into her thigh, harder and harder until the music stopped and then looked sheepishly away, stuffed their hands deep into their pockets and said sorry. Boys who couldn't reconcile the thing between their legs with the girl in their arms.

"It's a penis, Wade," she said.

"Oh, I get it." Wade turned the mold upside down to see what the cake would look like. He felt his ears burn. "I guess I've just never seen one this big."

"Well, that makes two of us." Charlotte winked.

"Yeah, dream on, eh?" His ears burned even brighter. He placed the mold back on the rack and checked his loaves in the proofer. The dough had started to poke its way up under the tea towels, the sight of which made Wade even more uncomfortable.

The next time an order came in for a specialty cake, Charlotte let Wade make it and they both laughed at the odd business of women. Wade added certain details to the frosting Charlotte had not thought of.

At first, Charlotte felt robbed of her time alone in the morning. The bakery had been her dominion for so long. The long quiet mornings, alone under the bright lights with the sound of the mixer churning and the room warming as the oven heated up. She always hummed or sang and knew she wouldn't have the nerve in front of Wade. In the summer she would sit out back and watch the sun come up. In the winter she wiped the condensation from the window and watched from inside. Her resentment at Wade came from the feeling of losing that time alone. But, he turned out to be a perfect assistant. He loved the feeling in the bakery at that time of day too and he and Charlotte worked in silence until their break. They never had to agree to do this, or discuss it, it just happened. Once Charlotte realized Wade loved the same things about the bakery as she did, she knew they would get along. Now that she was leaving she would even miss him. All the years she had worked alone, she never thought she would prefer to work with somebody and she was saddened she discovered this so late.

On his second day, Charlotte made each of them a cup of instant coffee and a warm buttered bun with apricot jam. They sat out back and watched the sun come up, beautiful as ever. Wade took off his hairnet and ran his fingers through his limp, blonde hair.

"This is the best part of being a baker," he said as he chewed. "You're always there, right when the bread comes out of the oven."

"Right you are. It is glorious, isn't it?"

"Glorious, indeed."

chapter seven

"Charlotte," Vi's voice came from the front before she swung through the door. "Did you see the list? And the picture June dug up? Isn't it a hoot?" The announcement for Charlotte's retirement and the accompanying list had been taped up next to Wade's certificate.

"I need to talk to you later about the dinner. We have to finalize things by tonight." Vi checked her watch. "Where's Doris?"

"It's not eight-thirty yet. She'll be here," Charlotte said.

"Why can't she ever be a minute early? Just one minute. I've asked her to be a little considerate and come early. It gets me all tense when she rushes in here on the nose of eight-thirty. I hate being frantic right at the start of every day."

"She hasn't been late or missed a day yet."

"That's not the point. Her sense of timing makes me tense."

The door flew open and Doris yodeled into the bakery, "I'm here, ready for duty." She blew one last puff of smoke out the door and let it swing shut behind her.

"Right on time," said Charlotte.

"Can't be late. It would upset the boss." Doris winked at Vi, leaned against the counter and shut her eyes. "Oh, God. I swear I will never tire of that smell."

The bread had just been pulled out of the oven. Charlotte broke a piece off for her and buttered it. "A little something to keep you going this morning."

Doris held it to her nose and let the steam rise into her face. "This is the sweetest thing of all."

"It's bread. It's what we do here. Bake bread. If you worked in a potato chip factory, would you think the chips were beautiful too?" asked Vi. She had not yet adjusted to the camaraderie developing in the back of her bakery and she didn't like the way Doris winked at her as though they were the best of friends. "If you eat that now, you'll be officially late. The front door should have been unlocked two minutes ago."

"I guess I'll have to save it for my break. I hope fifteen minutes is enough time to have a smoke and eat a snack. I'll have to be sure to hurry." Doris gave Vi an earnest look. "One of these days I'm coming in early to watch you guys bake bread. Start to finish. I saw it on a cooking show once and the guy was going on and on about how beautiful the oil was when he poured it onto the flour and he slowly mixed it in and the most gorgeous swirl filled the bowl, white and yellow. So they had the camera shot over the bowl, but the cable was on the fritz, so I couldn't really see it. I mean it. I'm coming in one day to see." She turned on her heel and disappeared through the swinging doors, leaving Vi behind with Charlotte and Wade.

"Honestly, if Barbara Richards wasn't such a dear friend, I would have fired that girl long ago." Vi picked up the broom and began sweeping the floor, bending awkwardly in her skirt and blazer to get under the table and then around Wade's feet. Little piles of dirt were placed every five feet and then she swept them all into one large pile by the back door.

"There, that will save you a little work later on," she said.

Every time Doris was around the shop, there was drama. She never approached any situation or conversation without acting, just a little bit. It wasn't that she was acting out a part, she was acting like an actor. It was one of her most endearing traits, Charlotte thought. When she was ten, Doris won second prize in a talent contest. She sang *Walking After Midnight*, the old Patsy Cline tune and walked away with the second prize, a set of cutlery. Her picture was in the paper the next day, her first taste of celebrity and she had been pursuing that taste every since. She carried herself with an air of importance which hung on her like an ill-fitting suit. Who could blame her though? Here she was working at the age of sixteen with all these adults who knew she had dropped out of school. She didn't want them to think she was stupid, which she assumed was the first thing people thought about her. She wanted so badly to prove she was smart, too smart for school and that was why she chose to leave and work instead. It was in her mind to prove that she could amount to something and for her the choice of acting was only the vehicle to the true goal, the one thing people here might respond to and that was fame. Doris didn't want to act so much as she wanted to be famous. Fabulously rich and famous. The ultimate dream.

Doris's mother, Barbara was president of the Norman Business Council, so Vi had thought the move to hire Doris would be politically beneficial, and of course a friendly gesture towards Barbara. Now, she could not clearly see how she could fire Doris without being shunned by the business community. So, Doris stayed and stretched the limits of Vi's patience, which meant Vi spent a lot more time in the back of the bakery, which shattered the calm routine Charlotte and Wade had worked out.

When her father died and Vi inherited the bakery, rather than sell it, she embraced the challenge of running it herself. She signed up for week long courses in business management and even once travelled all the way to Toronto to take a seminar in "Employer-Employee

Relations." She learned principles of TQM (Total Quality Management) and CQI (Continuous Quality Improvement), she swore there was a difference, one Charlotte never quite grasped but thought that was for Vi to keep straight. As far as Charlotte could tell the bakery ran in pretty much the same way it always had. Vi's greatest challenge was implementing something called the Team Approach, because she valued her own opinion above everyone else's and certainly was not about to include Doris, the high school dropout, in any decisions regarding the bakery.

Besides, she saw nothing but futility in the team building exercises the course instructor came up with. Huddled in groups around tables, racing to build a tower out of Styrofoam cups, paper-clips and coffee stirrers. It made her feel no closer to her appointed teammates. Vi felt the entire exercise to be a slap in the face of feminism.

"Why always towers? What have we been fighting for the last hundred years? Am I the only one who smells a rat here? As if racing to build a tower ever got anyone anywhere."

Vi grabbed a tea towel and began polishing the stainless steel cabinets. It was not possible to keep the stainless steel free of fingerprints. Wade did it at the end of each day when all the dishes had been done and put away and they didn't need anything else from inside a cupboard. To bother before then was futile. Vi chattered animatedly while she worked.

"The numbers are looking pretty good this month. Those cheese buns are a hit. They sell out by eleven every day." Vi attacked the cupboards with a furious scrubbing, around the handles, where most of the fingerprints gathered, while Wade and Charlotte tried to work around her and not be bothered by her presence. It was like having a big furry spider in the kitchen. Too big to squash without making a slippery mess and it made you uneasy as long as you knew it was there. They couldn't very well sweep Vi onto a piece of cardboard and flick her out the back door.

"I'm thinking of having a bun sale. Sometime soon. Not this week. There's too much going on. Maybe at the end of next month. That will give me time to come up with an ad. Something like: *We're on a Roll*, or, *Get Fresh with our Buns?* What do you guys think?"

"How about *Hot Buns Guaranteed?*" asked Wade while he waited for her to finish polishing the cupboard where the rolling pins were kept.

"Oh, heavens. You can never say guaranteed. People hold you to it. It's bad for business to guarantee anything."

Vi had also been toying with the idea of a Baker's Dozen card: buy a dozen, get one loaf free. But, she couldn't be giving away too much. That Senior's Day discount almost did her in every time as it was.

"It's like they can't buy a loaf of bread any other day. I better make sure Doris is checking ID. She probably thinks forty-five year olds are seniors. But, you can't argue with the numbers at the end of Senior's Day."

Charlotte followed Vi through the swinging door to the front.

"I've got to leave a bit early tomorrow Vi. I've got to buy a dress for Saturday. June's made an appointment for me at Rosa's."

"Oh, Charlotte, I can't believe it's this Saturday already." Vi leaned on the chair behind the cash register and fingered the edge of Charlotte's picture and sighed. Charlotte knew her leaving wasn't really that disappointing for Vi. She was pretty proud to have a baker with a certificate to display for the customers. Credentials were key. The bread was bound to be delicious if made by a certified baker.

"Listen Charlotte, could you drop in at the Driftwood and look at the room? They want to ask you about the layout."

"What layout?"

"You know, how you want the tables arranged."

"I don't care, as long as everyone gets a seat."

"Well, it's right on your way, just drop in and ask for Mitchell. He's great. It'll take a second."

What about my bad heart? Charlotte wondered. She was sure in all the fuss over her party, everyone had forgotten why she was retiring. Frankly, she forgot about it herself most of the time and wondered too, why she had to quit. She would pop in at the Driftwood and if Mitchell didn't appear within ten seconds, she would tell Vi he wasn't there.

"Doris, make sure you sell those Imperial cookies from the freezer first. Don't let any of the fresh ones go until those are gone."

The look Doris gave Vi, with a snap of her bubble gum made Charlotte thankful Vi didn't have any teenagers of her own to guide through life. Some people just didn't have the knack.

"And what did I tell you about gum?"

"Um, if you swallow it, it stays in your stomach forever?"

Doris needed this job and she knew Vi's limits exactly. If this didn't work out, if she didn't prove herself responsible enough to hold down a job, then her mom would make her go back to school. She hated that she still had to answer to her mother. Here she was holding down a full time job and her mother could make her go back to school the minute she messed things up. If Vi fired her, she would be back to sitting in Mr. Howden's math class, dying from boredom or changing in the locker room for gym class, and trying to think of an excuse to get out of the twelve minute run. What would her friends say, after Doris had gloated and boasted to everyone? On her last day she walked out of the school with her friends and turned and yelled at the building, "Thanks for nothing." Her friends giggled. They were all so jealous. None of their parents would ever let them quit and get a job. Doris was experiencing another dash of celebrity and it felt great. She vowed to follow Vi's rules and not get into trouble. Going back to school would make her feel like such a loser.

chapter eight

At two-fifteen, Charlotte hung up her apron and left for the Driftwood. On the sidewalk, coming towards her was Kuldip, with his plastic blue Pepsi cooler slung over his shoulder like a purse.

"Hello, Kuldip. Off to see your wife?"

"Oh yes. Everyday, Miss Charlotte." His eyes squinted into the sun. Four years ago he had to move Meagha into the care home. She had woken up one morning and only opened one eye. All morning Kuldip waited for her to open the other eye, until finally he asked her and she said she didn't know what he was talking about. The doctor diagnosed a small stroke and said it was normal for someone her age to experience small strokes. Since she seemed to be fine, he sent her home.

Later that evening, she dropped the spoon into the pot of soup she had been preparing for their supper and fell over sideways. The doctor said it was normal for a big stroke to follow a little one. This time Meagha had to go into the hospital for awhile to see if she would get back to the point of only having one eye open. But, she could no longer talk and her only way of expression was a mounting agitation accompanied by a mournful yowling and nobody knew what she wanted. The therapists moved her arms and legs, sat her up on the edge of the bed and tried to balance her there, to see if she could sit up on her own. She tipped over very easily. After two weeks they determined there would be little recovery. Papers were filled out and slid across a table for Kuldip to sign, so they could transfer Meagha from the hospital to the care home. With a heaviness in his heart, Kuldip signed where the social worker held her finger. Heartbroken, because Meagha didn't know when the ambulance attendants carried her out on a stretcher and drove noiselessly through the streets to the hospital, that the last she would see of her house would be the ceiling and a wall of family photographs, upside-down. At home, later that night, Kuldip lay on the floor of the hallway to the front door and looked up at the ceiling and the photographs and tried to convince himself he had not betrayed his beloved wife by letting the ambulance come and take her away.

"What happened to your arm?" Charlotte pointed at three round bruises on Kuldip's arm.

"Oh, my wife very strong." He grabbed Charlotte's arm and squeezed. "Like that. Very strong. Hee, hee, hee."

Kuldip often came home with purple bruises on his arm from where Meagha's strong and still mighty hand gripped. He visited everyday and had lunch with her. In his cooler, he packed familiar food. Meagha liked the smell. She couldn't eat it, but Kuldip ate while her dinner dripped through a tube in her nose, from a plastic bag hanging on an IV pole.

It was after his wife had been driven to the care home in an ambulance that Charlotte noticed the lights and the cooking in the night. Kindred spirits. What was it about the night? Charlotte felt less alone when she rose in the night to go to work, than she did all day, surrounded by Vi and Doris and Wade. She supposed she was drawn to the solitude, or had spent so many years alone she had developed a dependence. It was easy in the middle of the night. No blinds or curtains to draw or ringing phones to avoid, nobody knocking at the door to ignore. That was simple avoidance, not solitude. And there were such people who sat grumbling in a darkened room and avoided any intrusion into their misery. People who sought solitude eliminated the distractions. For this the night was perfect.

Perfect for Kuldip too, because the unoccupied space in his bed frightened him, especially at night. From a sound sleep his eyes would fly open when his hand strayed across the bed and found nothing there. When he slept on the sofa during the afternoon, no darkness and no empty space threatened to jar his heart, making his muscles jolt him upright and gasping. There, he could sleep, heavy and warmed by the sun and his cat. Sleep came easily and the softness of the sofa made him imagine he was floating all the way to heaven.

* * * * *

The Driftwood was the only hotel in town. A vast parking lot sprawled before its beige brick exterior. It was empty today, but by six o'clock Friday night, it would be hard to find a spot. A red neon sign flashed *vacancy* for most of the year. Ever since the town council approved the construction of the Norman bypass, most prospective visitors were re-routed around Norman at one hundred kilometres an hour.

The lobby of the Driftwood still smelled of stale smoke, as it had in the beginning, as though it had been built with the smoke saturated wood veneer salvaged from some other dilapidated hotel before the wrecking ball hit. As soon as she entered through the heavy glass doors Charlotte remembered the dark panelling and dirty yellow light and the thin, fibrous carpet under her feet. She walked over to the lounge. It looked a lot different in the daytime. She hadn't even noticed the windows before, having always been there at night when the heavy brown drapes had been drawn and the lights dim, except for over the bar. A few people sat at a table with six glasses of beer each in front of them. The bartender wiped down the front of the bar while country music twanged through the speakers.

The furniture looked the same. Heavy metal framed chairs with dark brown, mottled vinyl and square tables with pink and green and blue gum stuck underneath. There was a lot more neon and more beer signs. It never had been a classy place, but she always thought the live music brought a touch of sophistication to the night. Either nobody cared for live music anymore or more likely, no musicians could be bothered to play here. A pool table stood where the little stage had been. The stage was still used on weekends when the occasional country and western band rolled into town.

She and Ray and Andy used to play here Saturday nights, cramped up on the little stage, the sound of their three instruments against the clamour from the crowd. For a year and a half they had had a regular gig at the Driftwood lounge. No other bands ever played there so they became the house band by acclamation. A small poster had been taped over the bar: 'Live at the Driftwood every Saturday Night: The Hots!' Sizzling vapours shimmered above the letters of the word Hots.

Ray had been the percussionist in the high school orchestra and his parts rivalled Charlotte's for complexity. Often, they caught each other staring into space, concentrating only hard enough to maintain the three-four tedium of the *Blue Danube Waltz*. In their break, Ray got behind the kit he rarely got to use and Charlotte placed her bow on the stand and plucked her best catwalk rhythm to Ray's staccatos on the high hat. Once he got going, Charlotte had a hard time keeping up with him and their playing turned into a duel to see who would give in first. If he sped up, all Charlotte had to do was cut the time in half, until Ray noticed and told her she was cheating. This was

76

how the two of them flirted at first. Trying to out-jazz one another.

All the coy banter between Ray's drums and Charlotte's bass soon led to a real kiss, to an embrace and eventually to bed where they discovered what everybody meant by ecstasy. They explored each other's bodies with the wonder and amazement of exploring exotic lands. It developed so naturally, the extension of their friendship into something more physically intimate. This time in Charlotte's life was one of such simple bliss, she hardly noticed she was in love.

She loved her life and Ray was part of that. It was not a torrid affair, not a fiery union. They did not gaze longingly into each other's eyes and moon over each other everywhere they went. They enjoyed one another, in every sense. They were friends who did not want to step in the way of the other, and so talk of commitment, or true love or soul mates never entered the conversation. There was no need. There was a long way to go in this life and they knew any talk of getting married would have stunted them both.

Andy generally steered clear of the music room, but played the piano like a wizard. Andy's basement became their rehearsal room where they listened to his records and tried to get the main licks down. They turned the music up loud and tried to play along and sort out the notes and rhythms. Then, when they thought they had it, they turned the music off and put it together themselves. Their method seemed to work. As long as the music resembled something close to jazz they were happy.

After their basement rehearsals Ray and Charlotte would walk home through the cemetery, their arms draped around each other, comfortable as worn sweaters. They walked slowly and talked about the music and their Saturday night gig. Sometimes, if it wasn't too cold, they stopped and sat on the bench in front of Jack William Walter's grave. "Let's pay our respects to old Uncle Jack, shall we?" Ray asked.

"Sure, it's a nice night, why not?"

They sat and marvelled at the moon, big and yellow in the late summer sky, Charlotte with her legs curled up on the bench and Ray with his stretched out long into the middle of the path. It was here that they came up with the plan to go to Montreal for the jazz festival. All they had to do was work for a while after graduation and then they would take the train from Winnipeg and be there in time for the jazz festival. They could travel from there to Quebec City or Toronto or even hop a freighter for Europe. One of the things Charlotte and Ray did best was dream big dreams. If Ray had his way, Charlotte would travel the world with him, rolling her bass in front of her and they would busk their way across Europe.

"Easy for you to say with your sticks in your back pocket. Maybe I can learn how to play the bongos."

And he did buy her a set with a card that read, "Bongo lessons included. World tour to follow."

The bohemian life was within reach. After their tour of the world they could go to New York and live in the Village and check out the Saturday afternoon scene at the clubs. But for now they had the small version of their dream. The beer-guzzling crowd on Saturday night didn't care what they heard, as long as they recognized a song or two. People felt like they were out, doing something. Sitting in a bar, listening to a band, the weekend only half over.

The band played two sets, forty-five minutes each with about an hour between sets. They didn't get paid, but the manager allowed them two beer each and after that there was usually a table of drunk customers willing to buy drinks for the band. They played the standards: Billie Holiday, Cole Porter, Rogers and Hart. Charlotte tried to sing like Nina Simone, but could never quite get her voice to wail and sob, as only Nina could.

They played to a roomful of people getting drunk on beer for twenty-five cents a glass and loading their tables with endless baskets of pretzels. The band's signature song was a rollicking rendition of *My Baby Just Cares For Me*. They started off with Andy vamping on piano, then Ray came in on high hat, just gently and Charlotte would come in with her bass and they would vamp the intro until the crowd recognized their favourite song and started whooping. Then Andy would tease them some more and play a twenty-four bar solo before Charlotte even began to sing. They ended their second set with this song and left the stage feeling charged, on top of the world. Performing on that tiny, rickety stage, singing her heart out into the smoke-filled room, thumping rhythms out on her bass made Charlotte feel brilliant. An unreal charge filled the room. An exuberance emanated from the stage and filtered down to the audience whose spirits rose as the night closed in. She gave it her all, every night. Because, she knew this was it, the closest taste of fame she might ever get.

She never felt unsafe here. Ray and Andy stayed close and most of the people drinking in the bar knew her. By the end of the evening Charlotte's hair and clothing would hang thick with the stench of smoke, but she didn't care. It was the one night of the week she didn't mind being in Norman. The one night she felt extraordinary. Men would buy her drinks and offer her cigarettes and sometimes she even smoked one and tried to imagine what the clubs were like out there in the real world. Surely in New York they drank something other than beer out of glasses still hot and soapy from the dishwasher. And people dressed in suits and slinky dresses, rather than jeans and boots and shirts they had worked in all day. In the parking lot shiny black cars with gleaming chrome would be parked one after the other like a row of dominos, rather than the dented, dusty pick-up trucks which squealed in and out of the Driftwood lot all night.

Andy liked dressing up the most. Back from trips to Eaton's in Winnipeg, he'd show up on gig night in purple satin shirts and tight black pants. Ray normally wore a short sleeved shirt and jeans and Charlotte sat on a stool behind her bass, wearing a jacket and slacks with her blouse open and the collar folded over the jacket collar. She and Andy took turns singing. He loved to sing *Over the Rainbow,* because he said he'd never heard any male vocal interpretation he liked and thought it might be his ticket to fame. It turned out to be his ticket to the hospital, when a couple of farm boys slammed him onto the hood of their truck and broke his nose and collar bone, claiming he had winked at them while he was singing.

"Rhythm is everything in music, you can have a great ear and a knack for your instrument, but if you can't keep a steady beat, you're doomed," Charlotte's father used to say while they sat in his study and listened to recordings of Les Brown and Ornette Coleman.

"You start listening to the rhythm section and it's pure magic. Every beat of the high hat and every brush on the snare perfectly placed to bring the music alive. The bass and the drums, that's where the music begins and ends."

Once she started listening this way, picking out the bass line and the subtle rhythms of the drumsticks, Charlotte found herself mesmerized by the intricacies of the music. She found she could tune out different instruments and focus on one at a time. Sometimes barely perceptible as part of the ensemble, but when her hearing honed in on the bass, she discovered the music always hung perfectly over the bass line. No matter how simple or complicated the riff, the other players seemed to be all over the place, doing their own thing, but the bass held things together. Without that foundation the music made no sense.

Charles taught her to listen for the blue notes, those flattened notes between notes, the ones which don't really exist in musical notation. Jazz grew from these root notes, became the music it is, because of them. Like bending the truth, blue notes were bent, not quite true, ringing minor when the music cried for major, this tension gave the music its heart-wrenching appeal. Charlotte imagined musicians experimenting with these notes, stumbling upon them with a misplaced finger and then injecting them throughout the music, creating such a mournful sound, which reduced all the room to weeping into glasses of whiskey. These notes slowly merged into western music; a reconciliation of African influence with western music, and resulted in these hybrid notes. But, Charlotte preferred to believe it was an accident. Some grizzled old bass player, too drunk to stand up and play, his hands sliding all over the fingerboard producing sounds which for unknown reasons pulled his heart from inside him and in his drunken state he stood there, sobbing, playing those notes over and over again, tears cascading onto his hands, making them slide around even more, feeding into the heaving swells of sorrow in his chest and the tears which stung his eyes and wanting more and more.

* * * * *

"Ma'am?" Charlotte jumped. "Would you like anything ma'am?" The bartender was speaking to her.

"Oh, um. No thank you. I'm here to see someone about a party on Saturday."

"Banquet room is down the hall to your left."

"Thank you." She left. Vi could arrange the table layout. Suddenly, Charlotte felt too weak to wait.

chapter nine

C hildhood memories flitted through Charlotte's mind from time to time like a slide show. Scenes in which she appeared as a character involved in some event were captured in her memory as a static image with no associated emotion. She didn't remember being particularly happy or sad. She was a character from her past in the same way June, her mother and father figured in her memory. They were almost more real and animated in the events she remembered than she herself was. The parts they played were clear, made sense. But if she focused on herself, her thoughts became muddled and distracted. It saddened her to realize she couldn't relate to the child she had been, couldn't really remember what she was like, that little girl. When she looked at old class pictures, she stared at each row and didn't know anything more about herself than all the rest of the kids in her grade one class.

The memory of Charlotte's mother had faded more than her father's, partly a factor of time and partly a factor of space. Space was one thing never lacking between Charlotte's mother and herself. A stiff, cold space between two people which came about as Charlotte shifted into being who she was and away from the image of her mother's expectation. Thinking back, Charlotte realized she betrayed her mother's vision when she discovered her mother's real self. A fallacy unveiled and exposed to the scrutiny of the young. Charlotte's mother was a poseur and Charlotte eventually told her so. No trust can develop when the truth is told. The truth which was covered with a lie.

Charlotte knew her mother thought she had married beneath her. Florence spent her life grappling her way back to where she thought she rightly belonged. The point of her struggle was never quite clear to Charlotte. Her mother was born into the family of a prominent surgeon in Winnipeg and lived a privileged, ask-the-housekeeper-to-fix-you-something kind of life. Florence believed the role of children was to flesh out the family image, to add to the character of her highly respected family.

When Florence and Charles moved to Norman after Charles had been offered a position at the high school, she set out to teach herself a lesson. A lesson that Florence Weiss was not too good for a small town; she would make an effort to fit in and mix with the locals. But Florence found the women of Norman plain and a bit vulgar. She thought it distasteful the way they presented themselves in town with rollers in their hair and slippers on their feet. Their casual attitude and unsophisticated airs irritated her. The familiarity with which she was greeted, like a long lost friend, made her clench.

"Oh, hello Mrs. Weiss. And how are you getting on? And how are the girls? Settling into school all right?" The whole while they spoke, their darting eyes scanned the contents of her shopping cart. She knew these women all vied to befriend her, ingratiate themselves to her. She could see it in their plastic smiles. Hair piled on their heads and covered with garish scarves and lipstick stuck to their teeth. Uncouth. Well, she would have none of it. She felt insulted by it, an unfounded feeling, but present all the same. It made her feel as though she had to fight to retain her status, to show off her good breeding, lest she slip into the slovenly habits of the common citizenry of Norman.

Buying a house across the street from Mayor Weisenthal and his wife was not pre-meditated, but definitely a boon to Florence's cause. It was the movers who alerted her to the identity of the people in the stone house across the way. While they unloaded the truck, Florence strolled the grounds of her new home and cast glances across the street to see if she could detect a figure in the window, or the stirring of a curtain.

"See that house over there," she said to June and Charlotte, who sat on the lawn eating lime popsicles. "The mayor of this town lives there. He's a very important man, so it's very important for you two to be polite to anybody you see coming out of that house. And don't be seen tearing around the neighbourhood. We want them to know you've been brought up right."

"I thought we had to be polite to everybody."

"Well, you do. But be especially polite to our new neighbours. We want them to like us, don't we?"

While June nodded her assent, Charlotte already knew she didn't like those people across the street. She didn't care if they liked her or not. It was the first time she wondered about her mother and the funny things she worried about.

The day after the movers delivered the furniture, Beatrice Weisenthal delivered lemon cookies and bran-raisin muffins to welcome the new family. Her head, with its hairspray hardened, ash blonde hair, appeared in the window of their front door. A permanent smile painted on her face, a thin invitation to help out in any way she could, delivering the same speech and cookies she did for every new family in town. Beatrice had assumed the role of every-woman's friend ever since her husband was elected mayor. Her intention was not to actually make any friends, but to extend the hand of friendship, at an arm's length, in order to buttress her husband's career. But, in delivering the baked goods to the new Weiss family across the street, Beatrice had set in motion a series of cake and loaf exchanges, the end result of which would be a something approaching real friendship.

Florence saw Beatrice leave her house. She watched as Beatrice struggled with the plate and pulled the door shut and then watched her cross the street and walk up Florence's sidewalk. In the five seconds it took Beatrice to walk to the front door, Florence quickly settled herself comfortably on the sofa, listened for the doorbell and when she heard it, composed herself a moment, rose and walked to the front door to receive the mayor's wife. Her neighbour.

She accepted the baked offering as though it was a victory torch. The usual overtures were crooned.

"Ooh, don't these look lovely. The girls will make quick work of these."

"Well, it's just a small gesture to welcome you. I'm sure you don't have your kitchen unpacked yet."

"No, no. You're right. Everything is still in quite a mess."

"Well, you know where I live if you need anything. Just give me a dingle."

"I certainly will. And thanks so much."

Florence hoisted the plate of cookies over her head and waltzed them into the kitchen. The lemon cookies melted on Florence's tongue. The mayor had married an excellent homemaker. Amid the boxes of dishes, cookware and cutlery, Florence immediately seized upon the box containing her cookbooks and spent an hour looking for her recipe for lemon meringue pie.

If there was one person worth knowing in Norman it was Beatrice. So, the very next day, Florence made the pie and watched out the window until she saw Beatrice return from town. The clock counted down five minutes and then, Florence crossed the street, paused and marched regally up the walk of Mrs. Mayor Weisenthal's house. She peered through the front door. The hallway led through to the kitchen where Florence watched Beatrice unpack her groceries. The smell of bacon wafted through the screen. From where she stood Florence could glimpse into the dining room and living room. A silver tea service sat on the sideboard in the dining room and Florence could make out a piano in the living room. It was much the way she expected the mayor's house to look. It was the way she wanted her own house to look.

"Why, Florence, hello." Beatrice's voice startled Florence. She was calling from the kitchen. "I didn't hear the bell. Just a minute, I'll be right there."

"I'm just returning your plate," Florence called back through the door, hoping she didn't sound too nervous. Now she rang the bell. It chimed through the hall. "It's working now."

Beatrice unlatched the door and invited Florence inside.

"Mmm. That looks even better than the pies at the bakery. Please come in. I'll put the kettle on."

"Well, I thought I'd return your plate with a little something on it." Florence held the pie out for Beatrice. She padded to the kitchen in her stocking feet and Florence had a brief thought that it was not becoming of a mayor's wife to be in stocking feet.

Her offering having been graciously received, Florence entered into the mayor's house. Her feet sunk into the carpet. Everywhere she looked, the furniture gave off a rich sheen. Taking the opportunity while Beatrice was occupied in the kitchen, Florence looked around the living room.

Large clumpy oil paintings of bunches of flowers hung on the walls. There were a few watercolours, boats and docks and sunsets and loons, bearing Beatrice's signature. A low piano stood in the corner with an African violet and a potted fern on top. Charles wouldn't let Florence put anything that needed watering on their piano. 'It's not a piece of furniture, it's a musical instrument,' he said.

Beatrice's furniture gleamed and still smelled of furniture polish and Florence wondered if she did it herself or had someone in to clean. Surely she had someone in. The couch felt stiff and new when Florence sat down.

When Beatrice returned she had a pair of tan loafers on, which put Florence at ease. Her presence warranted loafers.

"Here we are. I couldn't wait to try your pie."

"How nice. I make tarts, too. Those are nice for parties. People don't expect that. Lemon meringue tarts. They're a bit fiddly, but well worth it."

They drank tea from dainty cups with saucers and took polite bites of the pie. The window to Florence's living room was clearly visible from where she sat. The house looked empty, just a blank window with no movement or sign of life behind it. She didn't like the look of the house. The shutters needed a coat of paint and the shrubs were dusty and scraggly. There was a lot of work to be done that Florence hadn't noticed before. Later, when she got home she would move a vase of fresh cut flowers to the table which sat below the front window and ask Charles to mow the lawn and trim the bushes.

At the mention of Florence's tarts, Beatrice invited her to a shower she was hosting the next week.

"It's for Karen McBride, my husband's secretary's daughter. She's marrying a high school teacher. Like you, Florence. Maybe you'd like to come and meet some of the ladies and let them have a taste of those tarts you mentioned."

All week, Florence tinkered with the recipe for her tarts, making batch after batch. Charles and the girls fed on them every night after dinner and were asked if they liked the ones they were now eating or the batch from the night before. By the end of the week Charlotte blurted out,

"They all taste the same. We want something else. I hate meringue. It gets those drops on it that looks like pus."

Florence looked as though she might cry. "You people are no help. I'm supposed to take these to a party where everybody will know everybody except for me. I want them to know I can cook."

She took the remaining tarts and stepped emphatically on the pedal of the garbage can. She made sure every last one slid off the plate into the garbage. "There. Are you happy now? No more tarts."

Nobody knew what to do. They all sat frozen in their seats, waiting for something to happen. Florence crossed her arms and glared out the window and wouldn't speak. The girls were too afraid and finally Charles got up and led them into the hallway to safety. When he re-entered the kitchen, Florence sat sobbing into her apron.

"I just want to make some friends for us, Charles."

"Well, you don't have to start with the mayor's wife. Maybe there's too much pressure."

"Start at the top, Charles. Always start at the top and work your way down if you have to. Now, tell me those tarts were alright."

"They were more than alright." He brushed aside her hair and kissed her cheek.

"Because you know, Charles, I am going to make a name for us in this town. By Christmas, I'll have the mayor's wife begging me for an invitation to our Christmas party." Florence was on her feet now, wiping her hands on her tear-stained apron. "I'm going to be the one to know around here. One day people will look right past Mrs. Mayor Hubert Weisenthal and see me as the one to cozy up to."

"I liked batch number two. The ones we had on Tuesday. Take batch number two."

* * * * *

Beatrice hosted dozens of showers for young brides and mothers-to-be. Who was engaged and who pregnant was found out through an elaborate network which involved the Norman Herald and someone working in the mayor's office. It was almost a full time job, just planning, shopping for and hosting the showers and Beatrice was glad when Florence offered to help.

"What you need is an assistant. A right-hand woman."

The two women spent long afternoons together, usually at Beatrice's dining room table, addressing envelopes, double checking guest lists and shopping lists. They kept track of gifts they bought and to whom they were given to ensure somebody and her sister didn't receive the same blender or casserole set. She and Beatrice became known for their elaborate decorations and decadent dainties. Life in Norman could not have turned out better for Florence. Not a week went by where she wasn't either hosting a shower with Beatrice or attending a shower. She was busy all the time and had aligned herself with Norman's elite. The mayor's friends were her friends. The first step had been taken.

"Girls," Florence said to them one day. "Sit down and listen. I have some exciting news."

There was a different look in their mother's eyes that day. A look June and Charlotte saw everyday among their classmates on the playground. It wasn't as easily recognizable in an adult, but the look was unmistakable. Florence had a secret. Their mother was up to something.

"Sit, sit," she said and put a plate of crackers with peanut butter in front of them. "Ooh, you're going to be so excited when you hear, girls."

"What is it?" asked June, her eyes wide.

Very earnestly, Florence sat down, leaned forward and fixed her eyes on them. "Girls, two weeks from Saturday, in this very house, we will be hosting a bridal shower for none other than Penelope Wilder. Now what do you think of that?"

"Who?"

"Oh, come now. How are you ever going to get along here if you don't know the Progressive Conservative party representative in your town? Penelope Wilder is the daughter of Joseph Wilder. You should know that. What do they teach you at that school?"

"Is that it?" Charlotte demanded.

"Is what it?"

"The surprise. Is that the surprise?"

"What do you mean is that the surprise? Of course that's the surprise. It's the most exciting news, don't you think?" A far away look came over Florence's eyes.

The kitchen fell silent. Charlotte shrugged at June. Suddenly, Florence jumped out of her chair and landed back in it with a pad of paper and a pen. Her face tense, her pen poised.

"Goodness, we have a lot to do. This is going to be such a good experience for you girls. Now, we have to begin with a list of people to invite."

"Doesn't Mrs. Weisenthal usually help you?" asked June.

"Oh, this time I'm going to give her a holiday. That's part of the surprise. You two can help me. Okay? Now, I had the most terrific idea. I read about it in a magazine at the hairdresser. All the guests bring gifts for one room of the newly-wed's house. Then at the end of the shower, the bride-to-be has everything she needs for the kitchen, or her bathroom, or the dining room. It's called a theme shower. Here's where the fun begins. We get to pick the room. What shall it be?"

"Can I go out and play?"

"Charlotte. Don't you want to help with the shower? This is much more fun than playing. You go around the house and count all the chairs we have and then report back to me. Now march! June is going to help me think of people to invite."

Six chairs in the dining room, one by the telephone, four in the kitchen, three big chairs and a sofa in the living room, five in all the upstairs, one by the sewing machine. Twenty chairs in all. Charlotte only had the vaguest idea of what took place at a shower and she could not get rid the notion that at some point during the party, water would be sprinkled over the guests and they would all go home laughing and dripping wet. She wasn't sure how her mother planned on preventing her precious furniture from becoming soaked and was a little dumbfounded her mother wanted all that mess in her house at all.

"Twenty chairs, twenty-four guests, not counting us. Perfect. Now which room should be the theme room? Let's think. I suppose the kitchen is the obvious one."

The stack of paper and lists lay spread across the kitchen table. June had a pencil in her hand and was scribbling on a piece. "The decorations," she told Charlotte. "Mom says we get to make the decorations, so I'm making a list."

"Now, don't you two say anything to Mrs. Wiesenthal. I don't want her to think she has to help. She'll be an invited guest, like everybody else."

Everyday that week and into the next, June and Charlotte came home from school and got to work on the decorations. They made bells made from styrofoam cups and tin foil. They cut pictures from the Sears and Eaton's catalogues of blenders, toasters, bowls, anything from the housewares section. These were glued onto cardboard and made into mobiles that would hang over the gift table and the food table.

Those kind of activities frustrated Charlotte. She found the snipping and gluing so fussy and she wasn't good at it like June. Things got lost in the stack of magazines or fell on the floor and then got crumpled when she tried to pick them up. The glue wouldn't work the way she wanted and she stuck pictures together that weren't supposed to go together.

"Can I do something else?" she asked her mother. There was no question she had to do something. "I don't like cutting and gluing."

Florence told her to count out the cutlery. "But don't smudge it. It's already been polished."

There would be streamers and balloons and a banner: *A Beautiful Bride, Penelope.* The kitchen turned into a mass production of sugary slices and cakes. The fridge was stuffed full and the counters overflowed. They ate nothing but sandwiches since Florence was too busy to cook. By Friday afternoon, everything had been prepared, cleaned, decorated. All the work seemed to have recharged Florence.

"You girls pay close attention tomorrow. You're going to remember this the rest of your lives." An exuberant laugh erupted from Florence. "Hot *hors d'oeuvres*. Nobody in Norman has ever been served hot *hors d'oeuvres* before. Ha. They'll be too shocked to eat."

Saturday morning, June was sent across the street with an invitation for Beatrice. She tried to sneak up the walk and slip it through the letter slot without being discovered. When she was halfway down the walk, she heard the door open and Beatrice's voice called her back.

"Hello, June. What's this?" She fingered the envelope suspiciously.

"Um, it's from my mom." Now, June felt like she was up to something too. She shifted from one foot to the other and tried not to give anything away while Beatrice opened the envelope.

"Your mother is a little late with her invitation. I'm not sure I can make it."

"Oh, please try. She's been so excited all week to surprise you. She really wants you to come."

As Beatrice's countenance darkened, the grin on June's face disappeared. Something had gone wrong with their plan because Beatrice didn't seem very happy at all to be invited to the shower.

"So, she really wants me to be there today. Is that so?"

June nodded her head vigorously.

"Well, tell your mother I wouldn't miss it." The door swung shut and June was left standing on the wide step staring at the brass door knocker wishing she could have a second try at delivering the invitation. It all wasn't quite right. Of that June was certain.

That afternoon, the girls wore their matching flower print dresses and had their hair tied up in ribbons. Each time the doorbell rang, Charlotte ran to answer it, while June cowered in the kitchen and pretended to arrange the cheese. All morning those words echoed through her mind. *Tell your mother I wouldn't miss it.* Slam. Each time they were delivered with more ferocity and the door slam became louder and the sneer on Beatrice's face more sinister. Women's voices rang from the hallway.

"Oh Florence, the place looks fabulous."

"What a terrific idea for a shower."

"Oh, I see you made your lemon tarts. They're famous by now."

"Your girls are darling."

Her mother breezed in and scanned the platters of food June had been preparing. "That's fine. Take it to the dining room. I think everyone is here. I don't know what could have happened to Beatrice. Did she say she was coming?"

"I told you. She said she wouldn't miss it."

"Well, she should know when the invitation says two-thirty, the bride is expected at three. Come and help with the coats."

At five minutes to three, Beatrice arrived. Her hair newly done, her dress perfectly pressed, her perfume perfectly expensive. She dropped her coat into June's arms and made her way into the throng like a queen greeting the commoners. Once people noticed who had arrived the din hushed as women tried to get close to her. It was as though they had been waiting all this time for her arrival and not Penelope's, who had to ring the doorbell three times to break the spell of Beatrice. All the while her guests hovered around Beatrice, Florence watched and waited her turn. What was it about this woman people so adored? They were making positive fools of themselves, fawning over her like some movie star. The whole room had sprung to life since her entrance. Or, perhaps it was just the wine. That had to be it.

Florence finally made her way through to Beatrice and was greeted with an icy stare. "Florence, how ambitious of you to host a shower all by yourself. And for the Wilder girl too. I wish you luck."

Luck? A pang of unease fluttered through Florence. Maybe she had taken on more than she could handle. It would be horrible if her shower flopped. Maybe she should have tried her plan with somebody other than Penelope Wilder. But, now it was too late and Penelope had arrived with her mother and all her bridesmaids. Florence said a quick prayer asking God to help her and prove to Beatrice she could do without her quite nicely. She had expected Beatrice to be impressed. Now it seemed Beatrice would spend the afternoon watching down her nose for things to criticize, waiting for Florence to fail. Well, she didn't need any luck. She had hot *hors d'oeuvres.*

The smell of strong coffee fuelled the chatter which filled the room. Florence gave June the job of folding the gift wrap into squares and Charlotte had to arrange the presents on the side table once they had been passed around the room. The guests smiled at them and told them one day they would be engaged or having a baby and people would honour them with a shower and how nice of them to be such good helpers. While the girls did most of the work, Florence floated from person to person, divining from each of them how fabulous her shower was. By the time the food was served, Florence felt lighter than air. Everything was going perfectly and each time a compliment was extended, she thanked the person loud enough for Beatrice to hear.

When one person decides to attempt to overthrow the reign of another, it is never without risk. Once a plan has been set in motion and the troops are on the battlefield, one can be certain a battle will ensue. When one attacks with hot *hors d'oeuvres* and delicate dainties, the counter attack will predictably be a mouthful spat into a napkin and a directive issued in a loud voice not to eat the meatballs, as they are a little off. The ace up the sleeve, the secret weapon, meringue tarts, even if they are flawless, will be left untouched on their platter along with every single morsel of food which has been prepared for the occasion.

With victory secured, Beatrice led the way out the door just one hour after the shower had begun. All the guests followed, muttering their thanks and slightly dazed from the turn of events.

* * * * *

"These meatballs are perfectly fine. Aren't they?" For the third time in a row, and hopefully the last, Charles, June and Charlotte ate their dinner with toothpicks and agreed the meatballs were quite fine, and the sandwiches and the tiny quiches. It wasn't over between Florence and Beatrice. They reached some sort of truce, if only for the purpose of keeping watch over one another and resumed their role as representatives of high society. Friendship turned business. Maybe it was better that way.

chapter ten

While Florence infused the population of Norman with her good breeding, Charles taught History at the high school. The French Revolution was his favourite subject and the one he threw all his energy into teaching. He loved to impart the gory details, as many as he knew, of the taking over of the Bastille in the sweltering heat of the Parisian summer. "If it's hot, it may as well be really hot," he provided as explanation along with the slides he showed of the Bastille up in flames.

In class, he performed as he lectured his students on the great uprisings and riots from the past. He would stop mid-stride and bellow forth a quote from some obscure figure whose place in history was determined by a single utterance of unexpected wisdom: "This is not a riot. This is a revolution."

When the class debated the meaning of privilege, "as was the preoccupation of the French government at the time," he divided them into the Noblesse and the Petit Bourgeoisie and sped from side to side to vehemently support each argument. With sweat beading at his temples and his sleeves rolled over his elbows, he would shut down the debate and proclaim: "Vive la France libre! Vive la revolution! Class dismissed."

To celebrate Bastille Day, Charles treated his class to red, white and blue cake from Olafson's and grape juice in Styrofoam cups which was supposed to represent red wine and all that it represented. The celebration had to be held on June 14, a month before the real Bastille Day due to summer break, and coincidentally Charlotte's birthday. A map of Paris in 1789 hung at the front of the room, with the Place de la Bastille marked by a tiny, cocktail sized flag of the revolution. The class previous would have been spent with each student making triangle hats to wear for the occasion. He brought in his record player and a scratchy recording of the *Marseillaise*. Thus, each year was capped, with he and his students standing at attention wearing the traditional hats of the revolution. As the song neared the end, the students threw their hats in the air and cheered three cheers for Charles.

Students come and students go. As a teacher, he learned not to make too much of any one student, knowing the information he taught held little relevance for them and the lives they would go on to live after graduation. This was the reason he made it entertaining. At least if he made it interesting, his students would remember something and hopefully gain some perspective, a broader scope with which to view the world. Any time a student approached their work with some interest and industry, he felt rewarded. Ask any teacher and they will tell you their greatest reward is a flicker of interest amidst the sea of blank faces and wandering minds. A question that predicts the point you are making and not the point made ten minutes ago. A teacher appreciates a thoughtful mind.

He tried not to think too hard about where his students ended up. Either they went on to work at the service station and made him feel like a failure, or they went on to become nuclear physicists and made him feel like a failure. He tried to focus on the year at hand, the one year and the material he had to teach in that time. At the end of the year he wished them all success and hoped they got everything they wished for.

If you get Mr. Weiss, it'll be a piece of cake. He's great. Sure, he knew what they said about him. Every teacher does. He'd rather be known as a softy than be utterly despised like Mr. Inglewood who thought nothing of throwing chalk and brushes at students and telling them they were stupid, when in fact, not even the brightest students could follow what he was saying. Then, there was Ms. Labelle who had students and staff alike convinced senility had set in as she stormed around the rows of desks in mismatched outfits with buttons askew and untied shoes, shrieking at her students to get out a pencil and get busy.

After every class, a group of students gathered around Charles's desk pleading for leniency. "Can I have an extension?" "Can you give us a hint about the test on Friday?" "Can I change topics? The one I picked is too hard." And so on. He let them have it, whatever they asked. He was there to teach, not dictate. What did it matter if they had a hint about the test or wanted an easier topic? Lessons would be learned either way. Students did not flourish under harsh rules and rigid methods. Teachers gain nothing by engaging in a power struggle with their students. The student wins every time, because win or lose, they can walk away, on with their life. With, or without the benefit of a teacher's wisdom.

* * * * *

By the time the girls were teenagers, Florence and Charles's annual Christmas party was a much-anticipated tradition. It was a splashy affair, a chance for them to invite all their friends and acquaintances and a chance for Florence to do up the house and her family for all of Norman to see. The preparations began a month before with an intensive organizational effort. The whole family gathered around the dining room table and the chores were divied up between them. Linen had to be ironed, crystal, china, silverware, washed and polished. The punch bowl came out of the box and Charlotte hung all the cups from hooks all around the big bowl. They played carols on the HiFi and got into their work with the help of the Ray Conniff Singers. Christmas was coming and the chores didn't seem so bad with the smell of shortbread to accompany them. With any luck, some of the cookies would be burnt or broken and therefore allowed to be eaten early.

By mid-month the first cards would arrive in the mail and they were strung up along the banister and placed on top of the mantle. Little by little, Christmas arrived.

Charles rearranged the furniture in the living room to make room for the tree and to create some space for the flow of guests. The house looked like the houses in *Better Homes and Gardens.* And like the houses in the pictures, one wondered whether anybody ever actually lived inside. In fact as the day drew close and the house was cleaned room by room, less and less of the house was inhabited. Once the dining room was clean, the French doors sealed off the area. Same with the study, living room, guest bathroom, they all became cordoned off. It all added to the current of excitement and anticipation for the festivities to come.

The decorating was left until the day before the party. Weeks earlier, just after the first snowfall, Charles and Charlotte drove west to a forest where they gathered pine boughs and pine cones. Among the towering pines were poplar and maple trees, stripped bare by the December wind, their leaves dotting the fleecy snow like flecks of gold and amber. Being outside on a bright, cold day this close to Christmas made Charlotte think of sitting in the living room, warm and cozy, next to the fire, flames dancing with the lights from the tree, plates of cookies and sweets and baskets of nuts and oranges all within reach. Christmas morning she would tramp through the snow to church in her warmest winter socks and boots, only her calves exposed to the sting of the cold. Her dress would stay hidden under her parka but, she didn't care. She just wore the dress because her mother made her.

The smell of the pine was strong and rich. They had brought a sled to help carry everything back to the car. Charles pulled while Charlotte walked beside and they sang at the top of their lungs: *Over the river and through the woods, To Grandmother's house we go.* Then, on the way home, Charles turned the heat in the car to full and the air blowing from the vents warmed quickly while they sang all the way home along with the carols on the radio.

The boughs lay in the snow by the back door until the night before decoration day when they were brought inside to thaw. June and Charlotte cleared the worktable in the basement and made wreaths and red velvet bows. Upstairs, they could hear their mother clicking on the kitchen floor as she took things out of the oven and placed them on the counter and then from the counter to the fridge. Directly above them, in the living room, Charles could be heard moving the couch. Suddenly a thud sounded above them. They heard Charles swear and then groan. Florence clicked from the kitchen to the living room.

"Goodness, Charles. What happened?"

"That damn couch weighs a ton. Jesus! Get it off my foot. It's on my damn foot." The carpet had rumpled up under the legs of the couch, and when Charles tried to lift it over, he felt a ripping and a pop in his shoulder, which caused him to drop the couch onto his foot. He slumped to the floor with the couch still on his foot. His face became ashen. Between Charlotte and her mother, they straightened him up. Got the couch off his foot and the carpet straightened, and settled him onto his easy chair.

"I think I pulled a muscle," he gasped. He clutched his shoulder and then his foot and then his shoulder again. He stamped his foot a few times on the floor. "Not broken."

He tried to move his arm a little, starting by making a fist. Sweat beaded onto his forehead.

"What am I supposed to do now with you out of commission?" Florence stood over him with her arms crossed. "The party's tomorrow. Try to move your arm again."

Charlotte wrapped some ice in a towel and pressed it onto his shoulder. "I'll move the couch. Should I call the doctor?"

"Oh, I hardly think it will come to that," Florence stated, her mind already back in the kitchen. She left Charlotte to tend to the couch and Charles.

"Keep the ice on it. I'll finish this. What is it with her and parties anyway?"

"Your mother is an entertainer, Charlotte. It's what she loves best. Let's let her have her fun."

* * * * *

The tree in the living room twinkled with little white lights. Florence had her shopping done and all the gifts wrapped and artfully arranged under the tree. The day of the party, the girls and Charles were kept busy with last minute dusting and wiping while Florence went to the hairdresser and for a manicure.

By the time Florence got home everything was prepared.

"Do you have to wear that thing tonight?" She asked when she saw the sling supporting Charles' arm.

"It's dislocated. I have to wear it. Yes. Doctor's orders."

"Will it be better by New Year's?"

"We can only hope."

Florence wandered from room to room, inspecting her work and fiddling with the decorations. Unable to rest, she moved the knives over an inch, smoothed out the linen tablecloth, picked at the candlewicks. She didn't stop until, at last, the doorbell rang.

The guests came after eight. The men wore V-necked sweaters with suede accents, their wives, gorgeous in dresses of velvet and silk, hair spun into neat, symmetrical shapes just that afternoon and a cloud of perfume wafting behind them like a swarm of bees as they moved through the room. Charlotte remembered how strange her mother appeared to her during the evening. Her shrill voice rose above the din as she mingled. Flitted from group to group and laughed in a harsh, forced way like she had a hair caught in her throat. Charlotte and June were designated servers for the evening. They moved through the crowd with trays of crackers spread with cheese and olives, spicy meatballs with colourful toothpicks and rum balls. Everybody drank: Harvey Wallbangers, Tom Collins', Rusty Nails, Gin Fizzes. Charles prepared all the drinks, and the ladies oohed as he shook their drinks with his good hand and stabbed maraschino cherries onto a plastic saber with the one in the sling. Charlotte had to keep the ice bucket filled so he could reach in with the tongs and drop cubes into the highball glasses.

Charlotte sat on the steps for a moment in the middle of the evening. She heard a voice, louder than all the rest carrying on about the sausage rolls in a way even the flakiest sausage roll shouldn't merit, and she tried to place it. Her mother broke away from the group, jammed a sausage roll into her mouth and when she spotted Charlotte she launched bits of pastry from her mouth and said, "Honey you should try these, they are absolutely divine," in a tone Charlotte had not ever heard.

"Who cares?"

She looked at her mother whose cheeks had become flush and her hair started to unravel. Maybe her mother didn't hear her because she didn't give Charlotte a second glance, she just kept walking and talking in a voice that wasn't hers, to whoever would listen. Her mother was being a phony. She hardly even knew anybody at her own party and had just invited whomever had been at the mayor's party last year. She would say "good-bye" and "Merry Christmas" to each of them at the end of the evening, after Charlotte or June had retrieved all the coats, and wouldn't see them the rest of the year. This discovery of façade did not surprise Charlotte but made her wonder when her mother had become so weak and so phony.

* * * * *

Florence was killed the next year, before Christmas, in the midst of preparations for her party. Her annual personal celebration annulled, cancelled, by a thirteen-year old boy behind the wheel of a pickup truck. Who, saw the keys dangling in the ignition, saw his dad poring over three-inch nails in the hardware store, slid over behind the wheel. He adjusted the rear-view mirror until his reflected eyes met his own. He'd watched his dad do it a thousand times. Grip the key in the ignition, turn, press the gas and listen to the engine roar. Ecstasy. Exhilaration. He had dreamed of this moment, rehearsed it in his mind a million times. The blood rushed through his ears and he curled his fingers around the wheel. His toes grazed the brake pedal and he pulled the truck into reverse. When he released his foot, the truck jumped backward into the street and accelerated. The boy grabbed the wheel and turned hard to the right causing the back end of the truck to spin towards the curb and slam into the display case of Olafson's bakery. Florence had stopped to look at the cakes on display when the truck skidded over the curb and hit the building with a sickening crunch and snapped Florence into the window. Thousands of glass shards twinkled like snowflakes on the frosted Yule Logs. As people gathered and watched, a thin stream of blood trickled from Florence's ear. Mandarin oranges rolled from her bag into the street. She lay face down, arms askew, her body on a bed of glass. Like salmon on a bed of ice.

Charlotte remembered exactly what she wore to school that day: her grey wool skirt, Oxfords, green knee-highs, a white blouse and her favourite pale blue mohair sweater. She remembered looking up and seeing her father's face at the classroom door, floating behind the glass, just beyond reality. They walked the empty corridors and he said something about an accident, her mother taken to the hospital. But, when they got in the car he drove straight home and for a moment the waves of sickness lifted when Charlotte thought maybe her mother had already come home.

The house felt cold and empty and smelled unfamiliar. Maybe they had walked into the wrong house and all this was really happening to somebody else. A cosmic error in their favour.

"Never mind your shoes," her father said. They went to his study. The whiskey stood open on the cabinet and her father found a second glass and poured her a drink.

"She was killed by a truck."

The whiskey burned her lips. Her mother had been dead at the beginning of math. All through the class, while Mr. Poloniak made jokes about long division, her mother was already dead. Charlotte tried to remember if she saw or felt anything different, if any change in sensation alerted her, tuned her in to events unfolding in town. Or, if her mother's voice suddenly whispered in her ear but, all she could recall was Mr. Poloniak at the front of the class: "Now, don't confuse 'Gesundheit' the German term for 'you sneezed on me' with 'goesinta,' the mathematical term. What 'goesinta' seventy-two, nine times?"

Then she saw her father at the door. At first she thought nothing out of the ordinary. She almost waved when Mr. Poloniak wasn't looking, but then he knocked.

Why would he knock? Didn't he see she was in class? He couldn't interrupt her here. Mr. Poloniak didn't know either what her father was doing knocking at the door. He let him in and they whispered to each other, then motioned for Charlotte. And that was it. She wasn't in math class any longer. She crossed over to another plane, a new place in her life. Someone knocks at the door and leads you from one place, down an unfamiliar corridor, to a different place.

"Drink it all in one shot, it tastes better that way." Tipping his head back, her father drained his glass and poured himself another. "I've tried calling your sister but she must be at work. We'll have to call her later or tell her when she gets here."

June would have been coming that weekend anyway, for the holidays. The fridge was full of food, the decorations in place. Charlotte had started on the ironing last night. June was bringing smoked goldeye from the city.

Her father was right about the whiskey. The way it warmed her from the back of her throat, down to her stomach. Smoky comfort. It was her first drink and she held out her glass for another. Florence's disapproving look flickered across her father's face. He poured, raised his glass and said, "To your mother." Tears filled his eyes. Tears which he blinked away as he pulled Charlotte towards him and held her. He cried silently onto her shoulder only for a moment. They sat together in the study, not knowing exactly what to do.

June arrived two hours later. She came yoo-hooing though the door, loaded down with bags of groceries and a box of wine bottles and was met by Charles and Charlotte, still in their clothes from the day, reeking of whiskey, their eyes puffy and red.

"What, what is it?" She stood in the hallway, with her coat still on, bags on the floor, her legs about to give way beneath her, father saying death came quickly and her mother didn't suffer. It simply couldn't be. Not now, just before Christmas. It was her mother's time to shine. How could she miss it?

The house rang with emptiness. Charles sat in his study and listened to Chet Baker. The television droned at June who sat on the sofa and clucked in disapproval from time to time. Charlotte kept busy in the kitchen packing and re-packing food, which the neighbours and church ladies had brought to the house. Tuna casseroles, beef stews, potato and macaroni salads, cookies, pound cakes, chicken soup, bread, rolls. It all tasted strange, this common food to which their taste buds couldn't adjust. They buried Florence on Monday afternoon. After the funeral people came to the house to pay their respects and eat the food they would have had at the Christmas party. It almost was like the party they would have had on the weekend, with the house decorated in garlands and lights, the aromatic coffee and the sweet scent of the Christmas tree. People dressed up, drinking wine and mingling. The food was delicious and abundant. Florence would have loved every moment.

* * * * *

Without the delight children brought to Christmas and without Florence's exuberant Christmas spirit, Charles, June and Charlotte tried to make the best of the season. On Christmas morning they opened the gifts which lay under the tree. Charlotte had put all the ones for Florence away in a closet upstairs. They opened the gifts Florence had picked out for all of them. Charles and Charlotte each got a sweater. On Charlotte's, Florence had pinned a small brass bass. Along with Charles' sweater she had laid an LP recording. A live performance by Duke Ellington and Count Basie and, remarkably, a record Charles did not yet have. He scratched his head while he looked at it and wondered how he could have missed hearing about it.

"Where could she have gotten this?" He asked Charlotte.

"She went to Winnipeg one day to do all her shopping and came back with it. I told her you didn't have it yet."

"Well, what do you know?" He turned the record over and over, unwrapped the cellophane and let the record slide from the sleeve into his hand. He examined it for scratches. There were none.

For June, Florence had purchased a covered skillet and an Italian cookbook, something practical for a woman on her own. June wasn't sure if it meant Florence was proud of her to need a skillet and cookbook or if she thought those items June would never think to buy for herself. They all sat in the living room and pondered the last gifts Florence gave them and tried to divine some higher meaning from what really were quite simple, but thoughtful gifts.

Over the holidays, many people came by, but none stayed long, not even removing their coat and overshoes, but standing in the doorway instead, allowing a chill to creep through the hall. They stayed to peek inside and make sure Charles and the girls had everything they needed. Just as the cold they had let in began to dissipate, the visitors turned and left and let another blast of winter into the house.

What a relief when school started again. The routine of school and work recharged them. They needed to know days like the one when Florence died, would not haunt them. Days like that were out of the ordinary. Their world would not shatter every day. For the most part their days were the same, predictable. Charlotte was in her final year at school and Charles, though he hadn't planned it, was too.

chapter eleven

C harles retired at the end of that school year. He had no enthusiasm for anything anymore and had a hard time capturing the students' attention the way he used to. The passion with which he used to teach had left him and his classes were dull and the students restless. He forgot about Bastille Day. On June fourteenth, the students filed into his class and each of them wore something red, white and blue, because they were expecting the usual celebration, and because they wanted to do something special for a favourite teacher. At first Charles didn't even notice. He stood before them, about to discuss the Battle of the Plains of Abraham, when one student raised his hand, waving the Tricolour. "Don't you know what day this is, Mr. Weiss?"

And then he saw what they had done for him. He checked the calendar and the class tittered; they thought he was trying to be funny. When he turned back to the class, their expectant grinning faces met his blank look.

"I forgot," he whispered. Charles sat at his desk, assigned reading and sat the rest of the time staring vacantly out the window. He didn't care anymore. It hadn't occurred to him until this moment. He thought he was still grieving, but this did not feel like grief. It did not feel like anything. He felt empty, without sense or need. The sudden loss of his wife had shaken him but he expected to bounce back. He had no doubt he would be exactly the same once he got over the loss. Everybody told him it took time.

He knew no life without her. Florence chose the path and he followed. It was simple, so simple. His life was made easy because of her. Had he really fallen in so easily? Was his whole life so wrapped up with Florence and her activities that he could not recall how he spent his days before this? He did not remember being so in love, so devoted.

And then it was over. On his last day, he packed up twenty-five years of papers, books, a selection of student essays once worth keeping, maps, charts, everything down to pencils, erasers, paper clips and tacks. Brought it all home and stuffed the fireplace full and watched it burn.

They planned a retirement party for him, but he didn't go. Maybe they had it without him anyway. Charlotte tried to prepare him for it after the invitation came in the post.

"Dad, they're having a party for you next week. A dinner."

"I can't go to a dinner. I can hardly eat my dinner here." How did they expect him to celebrate? What nonsense. He was retiring because he no longer was capable of following a train of thought and making sense of his notes. When he stood before his class, his mind reared like a spooked horse and wouldn't carry him farther. This was how he would be remembered and he didn't want to go to a party and make an ass of himself. They would have a fine time without him.

Charles didn't bother responding to the invitation. Instead, he sat in his study and played three chords on the piano over and over again, striking the keys and letting the sounds reverberate and twist around each other until they distorted. Somebody phoned to see where he was.

"We're all waiting for him." Charlotte had forgotten about it herself. She should have known by the sounds coming from the piano in the study that today was the day.

"He's not able to come." What else could she say?

Cards and flowers piled up in the living room. Charles left them for Charlotte to read and answer. He was done with the school. He wanted to forget about it. Even the night of Charlotte's graduation, he scarcely recognized the occasion. Ray picked her up and Charles looked surprised.

"Where are you two off to tonight?"

"It's our graduation. I'm done with school now too."

She hadn't expected him to remember. He picked at some lint on his sweater and wished them a good time.

* * * * *

Ray and Charlotte poured their energy into their work so when they left they would have money to last at least eight months. It was good to have a distraction from Charles's dwindling energy. She was anxious to get away and watched everyday to see if Charles' mood was improving. His sagging spirits and his unflagging bitterness made Charlotte nervous. The way he was now, she couldn't leave. He didn't know enough to eat even when the plate was there in front of him. He shaved at the end of the day when she came home and reminded him.

Norman felt empty to Charlotte that summer. Most of her friends from school left for university in Winnipeg or Toronto. The ones that stayed did so because they were pregnant or engaged. Charlotte worked hard at the bakery while Ray painted houses. Every chance they got, they poured over maps and planned their route. They calculated that they would be able to leave by early October. The 'Hots' planned one final gig, their farewell night. After that they would be off to see the world.

It was the one performance Charlotte, after an exhausting effort, finally persuaded Charles to attend. It was meant to jolt him out of his stupor so he would get back to normal and Charlotte could leave as planned. The end of autumn was approaching and Ray had already bought his backpack and was tossing things he would need into it. Charlotte hadn't made any preparations. Things were too uncertain. She begged Charles to please come to their performance. Perhaps had she left well enough alone, the night wouldn't have ended as it did.

"You know how hard it is for me to get out, Charlotte," he said from the easy chair, still in his pajamas, or already dressed for bed, Charlotte couldn't tell.

Charlotte puffed out her cheeks. "I'm tired of you never leaving the house. You sit in here all day and read every bloody word of the newspaper and then sit in front of the television and watch it all over again on the news. It's sick. When are you going to join the rest of us here in the world?"

Losing Florence had been hard on him but Charlotte thought Charles was drawing out his period of mourning so he could hide-out in the house and let Charlotte fend off the world for him.

"Come at eight-thirty," she told him. "I'll make sure you get a seat where no one will bother you. You ask me all the time about the band. This is the last chance to hear us. After tonight we're all going our separate ways."

"Even Ray?"

"Yes, even Ray."

Here, Charles paused. Somewhere far away in his mind he recalled Charlotte mentioning travelling with Ray. Where was it they wanted to go? Somewhere to hear some music. She hadn't mentioned it again and Charles assumed she had changed her mind. Young people changed their minds about things all the time.

"Aren't you going to miss him?"

"Maybe I'll catch up to him one day."

She could tell he was unaware that it was him who held her back. What did she think she was waiting for? Didn't he wonder why she didn't plan on leaving with him? The whole conversation made her nervous. She knew that night she wouldn't be leaving with Ray. And she knew if she didn't leave with him, the chances from that point on were slim that she would ever catch up to him at all. Who knew if she would even see him again?

"You better be there," was all she could say without getting upset.

She laid some clothes out for him and left for the Driftwood. Charles heaved himself out of the chair and pulled himself up the stairs. How would he get down there when he could barely move? His body had become so heavy lately. His once lithe figure now sagged and pulled his spirits down with it. Once upstairs, he had to sit and rest a moment on the edge of the bed. The mirror spanning the low, wide dresser reflected an image so absurd all he could think was, "What an old fart I've become."

He thrust his limbs into his clothes, drawing energy from mocking his reflection. Before he left, he forced himself to look once more into the mirror and straightened his tie. Compared to the old fart in the robe, he now looked positively dandy. With the moments passing as he prepared to go, potency coursed through his veins. Something he hadn't felt in a long while. His body woke up. With his hands he made fists and let go to feel the blood rush into his extremities. His hands on the dresser's edge, Charles did twenty knee bends and toe raises. To the flushed face watching him, he said, "I'm going out tonight. Gonna hear some swish music." With his index fingers he performed a drum-roll on the top of the dresser and strode out of the room. He was going to hear his daughter perform. It was the first glimmer of happiness he felt in a long time.

Before he left, Charles stopped in the study. The study belonged to Charles. His claim staked there by the teaching certificate on the wall and the RCA HiFi beside his desk. This was where no one could disturb him. Where he could retreat and ponder the circumstance of his life. Florence had placed a family portrait on the piano, so long ago. She found these personal touches important. Charles scowled at it from time to time. There he stood in his brown sweater and perpetually thinning hair, eyes cast downward, looking over his flock. The girls and Florence, smiling brightly at the camera, as though they didn't even know he was standing right behind them. The photographer had posed them this way, placing Charles above and behind the others, maybe thinking the man of the house belonged at the top. Or was it in the background?

When the girls were young, they knew to leave him alone when they saw the study door closed. If he left it open, they were free to peek inside. Charles didn't like to play in front of anyone. Charles played jazz all the time at the piano, but just for himself. It was all right to play for the girls when they were young, but once Charlotte gained an appreciation for jazz and was playing it herself, he felt more comfortable playing records than the piano for her. He still played, but with the door closed and when the house was empty. He would have felt like an impostor playing the pieces he made up for an audience. To him the imitation in his phrasing and expression was too obvious. Not at all his own. Unlike the geniuses who played from their hearts and were able to express themselves so movingly through their instruments, Charles only had skill enough to copy them. He couldn't help but think himself deficient in some way, unable to master the one true passion in his life.

Once, Charlotte suggested they play something together. Something from one of the records they listened to. But, it wouldn't come. Charles sat at the piano and tried to hear the melody in his head and nothing happened. The harder he tried to think of how the song went, the further it drifted away. Even when Charlotte put the record on and started playing along, his fingers couldn't find the right notes on the piano.

"Some days it just doesn't come, Char. And today is one of those days."

The truth was, he lost his nerve around other musicians. He never was able to concentrate enough to play with anyone. To follow their modulations and cord progressions and add his own to the arrangement. He didn't have it in him. But, he sat back and listened to Charlotte play along with the record and tapped his foot and smiled. She had it and it made him incredibly proud. At least she would experience the real thing from where it counted most. Right in the middle. Ask anybody sitting in the last desk of the second violin section if there's any other way to listen to music than to have it swirling and soaring all around you. You'll never want to sit in the audience again.

The lid creaked when he lifted it to reveal the keys. He sat on the bench and stared. The only thing that came to him were the cords of Heart and Soul. That catchy, simple tune everyone could play, even if they didn't have a musical bone in their bodies. Not even Charlotte knew he still played sometimes. He only played when she was at work. His playing had become rough and heavy. The lead in his fingers made everything he played sound forced and effortful. There was no joy in anything that came out of the piano when he played. It was as though he sat there to torture himself, made himself sit there and strike the keys, no matter what the music sounded like. He tried to make it as ugly as he could. Almost repugnant, so he couldn't stand it. He played until he reached his limit for self-loathing and then he would swing away from the piano and pass out in his easy chair.

His fingers fumbled over the keys and Charles felt the heaviness returning to his limbs. Better quit while I'm ahead, he thought and closed the lid again and rose to go. "Steppin' out, yessir. The man is steppin' out tonight."

There were several tables free at the Driftwood when Charles arrived. Charlotte sat at one with Ray, drinking a glass of beer. Not sure of his next step, Charles moved towards the bar. The tiny stage was cramped with instruments. The piano took up one corner, the bass the other and Ray's drums filled the remaining space. For all his love of music, Charles had rarely experienced a live show. Most of the live music Charles heard came from his own study. The radio and his records had to suffice though the live recordings he listened to carried much more spark and emotional purity than any studio recording. When he listened to the applause, he could guess the type of chairs in the club. Muffled and far away meant comfortable plush chairs, fancy club. Harsh and tinny, hard chairs, low-end club. Then, the smatterings of applause at the end of a solo, from different parts of the room, gave him an idea of the size of room. It really felt as though he was right there. So, this wasn't New Orleans or Chicago, but he imagined the ambiance at the Driftwood to be as seamy as the places where some of his favourite performers started out. He guessed the Driftwood to be an average sized room, though he wasn't sure how those vinyl chairs would filter the applause. The bartender placed a glass of beer in front of Charles and pointed across the room to Charlotte. She waved as she rose to meet him.

"You're looking sharp tonight," she told him.

"Well, you picked my outfit. How could I go wrong? When do you start?"

"As soon as I get those guys' attention to get on stage. Why? Are you getting anxious to get out of here already?"

She knew he was, but at least he had made an effort to come. He made her a little nervous, she was surprised to discover. She hadn't felt nervous in front of the audience in ages and now on the one night she wanted to stay cool, she had become jittery.

"I better get up there," she said to Charles. "Wish me luck."

Charlotte jumped onto the stage and thumped out a tune on her bass to get Ray and Andy's attention. Her hands felt slick with perspiration. Quickly, she wiped them on her pants. She had been avoiding Ray. Seeing him tonight made her choke up. Something was different tonight. The universe was shifting. Nobody knew how tonight would alter the course of their lives. Charles leaned onto the bar and watched.

Tonight, Andy wore shiny black patent leather shoes, which caught the lights from where they rested on the piano pedals. His hands were adorned with chunky glass rings, one amber and one green. The cologne with which he had doused himself wafted all over the stage and kept the smoke out of their eyes. Throughout the set Charlotte watched her father. Her heart leapt to her throat when she saw him there, tapping his foot a little, watching her, Ray and Andy. They had a good crowd tonight. People were happy to be off for the weekend and out with their friends.

The first bars from the band startled Charles. It was so loud. He moved a little farther down the bar. They were playing some bop tune Charles couldn't place. The three of them looked so professional, like real musicians. Not what he expected. Charlotte spoke from behind her bass.

"Good evening everyone. Thanks for coming tonight."

Gosh, it was just like the real thing. The murmuring crowd, not really paying attention, the tittering on the snare while Charlotte spoke. They played *Take The A Train*. Charles sat transfixed. He didn't know how to react each time Charlotte caught his eye and focused his attention on the bar instead. The crowd grew and people jostled around Charles to get at the bar. Drinks were passed over his head to customers behind him. None of them paid any attention to the music. The drums were too loud and Ray used his sticks far too much, not enough brushwork. Charles had a hard time hearing the bass. The flamboyant piano player distracted him with his flashy clothes and knuckle cracking touch on the keyboard. No finesse. The smell of popcorn was beginning to wear away any magic Charles initially sensed. He was certain nobody ate popcorn at the Savoy.

When he looked at the room through the haze, all he saw were drunk farm boys butting their cigarettes into each other's beer and tweaking the waitress on the behind when she brought them drinks. The ones who listened to the band, ogled Charlotte or jeered at Andy. Every so often a handful of pretzels or popcorn flew through the air towards the stage. By the time the band took a break, perspiration had soaked through his shirt and a lightheadedness threatened at any moment to turn into a headache.

"Everything okay, Dad?" Charlotte asked. "I was trying to get your attention, but you were never looking. You look kind of pale."

"Sweetheart, I don't think I can stay." The words choked him up. Was it her heart he was breaking or his own? Everything swam in front of his eyes and he couldn't bring Charlotte's face into focus. His hand shook when he lifted his glass to his lips and the rim clacked against his teeth.

"Come on. I'll ask Ray to drive you home. We don't go on again for forty-five minutes or so. I'll make you a pot of tea."

"No, no. I'd really rather walk. My head needs some real air. I'll be fine."

She walked him to the door. They stood a moment on the steps outside and breathed in the night air. "Thanks though, Dad. I know it was hard for you, but I'm glad you came for a little while."

"It's just not a good night, Char. Can you feel it? Not a good night at all."

She didn't know if he meant himself, the bar, Norman or the whole world. He kissed her cheek with such remorse, sadness shuddered through her and she worried whether the evening had set him back beyond repair. His body drooped as though something had pricked him and now he was slowly deflating. At the edge of the parking lot, he paused before he turned in the direction for home, deciding, perhaps, whether to go home or to walk as far as he could in the opposite direction.

Their second set was flat. The crowd became rowdy and beer bottles crashed to the floor and onto tables. A table of three young guys heckled the band. One of them got out of his chair and stood directly under Andy and shook up his bottle with his thumb over the top and tried to spray it on Andy. But, somebody bumped him and the beer landed on his own jacket instead. With beer soaking into his clothes, the boy yelled at Andy. "You're going to get it. You're a dead man." He waved his fist in front of Andy's face until one of his friends pulled him back to their table.

Distracted by her father's being there for the first set, Charlotte found herself even more unfocused now that he had left. Her playing was lifeless and for the first time since they had been playing here she wished the night was over and longed to be in bed. Thankfully, Ray managed to hold them together through the first two songs. While Andy sang Over the Rainbow, the heckling boys at the table close to the piano threw their empty bottles at him and shouted Queer! Faggot! One glass hit Andy on the side of the head and fell onto the keyboard, sounding an ugly chord.

"Don't Andy," Ray said from behind the kit when he saw Andy get up from the bench. "Let's just finish."

Ray started to tap out the beat for the last song of their set, even though they were only three songs into it. For about twenty bars, which seemed like forever, Andy sat with his arms crossed in front of him, his hands clenched into fists and scowled at the audience.

All the while Ray kept up on the snare and high-hat until Andy finally started to pound the piano with his fists. He and Charlotte exchanged worried glances. Things settled a bit when Andy decided to go ahead and play his solo. By the time Charlotte had to sing, *My baby don't care for shows, My baby don't care for clothes, My baby just cares for me,* he was playing normally, with his fingers, but with his eyes, he glowered at the crowd. They came to the end of the song and Ray stood up and said, "That's it folks. That's all for tonight. Thank you very much."

The manager turned a few more lights on to encourage people to go home. Ray and Charlotte packed away their equipment. "What a night," Ray said.

"God, it hasn't been this bad in a long time. Where did Andy get to?"

"Oh, he's around. Hopefully not picking a fight. Brother, those guys were assholes."

Once the drums and bass were packed up, Charlotte scanned the room once more, looking for Andy. "I don't know where he is. Let's just go."

But, when she and Ray got to the parking lot, Andy was flailing around in the middle of the three farm boys, his fists flying. "Come on you fuckers. Come on." He swung wildly at them.

One of them got in behind him and kicked him. "Faggot." Andy spun around, but was hit from behind by another one. Then the rest of them took turns winding up and kicking him, until he fell to his knees and covered his head with his hands. Charlotte screamed, "Leave him alone."

Ray ran over and tried to pull one of them back, but got an elbow in the head which sent him reeling to the pavement as well.

One of them hoofed Andy in the groin and he slumped to the ground. They hauled him to his feet and smacked his face into the front end of their truck. The yowl he let out nearly made Charlotte throw up. There was blood all over him and any time he tried to move, another kick was delivered, until he finally stopped moving.

"There, you killed him," Charlotte screamed at them again. "You can go now. You've fucking killed him."

The brief flicker of doubt cast across the youngest ones' face was quickly replaced by a sneer. "Good. One less faggot for us to worry about."

They got into their truck and squealed the tires all the way to the corner leaving the sickening odour of burning rubber in their wake.

Ray and Charlotte took Andy to the hospital, where they spent most of the night. There truly had been something sinister in the air that night.

chapter twelve

C harlotte watched and waited for Charles's grief to pass, but it hardened inside him like cement and Charlotte did not know if it was possible to pry it out again. Soup dribbled down his chin and he didn't seem to notice. He ate everything with the same methodical, automatic motions, like a machine, keeping a steady beat: spoon to bowl, dip, spoon to mouth, chew, chew, chew, swallow. Spoon to bowl, spoon to mouth, chew...and on it went. Those were the days he could eat. Sometimes the food would get to his mouth only for him to gag and spit it back onto his plate. It was not the taste of the food, but the taste in his mouth that made him gag.

Charlotte despaired over what to do. The time was drawing near for she and Ray to leave, to go on their trip that would open the world for them, and yet Charlotte could not abandon Charles. There was no way he could look after himself. After the night at the bar, something inside him had shut down. Maybe if Charlotte hadn't forced him to come things would have turned out differently. She pushed him into exposing himself to the world before he was ready.

Ray wanted to wait for her. "We can go to Montreal anytime and hear great jazz. We don't have to go right now." He stood in front of her in his work clothes, spattered with paint. It was supposed to be his last day and Charlotte knew he was anxious to go. It was all he ever talked about as long as she had known him. To get out of Norman and to travel and hear all the best music in all the coolest clubs he could find. He had always wanted this more than Charlotte and she wasn't going to hold him back. It was the only way she knew she could live with herself. She couldn't leave Charles and she couldn't ask Ray to wait. Who knew how long Charles would stay this way?

"Maybe I can meet you somewhere. We'll catch up to each other eventually." Even as she said it, as the words slipped out of her mouth she could already feel the opportunity slipping away with them. It would never happen. She felt it inside of her, a warning shift somewhere between her heart and her throat. That dream of the two of them tripping all over the world popped in an instant. As she felt it dissipate, she knew it had been as fragile as a string of daisies all along.

Winter followed autumn and then spring again. Each season bringing fewer letters from farther and farther away. And eventually no letters at all. The world had swallowed Ray up. For awhile Charlotte couldn't listen to any music and the house was dreadfully silent. She didn't go into the study where her bass lay and the records were kept. Despondent though she was, at least she kept busy. And she knew, wherever Ray was, he had better company than she would have been. There was no way she could have left. The five minutes she spent sobbing on Ray's shoulder when they said good-bye would have been nothing compared to the worry and sadness she would have felt had she actually left with him. She surely would have cut the trip short and ended up right back here in the end anyway.

The work at the bakery distracted her. It got her away from the house during the day. She went home at noon to make lunch for Charles and watched him eat it. When she left in the morning, he was still in bed and sometimes when she came home at noon he would still be in his robe and pajamas sitting despondently in his chair. He looked at her once and said, "I have nothing to do."

That was the worst. Faced with himself for the first time, he hated what he saw, what he allowed himself to become, or more truthfully, what he had prevented himself from achieving in his life. As a young man he dreamed of teaching abroad. In Africa or India, to walk to work along a dusty road to an open air, one room schoolhouse and teach children to read or multiply for the first time or to travel to the south of France or Italy. Maybe the notion was romantic, but people did it. People packed their steamer trunks and went abroad for years at a time. They wrote of their travels and made even the bleak view from their hotel room sound fascinating. They painted in their sketchbooks, detailed pictures of things they saw. Charles wanted to do that too. Before everyone owned an instamatic camera, travellers had to rely on a keen eye and steady hand to capture the images they wanted to remember. He thought, at least, he would stand at the Place de la Bastille before he died, even though nothing more than a few cafés and restaurants remained there.

But it never came to pass. He let the dreams go when he married Florence; came to his senses. He settled into life as a family man, buried and forgot any of the ambition he possessed as a young man and made the best of it. Now his wife was dead, his children grown and he had come to the end of his career without having accomplished one worthwhile thing. What Florence had given him, which he had been unable to provide for himself, was direction, a clear life path. All that was left for him now was a vacuum consisting of nothing but time, which he prayed would suck him quickly to the end.

One evening, Charlotte warmed some chicken soup on the stove. She dug it out from among the containers of food brought by neighbours after the funeral. As the comforting aroma filled the house, she could hear Charles swearing at the television. When she placed a bowl in front of him at the kitchen table, he picked up his spoon and let it fall into the bowl. Soup splattered all over the table and all over him. He scalded his hand.

"Shit," he shouted. "Why are you feeding me this shit?"

"Don't blame me," Charlotte said. "I didn't make it."

"I know you didn't make it," he roared. "Your goddamn mother made it. She's dead. I can't eat this." He took his bowl and threw it across the room at the sink. "And do something about that smell. It's making me sick."

After he had stomped all the way upstairs to his room, Charlotte walked through the house spraying air freshener into each room until the house smelled country-fresh.

Charlotte did try to talk to him. She knew he was in trouble. Sadness was supposed to be fleeting, its sting only temporary. Wasn't this going on a little too long? Was mortality not a condition of life? Till death do us part. What did people think that meant?

Charlotte sorted through her mother's clothes. After the funeral she had stuffed everything into boxes and stacked them in the basement where they stayed, unmentioned and blended in with the concrete walls. Each dresser drawer had been pulled open and emptied into a box. All Florence's make-up, bracelets, pins, rings, hair accessories, creams, lotions, nail polishes, combs, brushes. Charlotte didn't make note of what she was packing, she just wanted her mother's memory packed up and out of sight as quickly as possible. The years had gone by and Charlotte had ignored the boxes every time she washed a load of laundry, until one day, Charles spotted them and asked what was in all the boxes.

"I don't care what you do with it. She cared way too much about all those clothes. Who needs so many dresses? You don't have that many do you?"

"I don't have any dresses. I never go anywhere."

Charlotte would never use any of the dresses and June was another shape entirely. Charles watched for a while as Charlotte re-packed the clothes to drop off at the thrift store. The rest, the personal papers and letters, Charlotte put back in a box and left it in the basement. She left the photos where they stood. Hadn't they been taken for the sake of memory?

When she was done she said, "There, now you can take me out for dinner."

Charles nodded. "I think that's a good idea."

"You do?" This was unexpected. "I was kidding."

"I'm not. How about Chinese?"

"Sounds great. I'm going to get ready right now before you change your mind."

And they did go. Charlotte was astonished. They even walked there, arm in arm, to the Peking Garden.

They sat in a dimly lit booth. One other couple sat by the window leaning over steaming bowls of soup. The walls were painted red with swirls of gold and an enormous dragon spewed fire from its nostrils onto people's plates.

"Reminds me of my boss," Charlotte said.

"Probably reminds a lot of people of their boss," Charles smirked.

They ordered almond chicken, sweet and sour pork, fried rice and egg rolls. The food was served on little silver trays the waiter arranged on the table in front of them.

"It's such a treat to have dinner made for me."

Charles patted her hand and stared off into the distance. "Charlotte," he finally said. "Do you still think of becoming a music teacher?"

"What?"

"You said once you wanted to become a music teacher."

"I did? I don't remember. No, I don't want to become a music teacher. I'm used to working on my own. I wouldn't have the patience for it any more. Maybe at one time I could have done it, but not now." She honestly had no recollection of ever wanting to teach music. Play music, of course, but rehearsing a group of grade eight students through Pachelbel's *Canon* would be a pretty frustrating way to earn a living. She had witnessed Mr. Klassen's blood pressure soar when he had tried to teach the orchestra to play it in high school. Every time they played it, the ending sounded twice as fast as the tempo in which the piece began. There didn't seem to be one thing Mr. Klassen could do to keep the orchestra from careening uncontrollably towards the end as soon as the eighth note passage started. No, Charlotte did not have the patience for Pachelbel.

"I don't know how you kept your sanity teaching all those years."

Charles grinned at her and said, "I didn't, remember?"

"Well, I think you're getting it back. Your sanity that is."

"Here's hoping." He raised his beer and they clinked glasses and toasted their health.

The good mood and high spirits did not last. For about a week or two after their Chinese dinner, Charles's spirit seemed light and his countenance less cloudy. But he couldn't stop the bitterness from brewing inside him. It seeped out whenever he spoke of Florence. His shoulder bothered him more. "Ever since that damn party of your mother's."

"Dad, that was years ago. You were better a week later. I remember because you shoveled the snow after a blizzard New Year's Eve. How can it be hurting again now?"

"How should I know? It just bloody hurts. I can't help it."

* * * * *

The days bled into one another for Charles, the passage of time merely a merging of light and shadow. When his bed became too warm in the midday sun, he lifted the covers with enormous effort and sat on the edge of the bed. He sat there for a full twenty minutes before he stood up and reached for his robe. He made one stop at the toilet to pee and felt the backs of his legs tightening up with fatigue the longer he stood. The assault of cold water splashed on his face at the sink invigorated him only briefly. He hated the wet feeling in his beard but, the routine of shaving belonged to another life, another man. A life which required energy and focus and some kind of force propelling him along. How had he ever managed to shave every day, get dressed and go to work? And where did it get him in the end? Rambling through his old house, not shaving, not getting dressed and not going anywhere. And even that required an unnatural effort on his part.

He stopped at Charlotte's door and looked inside. Somehow she got up everyday and went to work. The bed was unmade. How did she still fit into that bed? They bought it for her when she was three and she barely filled half of it. It came with a white dresser she still used and stood in the same corner of her room as it had the day Sears had delivered it. On top stood a photo of himself and Charlotte in front of the car with a Scotch pine tied to the top. Snow banks piled high on either side of the driveway and more snow fell onto the windshield of the car. That was the day Charlotte had asked him if he liked being a teacher. She had been asking him all kinds of questions, intrigued by the business of being an adult.

"I like it well enough. It gets a bit repetitious, but there are ways of keeping an interest. Why do you ask?"

"Maybe I'll be a teacher. A music teacher."

She did say it. Of that he was certain. Charles lowered himself onto Charlotte's bed and stared out into the back yard. It was because of him she hadn't become anything. There was that fellow back then too, Ray. He was a decent sort. He left Norman after awhile, like most of the young people. Did Charlotte ever mention leaving? Everything was such a blur in his mind. All his memories jumbled together, he wasn't sure what he heard or what he thought he should have heard. She must have thought about leaving at some point. Especially after she didn't have the band anymore. He heard them once at the Driftwood.

Charles stood to look out the window and rubbed his arm. He didn't even mow the lawn anymore. A young kid came over every Monday to do it and Charles peeked out from behind the drapes to make sure he was doing it right. What a crotchety old man he had become. His mood used to be better. He remembered being reasonably content at one time. Now he was one of those people who complained if the mail was late or the paperboy cut across his lawn; the lawn he didn't mow.

* * * * *

Charlotte tried to engage him by talking about the news or things about the bakery. But, he hadn't the notion to respond in any intelligent way and didn't really pay that much attention. One day Charlotte was upset when she came home. Charles could hear her in the kitchen sniffling and blowing her nose. He sat where he usually sat, in the living room in his chair with his glasses, ginger ale and magazines all within reach. He had no reason to get up. The crying intensified and Charles finally hauled his leaden body up and went to the kitchen. She was at the table, her head in her arms and she clutched a tissue in her hand.

"Sweetheart?" He asked from the doorway, not sure whether he would be welcome any closer. "Did something happen?"

Charlotte wiped her nose. "Oh, I'll be okay, Dad. Old Mr. Olafson died last night. Vi didn't even tell me. She phoned in sick. I found out from a customer."

She broke down again for a moment. Charles moved into the kitchen and sat down beside her. He lay his hand on her arm.

"I mean, I know he was old. It's just upsetting, that's all. I'll be all right."

They sat awhile, at the kitchen table. Charlotte leaned over and rested her head on her father's chest, sniffling and dabbing her tissue to her nose. Charles put his arm around her and stroked her hair, feeling her head rise and fall with his breath.

It was one moment in time, one instant of understanding and compassion, not meant to be repeated or sustained, only experienced.

* * * * *

The spiral tightened the day Charlotte came home to find Charles sitting in his easy chair holding a wedding portrait of he and Florence. His hands shook and the picture fell to the floor. He fumbled around for it, leaning from the chair, his hand not able to connect. When he finally grabbed it his hand jumped so violently the picture sailed across the room and smashed into the television. Then he started crying and Charlotte didn't know whether to tend his tears or the shards of glass on the floor.

"What's going on, Dad?"

"Jesus Christ. I didn't mean to break it. I didn't mean it."

"It was an accident. We can get a new frame for the picture. It's still okay."

His hands still shook and he dug his fingernails into the arms of his chair to stop them. "Let go of the chair or you'll tear the fabric. It's all right, Dad. I'll put the kettle on."

His fingernails did tear the fabric.

The disease progressed sporadically after that. Some days he could not get his joints moving until well into the afternoon and had to be helped out of bed. Other days Charlotte walked with him on her arm around the block but he got going so fast sometimes, almost running and

Charlotte tried to hang onto his arm without tripping. She was afraid they both would fall. Doctor Wilson came to the house. He watched Charles walk, listened to his chest and tapped his knees with a rubber hammer. He held his finger in front of Charles's face and told him to touch his nose and then the doctor's finger.

"Get the hell out of my house," he yelled. With remarkable accuracy, Charles stuck his finger up his nose and shouted, "Do you still want me to touch your finger?"

chapter thirteen

"He looks frozen," June said to Charlotte when she saw her father from the hall, folded into his easy chair in the corner of the living room, an aluminum rolling walker in front of him. He sat at attention, in response to nothing in particular.

"Can he do anything?"

"Not much. It's quite a chore even getting him to that point."

"Listen, Charlotte, shouldn't we try to get him into The Pines?"

"There aren't any beds. He's on a list. It could be years before his name comes up."

They heard the walker fall. Charles sat stiffly in his chair, an empty look in his eye as though he hadn't noticed or heard the walker fall.

"He tries to get up sometimes. I think he forgets." Charlotte said, bustling into the room. She picked up the walker and put it back in front of him. "Better not try that again. You're going to fall. You're not to walk without me."

She never imagined how awful it would feel to have to scold her own father but he had become helpless. And it seemed to have happened so quickly. Now, June was here because of him, because he couldn't look after himself anymore. It was truly awful.

Then he started yelling, cursing her, his whole body clenching in sheer determination to lash out. He threw his walker down again. The "bloody hells", "goddamns", "motherfuckers" all running into one another in a garbled rant. He looked like a cartoon figure blowing a stream of nonsensical punctuation into a bubble. The yelling loosened up his body and he started swinging his fists into the air and it looked like he was trying to punch his way out of a giant plastic bag before it suffocated him.

"And you're the one he likes," June said.

"Don't worry, it won't last. I'll put a record on for him and he'll settle down. Hopefully he won't start crying. He does that sometimes. Something will set him off and he will well up and just cry."

This, for Charlotte was harder to get used to than the yelling. Charlotte didn't mind his cranky days, but when he cried, she couldn't look at him and couldn't console him. The rigidity would leave his body and he would slump forward his face in his hands, shaking the tears from his eyes, his nose running shiny rivulets to his lips. He tried to stop but would sniffle and snort for a long time after.

"Do you think he'll know me?" June asked.

"One way to find out. Some days I don't think he recognizes himself."

When June came into the room he started yelling again and shaking his walker.

"Dad," she said and walked towards him. "Dad, it's me, June. I've come to stay for awhile."

"Stay where?"

"Here in the house. To help you out while Charlotte is at work."

He stared at her, a hard stare. Finally he blinked and looked away. "Did she tell you to come?" He was looking at Charlotte.

"Yes, I asked her to come. I thought maybe you'd be happy to see her."

"I don't need any help."

"Well, I do," said Charlotte. "June came to help me, not you."

They sat by him in the living room and listened to a record. The only sound Charlotte could focus on was the scratch in the record, which opposed the beat of the music and made her temples throb.

One morning, after he had been washed and dressed, June led him to the study and sat him at the piano. Finding different things to distract him was not an easy task. She took his hands and laid them on the keyboard. With her hands over his, she pressed his fingers into the keys. His back curled forward towards the keyboard and his skinny wrists and long fingers extended from the sleeves of his sweater. He had become one of those frail men, who shivered at the slightest shift of air. He hunched over the piano and let his fingers hit a few notes. June always waited to see if anything he strung together sounded familiar, but he seemed to forget he was playing and sat with his hands in the ready position, suspended there as though in his mind he was preparing to perform the Brahms concerto. Sometimes his wrists tired from hanging in the air and his hands would fall onto the keys and make him jump with fright.

June stayed the summer and struggled with her father's uncooperative body. In and out of bed, on and off with clothes, up and down the stairs. Thankfully home care sent an orderly every Tuesday to help her get him into tub. They had all the bath-bars and seats installed but, most of the time when he understood to hang on, he couldn't signal his hands to let go again and June had to pry his fingers away one at a time, astounded by the strength which remained in his brittle frame.

By fall a bed had come up at The Pines. He had to go and they had to tell him, somehow.

"Dad, June's got to go back to the city soon and there's a bed available at The Pines." No use pretending or skirting around the issue hoping he would guess. June had to work in the city and he could no longer be left alone. Charlotte and June had seated themselves far enough away so if he threw anything, it wasn't likely to make contact.

"Dad?"

He didn't throw anything. Didn't glare at them or flush with rage. His eyes travelled around the room and then settled on the view out the window of the birch tree from which the girls used to peel bark in big sheets. He remembered the leaves it shed in the fall which were such a nuisance to rake but made the softest pile for jumping. Forty-five years he had lived in this house and now, when he was most vulnerable and afraid and as his body gave up on him, his mind could no longer decipher the world and not even the familiar scene outside could anchor him.

"I'd rather die," was all he said.

* * * * *

They drove him there in June's car and wheeled him inside in a wheelchair. The nurses settled him into his new bed and spoke in cheery voices which grated on the ears and made Charlotte irritable. Charles didn't seem to notice. He lay passively on the plastic mattress and let them turn him whichever way they wanted. After June and Charlotte sat in silence with him for an hour, they finally left and drove home for supper.

"Don't worry, he'll snap out of it," Charlotte had told June and urged her to return to the city. "In a few days he'll be used to the place and everything will be fine."

The next day when Charlotte stepped into his room, she found Charles half way down the bed. The top part of the bed had been rolled up to get him into a sitting position, but he somehow had slid down and his feet were pressed up against the footboard.

"Oh, Dad. Look where you've gotten to." She lowered the bed down and hoisted him back up. "I brought something for you. From home." On the dresser she placed his print of *Liberty Leading the People*. "There, that should inspire you."

His dinner came on a tray. A thin slice of beef with gravy, two small potatoes, string beans and tinned pears. "It looks just like airplane food. Open wide and pretend you're flying off somewhere."

The fork of food hovered in the air before his pursed lips. "Come on, Dad. You need to eat. It can't be any worse than my cooking."

Charles turned his head towards the wall.

"Just try some. Let's pretend we're on a plane. Where do you want to go?"

Charles opened his mouth and croaked, "Hell."

"Very well. Hell it is. I'm sure we can get a cheap flight."

After half an hour of spearing different combinations of food onto his fork, Charlotte gave up. She helped the nurse get his pajamas on him and kissed him goodnight. "I'll be back tomorrow."

"I'll be here," he said.

* * * * *

One by one, he turned off his senses. His heart beat inside him and his lungs took in air, but he had left his life behind. Failure to thrive, they called it and wrote it in his medical chart. Wanting to die. Giving up. Giving in.

The last conscious act of will: letting go. Do not interfere.

It doesn't take long to die, once you decide and stop fighting and struggling to live. You're really already dead, it just takes awhile for all systems to respond and then they slowly shut down. Sometimes it only takes a few days.

For Charles, it took six days. Each day Charlotte visited and each day there was less of him than the day before. His eyes grew cloudy and he rarely opened them. He couldn't open his mouth and his tongue grew thick and yellow-coated. The nurses did their best to keep him comfortable. Charlotte sat beside him and held his hand and felt a slight pressure in return. "Dad, can you hear me?"

His eyes opened, only for a moment and for the first time in days, they seemed clear. His lips moved but they were so dry they wouldn't part. Charlotte dipped her finger in the water glass and rubbed them with some moisture. All the while Charles stared fixedly at her. He didn't let go of her hand and squeezed harder.

"You're going now, aren't you?" she asked quietly, not expecting an answer.

"It's okay, Dad. Everything is going to be okay." She kissed his cheek and laid his hand back on the sheet. Gently, she reached over and closed his eyes and regarded him a moment. People really do look like they're sleeping when they're dead, she thought.

chapter fourteen

FOURTEEN

I t was less than a week until the retirement party. Tiffany flitted mosquito-like around Charlotte, whose eyes darted after her and whose hands resisted the urge to swat her. Perhaps, had she kept her bridesmaid's dress, the one intended for June's wedding, she wouldn't have to stand here right now, on a stool in the middle of a room full of mirrors while Tiffany buzzed about with a mouth full of coloured pins. Tiffany had been assigned to help Charlotte choose a style of dress and suitable fabric. Haute couture in rural Manitoba. First Charlotte had sat in a room with a stack of fashion magazines and was left there to look through them to see if there was a dress she thought would suit her. She wondered if the models in the pictures ever had any difficulty finding clothes to suit them. Maybe her measurements were still on file somewhere. She could ask Tiffany to look those up and work from them.

Finally, after scanning the glossy models and not seeing anything she could imagine herself in, she took a piece of paper and sketched out a simple blue dress, with a belt at the waist and a dip at the back of the neck. She showed it to Tiffany when she returned.

"I want the dress to look like this."

"Well, I think we can make that. Didn't you see anything in the magazines? It's a fairly simple dress. I can see how it would suit you. Let's find some fabric."

Charlotte settled on a bolt of shimmering deep blueish-turquoise and chose three round vanilla buttons for the back. She thought briefly of having button snaps put in, symbolic of the electrodes which traced the beating of her heart. Tiffany convinced her this was the place to jazz up the dress, and her use of the word 'jazz' made Charlotte believe her and so she chose the buttons instead.

"You'll look fabulous in this dress. A real knockout!" Somehow Tiffany was able to talk with all those pins fanning out from her mouth. Charlotte waited with great anticipation for her to suck one back and render herself mute. She was draping and pinning tissue paper over Charlotte's frame. With her giant scissors, she cut the paper out in crude shapes of Charlotte's body. A suit for a life-sized paper doll. All it needed was the tabs to fold over Charlotte's shoulders and around her waist. At the cutting table, Tiffany cut out pieces of the fabric in the shape of the dress and brought them over and started to pin them together on Charlotte.

Tiffany pulled a pin from her mouth without disturbing any of the others. Charlotte didn't like the feeling of Tiffany's hands brushing against her legs while she tucked up the hem. It reminded her of that same uncomfortable feeling she had the time she had sex with Arnie Zacharias.

Tiffany wore a suit of pale tangerine and stockings with seams up the back. Smart, Charlotte thought, she's going for smart. Rhymes with tart.

"Would you like it about knee length?" Tiffany asked.

"Smart. What length is smart?"

"Well, I guess about the length of my skirt. Let's try it there."

"Hmm, I thought so."

It happened when she was twenty-three. Ray was long gone and Charles moped around the house. She thought she did it for fun, but really, she was just lonely and thought Arnie, an old school friend, would be better than nothing at all. They went to his apartment which was decorated exactly as his basement bedroom had been at home. Surrounded by football pennants and crumpled photos of half-naked girls on motorcycles.

She had brought two rubbers and made him roll one on top of the other. She wasn't about to take any chances.

"Like getting the dentist to freeze it," he said, as he fumbled with the condoms.

"You're pouting might make me lose interest. It's not very attractive," she said. Boredom was setting in and they hadn't yet begun. He kissed each of her breasts and then abruptly slid into her and that was the end of any attention Charlotte was going to receive.

It was more arduous than she imagined and Arnie's repetitive, ineffectual rubbing wore on her. He took a long time. So long that she had time to ponder if this might be Arnie's first time. Surely it wouldn't take him this long if it was. His glasses kept fogging up and this unnerved her. Each time she opened her eyes, there he was thrashing above her, staring at the wall behind her through the condensation on his lenses. The sheer effort on his part, the strain she felt through his arms, the gasps for air and the sweat which poured from under his arms, just to keep pounding into her like a piston.

Arnie's leg hair itched against her skin and his urgent thrusting made her feel like one of those football practice things, buffers or whatever they were called. He bucked and grunted and Charlotte hoped he was all right. He had a piece of her hair in his mouth and champed at it while he ground his pelvis into hers. Christ, this had to be stopped, she could endure no more. It seemed so pointless. Charlotte shifted beneath him and pulled her leg free. Slowly, she scraped the thick callous on her heel along the back of his thigh. It worked. His head fell into the pillow. He shrank away from her and rolled over. "Sorry," he mumbled.

She left him lying in bed, his face to the wall. Her hair was still damp where he had been biting it. The thought of his spit in her hair made Charlotte queasy. She had to breathe with quick, shallow breaths so she wouldn't gag. If only she had left well enough alone, she could have basked in the afterglow of Ray. But now she had Arnie in there to skew her memories and mess with her fantasies, maybe for the rest of her life.

* * * * *

"How's that?" Tiffany asked. She had finished pinning the fabric around Charlotte's knees and stood back to look at the hem.

"Well, it's shorter. What else can you do with it?"

"Oh, well, we'll tuck it in the waist and bosom according to your measurements."

"Hmm, my bosom, yes."

"And I can make you a belt from the same fabric. It will be stunning."

"What colour is this anyway?"

"*Oceana.* Isn't it gorgeous? Can't you just picture the ocean?"

"Hmm, with my weak heart and all, maybe I should get something with a little less salt. Do you have anything in *Fresh Water?*"

"What? I don't think we have any of that right now. This looks great on you. The blue really brings out your eyes. I'd really stick with this if I were you."

Her eyes did look startling in the mirror. She only looked for a moment, because Tiffany was looking too.

"That's why I came to the experts. *Oceana* it shall be."

"An excellent choice." Tiffany unpinned Charlotte's dress and lay the pieces back on the cutting table. "Come back tomorrow and we'll do a second fitting. I'll have it sewn together for you by then. You're going to look fabulous."

When Charlotte left, she felt no more stunning or gorgeous or fabulous than she had earlier. Those magazines Tiffany had left her with. What woman wouldn't want to look like any one of the photos? Imagine it possible, that somehow the right dress would melt away the rolls of fat which had accumulated over the years; one for every forgotten dream. How many of them stood in front of that mirror while Tiffany slung fabric about and watched themselves, waiting to be transformed into the sly, alluring sylph they had become in their mind's eye? Watching, watching, believing they had it in them to slink into a contoured gown and emerge a minx. Waiting and waiting, while nothing happened, the fairy image in their heads spiralling away suspended in a mist, as a familiar, lumpy, worn-out figure emerged in the landscape before them.

* * * * *

Charlotte took a shortcut through the park. A clump of pigeons had been feasting on a fallen donut and created ripples around Charlotte's feet as she waded through them. Just ahead, a couple walked in an awkward embrace along the sidewalk. Not lovers, they walked too awkwardly, like two teenagers in a three-legged race. One seemed to be helping the other along and they travelled quite slowly so, in a moment Charlotte was behind them. It was June and Kuldip. How could she have mistaken them for teenagers? June held her hand over her left eye and Kuldip had hold of her arm and propelled her along. June had hung her purse around her neck and appeared to be limping.

"Slowly, slowly." Kuldip hung onto June as though her training wheels had just come off.

"What happened to you?"

"Oh, Charlotte."

June dropped her hand and revealed a red welt on her cheek. She honestly looked as though she would burst into tears at any moment but had to put on a brave face in front of a stranger.

"Oh, Miss Charlotte, she is very bad." He made pushing motions with his free arm towards June. "Bad boys push her down."

He shook his head and reclaimed June's arm.

"What? What boys?" People didn't push other people in Norman. Who would have done this?

"Oh, it was just some youngsters playing ball. It was nothing. I'm sure I would have been fine but, Mr., er, Channa insisted on walking me home."

"Well, thank goodness someone was there."

Their procession moved with tiny steps up Elm Street – June in the middle and Charlotte and Kuldip on either side, balancing her between them.

"Okay, I'll be fine. Charlotte will take care of me now. Thank you for walking me home." They had arrived at the house. June pulled her arm away from Kuldip. She kept her face covered and went up the steps leaving Charlotte with Kuldip on the front walk.

"Thank you, Miss Charlotte. Very bad. I'm so sorry. Bye bye." He waved at her.

"Thank you Kuldip. You are very kind. Why don't you come through the back? It will be faster for you." He followed Charlotte through the gate to the backyard and slowed to have a look around. Charlotte could tell he was looking for something to admire on the monochrome plain. It was not much compared with the dense growth of vegetables and flowers in Kuldip's garden. The lawn was kept trim and some bulbs poked through each year, though they were becoming fewer.

"No garden?" Was it disbelief or incredulity? All this space, rich black soil and perfect summers. What was

Charlotte's excuse? "Come, I give you tomatoes. Beautiful tomatoes."

He had some ripening on the windowsill. They were warm when he handed them to Charlotte. Such a funny little man, his skinny legs and big white running shoes, perfect tomatoes and a falling down porch.

"You have a beautiful garden," Charlotte told him.

"Oh, garden is beautiful all by itself." With a look of satisfaction, he looked down from the porch over the bounty in his back yard. He spotted something among the rows of zucchini and trotted down the steps to resettle some earth.

"Thank you for the tomatoes."

"You need nice tomatoes. Very good."

Charlotte carried the warm tomatoes across the lane. They seemed to pulse in the palms of her hands with an energy all their own.

* * * * *

"Of all the people to come to my rescue," June fumed. "I was fine until he came along and panicked. I don't like that smell that comes from his house. Curry. I don't care for it. It makes the whole neighbourhood smell like a slum."

Charlotte frowned. "As if you have any idea what a slum smells like. Besides he's lived here longer than you."

"Get me some aspirin, I'm getting a headache."

They had been living here, both of them, for eight years now. June got fed up with Winnipeg after thieves broke into her apartment twice in one month. When June pulled into Norman she had two bags and one cardboard box with her. Her clothes, some books, her hairdressing equipment and the flower print curtains from her kitchen window. With two trips from the car to the house, she had moved back home. She hung the curtains in the kitchen and announced, "There, that will make me feel at home."

chapter fifteen

The steam rose around Wade as his skin turned to bright pink under the water. The pads of his fingers became wrinkled. Sweat beaded up on his face and rolled into his eyes and ears. Each time Wade saw his naked body in the bath or tried to coax some rigor into his lifeless penis, he wondered what he was doing, back in the place he had left. *Gone to the city to find himself.* He supposed that much was true. Not a lot of soul searching and self-discovery is possible close to home. It's too easy not to bother. To play the role people expect, the one you're good at, the one your parents coached you for. Moving away allows you to reinvent yourself, to try on the personalities which have lurked beneath the surface for years, like trying on costumes from the dress-up box. In the city you can go out in your costume and nobody looks at you funny.

His return to Norman was almost a year ago. It was different to just come home for a visit. Seeing all the people you left behind, making them believe you had something they lacked which gave you courage to live in the city, to dodge the dangers and overpower your fears. When they see you in town they think you look bigger than the last time they saw you. You strut through town, confident and sure, but the only thing you are sure of is having experienced something they haven't. Maybe for the first time you've experienced yourself and you wonder how anyone can stand you. Anybody who moves away from home to live in the big city knows it's no big deal. So, you don't talk much about it, you just swagger more. When you move home for good, you lose the right to swagger.

In a place like Norman, your conduct can be deemed unacceptable by people who hardly know you, before you ever have a chance to defend yourself or explain. Nothing specific ever happens, you just gain a sudden sense of unease in the pit of your stomach that somewhere along the way, you turned a wrong corner and have upset everyone. You have stumbled into territory where nobody is comfortable, having led everybody there and they are screaming at you to let them out.

He wished he could, but it wasn't up to him to protect people from their thoughts. It was only himself he had to protect, especially in this town.

Winnipeg had changed two things in Wade. He had taken up smoking and discovered men. One led to the other. Except not all at once. He started out with a girlfriend, Laura. They met at college. She was in the journalism program and took her work very seriously. Most of the time they spent together was in the cafeteria, since when she wasn't at school, Laura was working on her assignments. She loved to say she had an assignment, even if she was just re-copying her notes. When they did go out, Laura engaged everyone they met in conversation, practising her interview skills. She talked to people taking tickets at the theatre, taxi drivers, bus boys, bank tellers and pretended to be fascinated by whatever they said. Or maybe those people really did fascinate her. It was hard to tell with journalists.

With Wade she was more interested in making out than talking, and she liked it to be fast. It was an exercise, an assignment, one more experience she needed to get down in detail, but it had to be concise because there were other things to do. "There, that was nice. That was good," she would say, already out of bed and stepping into her panties. "Where can we go now?"

Wade could easily blame his problems on her, but what happened to Wade would have happened one way or another anyway because Wade was gay. Around the corner from his apartment was a gay bar and it was only a matter of time before his curiosity would grab him by the collar and drag him over there. It was a convenience that Laura was so busy all of the time that Wade could even get into a bit of a routine going to the bar.

She used to stand at his window and comment on all the guys on the street below. "Oh, God, the queers are here again. Why did you take this apartment? People might think you're one of them. You have to walk past that place every day."

He didn't think she ever would find out since he would go and stand beside her and make the same kinds of derisive comments. "Those pansies wouldn't last ten seconds where I come from. They'd have the shit kicked out of them so fast."

"Well, what do they expect, dressing in those cut-offs with their ass cheeks hanging out and looking at other guys' asses. Any normal guy would beat the crap out of them for that."

For weeks he watched groups of men milling about outside the doors and filing in and out all night. On his calendar he circled a day, a Saturday and resolved to go on that night. He bought a pack of Cameos and practised smoking all afternoon. By the time he stood in the cold air outside the unmarked door, he could exhale a smooth blue stream of smoke without coughing. He felt cool.

* * * * *

The room pulsed with bass from the DJ booth and lights spun around, flashing red and green off the walls. His heart pounded in his chest and he was sure everyone was watching him. Men danced, men played pool. They hung around the bar and watched the doors to the bathroom. Wade had a seat at the corner of the bar where he could lean against the wall and view the whole room. Nobody talked to him and he hoped he wasn't giving out any signals. From where he sat he could watch the men cruise the bar. They were easy to spot, the ones who never sat still but kept walking past the bar, around the dance floor, at the periphery of the pool table and then back again, like circuits in gym class. Television screens beamed pornographic videos into the room. They weren't allowed to show real porn, only one guy per video, whacking off in bed, in the pool, off of the top of a tractor or performing a solo strip tease and shooting his load into the camera lens. Wade tried not to look anyone in the eye while at the same time tried not to watch the videos for more than ten seconds at a time.

At the end of the night the drag queens took over the floor. Blonde wigs, tight dresses, high-heeled shoes and bodies shaved smooth. They lip-synched to bass-boosted Dionne Warwick and Gloria Gaynor and strutted around the dance floor, laughing at their friends and tugging at their hems. People sat in a semi-circle around the dance floor and waved five dollar bills at the dancers. Five bucks and a kiss on the cheek from the lady of your choice. It was meant as a joke, really. How could you make a living doing drag shows in the middle of the prairies?

He went home alone but he was so excited he couldn't sleep. His phone rang at two in the morning.

"Where were you all night? I finished my assignment and wanted to go dancing."

Wade's tongue felt thick in his mouth from the beer and the cigarettes. His ears were still pounding from the loud music. "I went out."

"Where?"

"Out for a drink." He was a terrible liar, so he tried to stick to the truth.

"Where?"

"Just out, okay? Want to do something tomorrow?"

It was a close call and Wade should have made up his mind right then. Laura or the bar. Come out, come clean. But, he wasn't ready. Not nearly ready. He only came to terms with all those tangled emotions a short while ago. Sure, all through high school he knew there was something not normal about how he reacted around guys and how he didn't really react to girls. It took him awhile to figure out that that probably meant he was gay. One night at a gay bar was a start, but it wasn't enough to tell if he really was gay or not, was it? There was a long stretch of road between deciding he might be gay and knowing for fact. It came down to sex. He had to try it before he could be sure. And even then, weren't people supposed to fall in love?

After the first night, Wade went almost every Saturday. Suddenly, he had assignments for school too and couldn't go out. He became one of those men in the bar who lived double lives and there were lots of them. They had their one night, where they excused themselves from their straight life and stepped into their secret life.

Wade soon discovered he loved men. The way they smelled, sometimes of soap and tobacco, sometimes of sweat and sex and whiskey. The way they walked, hands in pockets, in the air, clasped behind their backs. The way hair grew in to outline the beard, so you could imagine what he would look like if he grew one. The way they flirted, with their whole bodies, their narrow hips, ready to be gripped like dumbbells; soft lips on a rough face and questioning eyes. Soon people started to recognize him, as he did them, the regulars. He looked forward to sitting at his place at the bar and watching the familiar faces drift in. They looked at him and sometimes nodded. He sat and smoked and pretended he was in a movie, different movies all the time. James Bond-type movies, where he had to infiltrate the gay scene and stake out a bar in order to bring down some mobster. Or an Indiana Jones quest for ancient treasure and the bar was where he was to meet his connection. Sometimes he was an undercover cop staking out a drug ring. He lurked about in the shadows of the bar trying to look a little dangerous.

"You a private detective or something?" The bartender asked him while he wiped down glasses.

"Me?"

"You've been sitting in that spot every weekend for the past four weeks. You come at nine-thirty, order a Blue, light a smoke and scan the room. You leave after the show. Never talk to anyone. No one knows you. If you were here for the meat, you'd have gotten some by now."

"What?"

"What are you looking for?"

"Nothing. I'm just out for a drink."

"Mark." He extended his hand. Wade took it, resisting the urge to wipe his hand on his pants first.

"Wade. Pleased to meet you."

"Wade." Mark opened a Blue. "Can I buy you a beer, Wade? Anything you want to know about anyone here, you just ask me. I know them all."

The more Wade drank, the chattier he became, asking Mark about the men in the club, one after the other. Mark did know them all: the floozies, the flirts, the married ones, the ministers. Wade would point out who he liked and asked if they were available. To which Mark raised an eyebrow and said, "Available? These are gay men, in a bar on a Saturday night. They're all available."

"What about you?"

"Me what?"

"Are you available?"

"Depends what for."

Images of Bond in his tux, Indiana Jones in his sweaty cotton shirt flitted behind Wade's eyes. The smoky bar, the buzzing crowd, lights flashing all around him. Now or never. He sucked on his beer and smacked the bottle onto the bar. "A nightcap perhaps?"

Mark struck a match and held it out for Wade. "Perhaps a nightcap. Yes, but only one. I can't get into the habit, you know. This is my job."

Wade couldn't help but feel giddy and smug the rest of the evening while he waited for Mark. To hell with cool. He was crazy with glee and had to force back the surge of excitement that rose repeatedly from his stomach like a bad case of hiccups.

Back at Mark's place, they listened to music, smoked a joint and didn't bother with the bedroom. Wade left an hour later feeling like a man. The teeth marks on Wade's shoulder made him feel incredibly proud. He crawled into bed at five in the morning and fell into the most delicious sleep. The only problem was hiding out from Laura until the teeth marks faded. The only other problem was that Wade went back every weekend for more.

Keeping a secret over a sustained length of time is like holding your breath. It will eventually kill you. With Wade going to the bar every weekend and making excuses to Laura, it was just a matter of time before the inevitable happened. He fell in love.

Beautiful, sexy Graeme, with his limp black hair and languid fingers. His nails looked like he had spent the afternoon at the salon getting a French manicure and when he spoke his fingers moved like willows in the wind. When Wade asked Mark about Graeme the night he came to the bar, Mark said, "You're on your own buddy. I've never seen him before. But I'd say you'd better act fast. He'll be snapped up in no time."

Graeme came over to the bar and ordered a double scotch. He picked up his change while Mark watched, waiting to meet his eye and give him a dirty look. "Those dimes are pretty hard to get a grip on, eh?"

Then to Wade he said, "Shitty tippers make shittier lovers. You might want to think twice."

They both watched Graeme from the bar. He took the drink over to another guy and handed him the change. "Aha, he's not a shitty tipper. He doesn't drink." Wade was hopeful once more. "Only one way to find out. Give me a beer."

"He's with someone," said Mark.

"Yah, a shitty tipper."

"You've got guts, man. I'll give you that."

Graeme accepted the beer. The way he studied the label made Wade feel for a moment as though he might give it back and ask for something else. "I'll catch you later," he said. "Thanks for the beer."

How cool. Wade sauntered back to Mark, grinning. "He said he'd catch me later."

Wade watched Graeme's friend leave and winced when they embraced. At least Graeme didn't leave with him but came over to the bar. "Sorry it took me so long," he said.

They stayed at the bar until it closed and then walked to Graeme's car and he invited Wade to his place. This was how most Saturday nights ended for Wade. Except this night, he didn't have sex. No urgent, frantic grappling sex followed by a drive home by a ghoulish cabbie working the night shift. They talked, drank some red wine and when they finally went to bed they slept. In the time they spent not having sex, Wade fell in love. Or the closest thing to what he thought love felt like. It made him feel weak and vulnerable. He wasn't sure he liked it, but Graeme assured him he felt the same way. They slept wrapped around one another. When Wade turned over, Graeme followed and curled up snug behind him and held Wade close to his belly. It was the most wonderful feeling Wade had ever experienced.

He awoke to the smell of fresh peaches and the voice of Julie London, with the sun streaming onto the bed. His eyelids stuck to his eyes and the red wine from the night before still tasted tart on his tongue. The frost had crept almost halfway up the window but the covers kept the warmth in. Graeme sat beside Wade and they ate fresh slices of peach, the sweet juice a salve for his parched mouth. They stayed in bed all day while the heaters hissed and forced the frost farther up the windowpanes. At five o'clock, Wade pulled his clothes on and drove home, thinking of nothing but the kiss Graeme gave him at the door. A real kiss, the kind which lingers for days. The thought of that kiss still made him quake.

* * * * *

At that point it would have made sense for Wade to break up with Laura. And he was going to. He spent days, a few weeks actually, trying to think of a way to do it, without telling her what was really happening. In the meantime, he juggled valiantly. He had a boyfriend and a girlfriend. The situation was absurd. Graeme wanted to know why they always came to his place and never to Wade's. Laura wanted to know why he didn't have time to meet her parents. His girlfriend wanted to marry him and his boyfriend wanted him to move in. Two equal and opposite forces resulted in stasis. He was caught between two worlds, weighing the merits and drawbacks of each, truly tormented over his decision. Then one morning the phone rang and it was his mother about the job at Olafson's. The escape hatch had opened. It was time to run away.

* * * * *

And here he was, soaking in the tub in his drab apartment, in Norman, Manitoba, not wanting to stay in and not wanting to get out. Not knowing what he wanted and becoming irritated by the necessity of making a choice.

This was his reward for his indecision and a lack of conviction.

The phone rang and Wade jumped dripping from the bath.

"Wade, it's me." His mother was on the phone. "Amanda has pneumonia again, I'm going to run in to Winnipeg for a few days. Can you check on the house for me?"

Amanda lived in Winnipeg at the St. Amant Centre. She got pneumonia about three times a year, which seemed to remind his mother to go and visit. Wade didn't go anymore. His mom didn't mind and Amanda wouldn't know one way or the other.

He didn't like the smell at St. Amant. A mixture of baby powder, drool and apple juice permeated the hallways lined with wheelchairs. The people in the wheelchairs all looked grotesque and deformed and needed padded bolsters to hold up their heads and foot rests with straps so their legs wouldn't stick straight out. They had bulky diapers in their sweat pants and chewed on terry cloth bibs. One girl had tubes on her arms to keep her elbows straight and her hands away from her mouth so she wouldn't chew through her fingers. For Amanda's twelfth birthday, her first birthday at the centre, he and his mom bought a double chocolate cake from Safeway with "Happy Birthday Amanda" written in pink frosting. They lit twelve candles and all the ward staff sang *Happy Birthday* with them. Amanda started to howl and bite her wrists. In the end she calmed down enough to lick some icing from a plastic spoon, while everyone else ate real pieces of cake.

Wade didn't think much of all the equipment and the wheelchair when Amanda was still at home but, when he saw so many kids like her all at once, he felt ashamed to have a sister like that, because he didn't like her. She was twelve and still wore a diaper and waved her hands around all day and grunted. That's all she ever did. When she turned eighteen they moved her to a place for adults, as if it would make a difference. Maybe they thought it was important for her to be around people her own age. Where they could rent R-rated movies and park all the wheelchairs around the television. It wasn't like Amanda could go get a job at Safeway now that she was an adult. Did it really matter to her in which institution she spent her life?

His dad hadn't liked her either. He took off, couldn't even look at her when she was born, just took off. The day he left, Wade saw his mom as he rounded the corner on his way home from school. He ran up the street. There were fresh baked Ranger cookies; she let him have as many as he wanted. When's Dad coming home? Her pursed lips bent to kiss him with a thin smile. Her hand gripped his shoulder and guided him to the kitchen table. She held him from behind by the shoulders and sent sobs into his body, he could see the ripples they made in his glass of milk. He felt like he was in a cocoon, the kind he made in his bed out of the blankets, with his mom standing over him like that. They stayed this way until Wade ate the last cookie. He left her standing in the kitchen and went outside to play. When he came back, they ate shepherd's pie on folding tables and watched *Dukes of Hazzard* on TV. It wasn't so bad.

Most of his life he felt like Amanda's older brother, when really she was supposed to be watching out for him, bossing him around like Paul Frechette's sister Evie did to him. She made Paul sit in his room and do his homework with no TV when she was in charge. Or made him vegetable soup and cheese slices and told him he had to sit at the table and finish everything before he was allowed to get up, even though the beans in the soup made him gag. Wade's mom paid Evie to look after him on the days she took Amanda to Winnipeg to have her wheelchair fixed. Evie walked to and from school with them and made them hot dogs and chips for lunch. After school they got cookies and milk and hung around Evie's bedroom door listening to her on the phone until she caught them and chased them all the way to Paul's room where they slammed the door in her face. They laughed when she screamed at them through the door and threatened to lock them in the basement. Paul and Evie didn't have to be careful with one another, or learn about wheelchair brakes and seizures.

Wade learned how to hold the special spoon so Amanda wouldn't gag when he fed her and learned to squirt medicine from a syringe into her mouth. His mom always told him he was a good brother and Amanda was lucky to have such a special brother. She never tried to tell him he was lucky to have a sister like Amanda. He wouldn't have believed her anyway.

Paul liked to try the wheelchair when Amanda wasn't in it. They took turns strapping each other in and pretended they were racecar drivers. Wade would push Paul all around the house, tipping the wheels up on one side at the corners. One day the chair tipped too far and with Paul strapped in there he couldn't brace himself and broke his arm.

"It's a good thing it was his arm and not Amanda's wheelchair. What would we do then?" His mother said. Amanda didn't seem to care when Wade wheeled her around like a race car driver. He did it mostly to get a reaction out of her, some sign that there was a person in that pale, purplish body. Her skin looked untouched, always clean and powdered and smooth. No rough spots, no sores or scrapes. When Wade held her hands they felt wet and cold because she had them in her mouth so much. Sometimes he got the shivers just looking at her dusty, bluish skin.

The school didn't have any ramps, so Amanda couldn't go to school with Wade. What would she learn there anyway, sitting in the room gurgling and spitting? She spit when she got upset. She couldn't learn colours or numbers or go out at recess and play four-square. In the city kids like Amanda went to school with all the normal kids. Wade's mom always said she wouldn't want Amanda to sit all by herself in a class full of kids running around. They were passed along from grade to grade without any more smarts than when they were born. They sat in their wheelchairs, with their diapers and bibs sopping wet while the teacher stood at the front and taught the class about Voyageurs and the history of Canada. The other kids in the class learned to ignore them like a spot on the carpet you don't see after a while. Thankfully, Wade didn't have to sit in school and ignore Amanda, or hear other kids talk about her. He was happy his mom decided to move her to Winnipeg. Amanda didn't know the difference anyway.

The Christmas parties at the centre were the one occasion for which Wade used to make the trip with his mom. Mostly the Christmas party, with the blinking lights from the tree and the noisy music resulted in nothing more than a lot of screaming and high decibel levels of stimulation. The staff tried to generate a festive feeling by clasping little hands onto a set of jingle bells and helping the kids to shake along to the beat of the Raffi Christmas album. By the end of the party, only a few kids remained, the rest having either seizured, vomited up their tube feeds or shrieked at such a pitch it threatened to result in more seizures.

Wade and his mom sat on either side of Amanda and just tried to keep her calm. Wade tugged and stroked her ears while his mom rubbed her arms. Most of the time she was one of the few who made it through to the end of the party and for some reason this made Wade extremely proud of her. Sometimes she even gurgled at the staff when they told her what a good girl she had been. Then Wade would wheel her back to the elevator really fast and sometimes she almost laughed.

The last time he saw her was while he was studying in Winnipeg. He met his mom at the centre one day. He hadn't seen Amanda since the time he was learning to drive and his mom let him drive the car on the highway all the way to the city.

By this time Amanda was close to thirty. It disturbed Wade to see his sister as a grown woman, with breasts and pubic hair under the pale yellow sweat suit she wore, and that bulky diaper. A stack of adult sized diapers sat on her night table, right there in the open. It had been different seeing her when she was a child. At least she still looked a bit cute. Now she just looked severely disabled. During their visit, Wade's mom wanted to pack Amanda up and take her to the mall. "Let's get her out of here for awhile."

"Mom, what's she going to get out of the mall? She doesn't care. Let's just take her outside, into the fresh air." The way people stared at people in wheelchairs made him sick. When they realized their piteous smiles weren't registering with Amanda, they would look up at him as though their pity went out to him too, for having the courage to bring a handicapped person out in public. Thankfully, his mother agreed and they took Amanda for a walk along the river. They stopped in a sunny clearing and Wade took off Amanda's shoes and socks and let the grass tickle her feet. She closed her eyes and held her face into the breeze and hummed and smacked her lips. It didn't take much to make her happy.

SIXTEEN

chapter sixteen

"Well Charlotte, I hope you like Chicken Divan." Vi appeared through the flapping door. "We had to make a decision, Saturday's not far off you know." She circled the kitchen, watching Charlotte and Wade work. Her heavy perfume tainted the aroma of the baking bread. Charlotte and Wade crinkled their noses at the same time.

"I'm not sure I know what Chicken Divan is."

"It's a chicken and broccoli casserole and I think it's served with pasta or rice. It's very light. I spoke with the chef about that."

"We're having casserole?"

"Well, you wouldn't make up your mind. It's fancy casserole. It's not made with cream of mushroom soup or anything. I don't think."

"I'm sure the chefs at the Driftwood use nothing but the finest ingredients from the IGA. Are we having pigs-in-a-blanket for appetizers?"

"Oh come on Charlotte. June and I are doing our best for you. It will be a special night."

As long as the showcase shelves looked full and delicious, Vi wasn't concerned with how they got that way. She liked to check up on Wade and Charlotte and watch what they were doing but had no real understanding of how they created the baking which stocked her shelves. All she knew was whatever Charlotte put into those cheese-sticks that sold out before noon everyday better be passed on to Wade. One best-selling product to get people into the store was essential. They always bought something else. Since Vi had taken over the bakery, the customers had seen a slow but steady rise in the prices. The dream cookies now cost almost a dollar each. Who would pay a dollar for a cookie, Charlotte wondered, but at the end of each day, the shelves lay bare. The day old stock went quickly the next morning.

"People will pay for superior products, Charlotte. And this bakery offers that. Quality."

"This is the only bakery in town, Vi. People will pay for convenience too, but they don't like it. It always takes a week or two for sales to pick up again after you've raised the prices. You're lucky I'm so good at what I do."

Vi was silent a moment. "Yeah, well. I guess we're lucky to have each other." She pursed her lips. "At least they haven't come to board us up yet."

Charlotte noticed the change in Vi not too long ago when two small businesses went under within one week. The balloon shop and the tanning studio. Granted, balloons could be bought anywhere and for a tan you just had to step outside, but still, the news weighed heavily on Vi. It was hard to convince people to get their balloons and their tans in Norman. Even though no one wanted to live in Winnipeg, they sure liked to shop there. A bakery was one enterprise that still stood a chance. It was one of those things where bigger wasn't better and people didn't want a huge selection of stale baking, but a small selection of fresh cakes and the possibility that their bread would still be warm from the oven by the time they got it home. The bakery was in no danger of closing. But still, Vi and her fellow business owners got scared every time one of their own went under. They hardened their resolve to stay open and to make downtown Norman a place where business boomed. It was after these closures that Vi cut down on certain expenses and made sure not to raise her prices. She offered specials and told Charlotte to use fewer raisins and chocolate chips.

"By the way, how's the dress looking, Charlotte?" Vi rubbed her thumb over a stain on the refrigerator. "The girls at Rosa's are so talented."

Charlotte was tempted to tell Vi she had designed the dress herself, no help from Miss Tiffany. "You could say that. It's bluey-green."

"Like turquoise?"

"I guess so. Anything special orders today, Vi?"

But, Vi had already flapped through the doors to the front of the bakery because the door chimes had rung. She liked to see what people bought, which items sold out first and whether to get Charlotte to put some buns in the oven to warm close to the end of the day to make them seem fresh for the dinner table.

When Charlotte peered through the window of the swinging door, she saw Vi talking to a customer. She had her eye on Doris at the till. The numbers hadn't been adding up lately and Vi's number one suspect was poor Doris. She had hired Doris three months ago as a favour to Doris's mother. Doris was about the same age Charlotte was when she began at the bakery.

Charlotte watched her from behind the door; her thin blonde hair falling over the cash drawer, her blue glossy fingernails picking away at the coin rolls, her skinny legs always bruised, rising out of the most monstrous shoes, like saplings growing out of cement blocks. Her eyes encircled with dark liner, so no matter what her mood, they glowered at everybody.

Charlotte checked the display every morning, but had let Doris take over the design and decoration. Sometimes, when Charlotte watched Doris arrange the display case, she thought of her mother on the other side of the window, looking in. Beyond the image of her mother was the traffic in the street. It was easy to see how it could have happened. Such a tragedy, but thankfully one that had never been repeated. There was no way to spare the cakes or the person, should a truck come along and knock them into the bakery while they peered through the window.

By this point in her life Charlotte had outlived her mother by twenty years. Her mother had been forty-three when she died. It was a violent way to die, unexpected and unjust. But, as so many people told Charlotte in the days after, Florence was doing what she loved. Or they said, she went quickly, wouldn't have known what hit her. Her last thoughts would have been of her party and her heart would have been at peace. Those things may all have been true, but Charlotte knew her mother would have been horrified to be sprawled on the pavement for all to see. To die in such a public way, with people who didn't even know her stopping to gasp and stare. Charlotte imagined the crowd of people standing there, feeling that rush shudder through their bodies, almost no different from the rush they got when they saw a dead dog or cat lying in the middle of the road. It was this lack of dignity in the way her mother died that troubled Charlotte most. No matter how Florence conducted herself through life, her struggles were not insignificant and certainly deserving of a little self-respect at their end.

* * * * *

Doris was good at the decorating and it gave her something creative to do. Besides, Doris was pleased to have something else to add to her resume: window display design. Already her resume listed tap and jazz dancing, roller-skating, figure skating, voice training, acting lessons, badminton and judo as her special skills. She had brought it in one day to show Charlotte before one of her auditions in Winnipeg. When Charlotte asked her where she had done all of this, Doris said it didn't matter if you only took a year of tap or just sang in the school choir. You had to put everything on your resume in case. Some people included things like sky diving, even if they never jumped out of the plane, but took the class on the ground. Actors had to be multi-talented if they wanted to get anywhere.

Doris did put a lot of effort into the displays, more than Charlotte ever had. She cut out paper flowers and seasonal decorations to scatter among the rows of cookies and sticky buns. At Thanksgiving she came in with maple leaves and a pumpkin to arrange around the pumpkin tarts. When Charlotte told her she had a good eye, Doris beamed. Later, Charlotte overheard her telling her friends how she was in charge of the display case.

Doris knew Vi watched her; didn't trust her and thought she was stealing out of the till. Vi was sitting on her stool at the end of the back counter, with a pencil in her mouth and the adding machine plugged in. Doris waited with her hand resting on the open cash drawer. Vi looked up from her work and Doris pretended to slip something into her pocket. Out of the corner of her eye she could see Vi shift uneasily in her chair. At the end of the day she would go over her stupid tally sheet a hundred times and wonder why it all balanced out. If she came over to ask Doris about it, all Doris had to say was, "Don't ask me. I failed math."

Everyday for the past week, Doris studied the photograph of Charlotte with the retirement announcement under it. "How old are you here?" Doris asked Charlotte.

"That was taken on my eighteenth birthday."

"I hope I'm not still working here when I'm eighteen." Doris quickly looked down. "Sorry."

"Well, it's not for everyone. You'll save up some money and move down to Winnipeg."

"Yeah, I hope so. Maybe I can get into acting down there. I've already done some modelling you know. I took a class."

"Sure, anything's possible. You're young." The glossy photo-articles in *People* could feature someone like Doris, once she made it. A simple girl from a hard working family, who supported her classes even though they couldn't afford it. And now they are oh so proud of her, living like a princess and bestowing on her family prestige and lavish gifts. The generic bio would say:

> *Doris Richards, raised in the small Manitoba town, Norman, dropped out of high school to work in the local bakery. Mother, a business woman. Father, an electrician. They say, "Doris is a born performer. She always loved the stage." Now Doris spends her time between shoots at her mansion in Beverly Hills and a condo in New York. All this from such humble beginnings and she's so down to earth! Though she does profess a weakness for limousines and caviar, but she's earned it!*

And there would be a photo of her with her cute husband in their colonial style kitchen enjoying some plebeian task, like making soup, to show she had married well and hadn't changed a bit.

* * * * *

"I'll show you guys how to walk like a model," Doris offered one day. They were behind the bakery, Wade, Doris and Charlotte, on their break. Two chairs and a milk crate had been arranged by the back door many years ago. The sun cast its warming rays onto Charlotte's face. She sat leaning back, with her head tilted towards the heat and let the sun soak into her skin. Beside her was a milky cup of tea and a warm buttered roll with orange marmalade. Wade and Doris smoked cigarettes.

"Here, hold this." Doris gave Wade her cigarette and turned on one foot.

"It's like this. You have to put one foot in front of the other, like on a balance beam, except you have to take a full stride, you can't look like you're about to fall off. And straight wrists." Walking down the alley, fists on her hips, her pelvis propelling her entire body forward, Doris strutted down the runway into the bright lights of her future. At the end of the alley, she pivoted right around on one foot and sashayed back to the crates, her eyes focused somewhere on the wall behind them. She took her cigarette from Wade and leaned against the building with one knee bent behind her. "Like that. Try it."

She held Wade's cigarette for him as he slung his leather jacket over his shoulder and slouched along the alley, one hand thrust in his pocket. He flipped his head, like the models do to make their hair fly around, except his hairnet kept his hair in check.

"Here, give me your jacket and try again. Oh, it's heavy," she said when Wade handed it over. "Stand up straight, no hands in your pockets. They teach the guys different ways of walking. Like the balance beam thing. I don't think boys can walk like that because of their hips. Anyway, they don't want the guys walking like girls. It would look prissy."

"No, you wouldn't want that," said Charlotte. Doris had draped Wade's jacket around her shoulders and began puffing on his cigarette.

"Oh, I love the smell of smoke and leather. Are you going to try Charlotte?" Doris asked.

"I'm on my feet all day, I'm not about to go for a walk on my break. Besides, I've never walked prissy and I don't want to learn now."

"It might help you for your big night. I heard you were having a dress made. You can't just walk any old way in a new dress."

"I'll keep that in mind. You could put modelling instructor on your resume then."

"Hey, you're right. I think I will anyway, because Wade walked. Say Wade, how much was this jacket? I'm saving up for one."

"I don't know. Three-fifty or something."

"How does it look on me?"

"All right, I guess. Not as good as it looks on me though. Give it here."

Only Charlotte saw Doris' quickly hold the jacket over her nose before she relinquished it. Wade was distracted by the lipstick on his cigarette.

The three of them went back inside. Charlotte saw Vi out front talking to Sharon Douglas from the *Norman Herald*. Sharon was a reporter with the *Herald*. She too belonged to the Business District Council, a group of local business people who had meetings to discuss their rights as business people. The Business District Council lobbied the Town Council for money to have signs put on all the lampposts on Main Street declaring it the Business District. It was just the sort of thing the town needed to distract people from the fact that businesses were closing rather than expanding, the way an official business district would imply. The council was in the process of raising funds for a Business Centre to be built at the end of Main Street where right now a vacant lot provided young people with a place to drink beer and litter. They needed a place to have their meetings, they argued. Right now they took turns at each other's houses and that wasn't very professional and besides the host did not need the added stress of hosting.

What Norman needed was actual new business establishments, not a bunch of people trying to delude others into thinking the town was prospering. The number of dusty, vacant buildings was growing and the big grocery stores were advertising "Winnipeg prices!" The apartment blocks all had vacancies. There were houses for sale on every street. The town was dying from an undiagnosed affliction. Something was sucking the life out of it and though Vi and her people had every interest in saving it, in plugging the leaks and injecting the B12, they couldn't put their finger on the problem and focused instead on saving themselves.

Vi was always running off to her BDC meetings, where Charlotte imagined the members tried to out-dress and out-busy one another. All of them arriving late at various intervals toting their slim briefcases and paper cups of black coffee, apologizing for their lateness, but claiming to be so swamped they didn't know until the last moment whether they would make it at all. What the meetings were about after the blue and yellow signs went up was anyone's guess. Mostly the group was made up of women. These women darted about town in creaseless suits with pert jackets and skirts, just enough above the knee. Their legs always clad in a fashionable, complementary colour of nylon, shoes which at first glance looked sensible, but the sinew and bulk of the calf muscles gave away the effort involved in clicking around in them for a full day. Their make-up gave them flawless visages which by the end of a frantic day would be cracking and peeling like cheap paint.

"Charlotte, Sharon is here to interview you for the *Herald*," Vi swung through the door with shiny Sharon gripping her valise, behind her.

"What interview?" Charlotte asked. She meant to get home early today.

Sharon chimed in. "We're treating it as a general interest piece. It's going to appear in our lifestyles section next week."

"I didn't know you were coming today. I have to get home early."

"Aw, come on Charlotte, I wanted to surprise you. Do something special for you your last week." Vi said as a tight smile spanned her face. It looked like someone had hooked either side of her mouth and was pulling from behind. "Don't you want to be in the paper?"

"What for?" All she needed was an account of her failing heart to be in the Lifestyles section right next to the "Ask a Doctor" column. She could just see the heads nodding over the brim of their morning paper, *probably all that butter she put in the pastry.*

"Do you really think people want to know how bad baking is for your heart?"

"Sharon's agreed not to discuss your health. Just you in general."

"Yes, that's right. Your life, your career here at the bakery, your service to the Norman community for the last forty or so years." Sharon looked hopefully at Charlotte and then threw Vi a questioning look. It was clear Vi had not intended to forewarn Charlotte and now Sharon's feature article was in jeopardy.

The tape deck squeezed out strains of Dexter Gordon. The cinnamon buns were ready for the oven. Whatever.

"What would you like to know?" Sometimes it was easier to give in than to fight. Let them have their fun.

"Well, how does it feel to be retiring?" Sharon's long eyelashes batted at Charlotte. "Oh, wait. Can I tape this?"

She pulled a tiny tape recorder from her briefcase and placed it on the counter. "Do you mind? It will help me later when I write the piece."

Charlotte paused. How did she feel? Did she want all of Norman to know? Did they want to know? Who read things of general interest? The general public, she supposed. The public who one day too, would be retiring from jobs they loved and had worked hard at. They wanted to know how it felt, to know the right things to do.

"Not the greatest," said Charlotte. "Pretty crummy, actually. But not insurmountable."

The eye batting stopped and Sharon scribbled it down. Sharon fumbled through the rest of the interview. At the *Herald* they tried to keep the general interest section light, positive. How could she print these answers? People looked forward to their retirement, didn't they?

"And what has been the most rewarding part of your job?"

The questions had preconceived answers. Charlotte felt like a sham. She had read the interviews in the lifestyle section. Everybody in Norman loved their job, their families, their life. Norman, where seldom is heard a discouraging word. Didn't anybody ever have a bad day? She didn't know what to say. What was the most rewarding part of Sharon's job? Asking questions nobody wanted to answer? She wanted Charlotte to say she could hardly wait until Monday morning when the day stretched out before her, that the most rewarding part of her job was to meet people and feed them fresh-baked, wholesome bread. Should she tell her the most rewarding thing was how she got to do the same thing day in and out and she got so good at it she hardly had to think about it anymore. That some days she amused herself by closing her eyes to see how much she could get done without seeing her way around? That on other days she didn't consult one recipe just to see how things turned out, and put them on the shelves to sell without even tasting them?

"Having a hot, well-earned bath at the end of each day. That's pretty rewarding." Charlotte cringed even before the next, inevitable question.

"What are you going to do, now that you're retiring?"

The past month Charlotte had spent wishing this week would never arrive. Not because she wasn't looking forward to the rest, but because she feared the open-endedness of the rest. She never had to work again. In the past Charlotte spent her vacations at home, resting, sleeping until seven and puttering around the house. After a week she was ready to go back to work. Until now, she never woke up wondering what to do. But, all this month, her first thought every morning as her feet hit the mat beside her bed and her toes crawled into her slippers, she wondered how long it would take before her retirement stopped feeling like a vacation. She imagined waking up a bit later, having coffee at home rather than in the company of the rising loaves. And then feel her heart speed up and hope the caffeine didn't kill her. Maybe she would take up some imaginative ways to tax her heart, now that she didn't need it for work anymore. Jogging up and down the stairs, line dancing, timing how long she could hold her breath. Maybe June would join in for that one. Like old times, when they were kids. Or hyperventilating into a paper bag and then giving each other bear hugs until one of them passed out. They could have no end of fun, now that Charlotte had a bad heart.

Frankly, after the morning coffee, Charlotte's imagination shut down. Shut down, because when she looked up from her coffee, June was sitting there, an expectant and condescending look on her face, watching to see the fear in Charlotte's face. The fear of the empty day.

"What are you going to do today?" she would ask in that tone which Charlotte learned to recognize and despise when she was eight and June eleven. The tone of voice that no matter what the reply, she was wrong, or stupid or go ahead, what do I care? Waiting for Charlotte to give in and ask what June was doing and beg June to take her along. Imagine, Charlotte joining June's Easy-Does-It Fitness class where they sat in a circle and waved their arms about to saloon-style piano music or batted a ball at each other with their canes. June didn't even have her own cane. She borrowed one from somebody.

"Don't you have to be in a wheelchair to join that club?" Charlotte had asked.

"It's perfectly legitimate exercise. I feel energized after the class."

"I've seen them in there whacking a ball around the circle with their canes. Honestly June, you really shouldn't join until you legitimately need your own cane."

"Well it's too strenuous for some of them and they are happy to lend me a cane while they sit out and catch their breath." June had already put herself on the waiting list for Elmdale, the seniors' apartment block beside The Pines care home. She tried to get Charlotte to put her name on too, but Charlotte refused.

"They'll find me dead in my own house, thank you very much. I'm not going to spend my last days sitting out a round of balloon toss while some healthy impostor helps themselves to my cane."

"Fine."

Perhaps she and June would sort things. Lots of people once they retire sort through things: photographs, letters, scraps of fabric, jars of spices that haven't been used in years, recipes, clothing, expired passports. They smile fragile smiles and say they didn't know how they ever had time to work. She and June could read the letters they used to send home from camp. About the salty food and what they bought at the canteen with their spending money and the wiener roasts they had around a bonfire. Maybe once the things got organized she and June could take a cruise vacation. They could buy bright sun hats and airy dresses and stand on deck throwing crumbs to the gulls. June may find a husband; find a husband and move out and let Charlotte be. Perhaps a cruise was not a bad idea.

"Maybe I'll take a cruise," she told Sharon who smiled and finished the interview before Charlotte could say anything more.

chapter seventeen

The kitchen heated up and the grinding of the Hobart lulled Wade into the routine of the morning. He looked up with a start from the loaf pans. It was still dark outside and in the window of the door, instead of his reflection, he saw Doris's face behind the glass. At first, he didn't know what he was looking at and wondered why his reflection looked so odd. He frowned at the image and Doris rapped on the window.

"Jesus, you scared me. What are you doing here so early?"

"I came to watch you make the bread."

"It's almost finished. It's already four-thirty."

"Oh, well, maybe I'll have a coffee and watch whatever else you have to do. Can't you make some extra?"

"I still have to do the whole-wheat. It's not as pretty, but you'll see."

He pulled the aluminum bowl from under the hook and placed the dough on the table. Returning the bowl to the mixer, he poured the flour in and with his hand created a well in the centre into which he poured the oil.

"That's it. That's what the guy on television said was so beautiful, the flour and the oil. Ooh. It is beautiful. Don't you think?"

Wade added the water and yeast and flipped the switch.

"Aw, you wrecked it."

"You wanted to see how bread is made. This is how it's done."

"But I came for the beautiful part. It was so short. Can't you do it again?"

"I'm taking a break." He wanted her to notice how he hadn't measured anything. Did it all by look and feel. Already he knew in his haste to impress her he had added too much flour and if the bread were to be salvaged at all he would have to let the machine work the dough for at least half an hour. Doris followed him outside. They both lit their cigarettes and Wade let Doris sit on the good chair. She was here for the really beautiful part, he thought as the sky in the east turned a delicate pink and the chatter of the birds grew louder and louder, soon to be drowned out by traffic.

Doris rested her feet on the edge of the crate on which Wade sat. Too close, her toes almost touched his thigh. Inside the door was the bag of dog food. Wade picked up the tin plate from the day before and rose to fill it.

"What's that for?"

"Oh, it's for this stray dog. We feed it back here. He eats when nobody's around, though."

"That's sweet of you."

"We better go back in." Wade shook the plate, hoping the dog would hear and placed it on the ground. "He won't eat if we're out here. You can watch me make the rest of the bread."

Back inside the bakery, Charlotte had lifted the mixing hook from the bowl and had slapped Wade's dough onto the table.

"I don't know what's with this dough," she said. "It's been in there for twenty minutes and it's not giving at all. I'll have to put it back in for a bit I guess."

Wade busied himself feeding pastry dough through the sheeter and hoped Doris would think making bread dough always required such flexibility. More of an art than a science. Perched on a stool in the corner, Doris observed Wade and Charlotte at work. She took her sweater off. It was warm enough for just a T-shirt. A spare apron hung on the wall so she reached over and put it on.

"Can I do something? I want to try the rolling pin."

"Are you sure? You might like it so much you'll forget all about being an actress," said Wade. He handed her the rolling pin. "Go ahead. Give it a whirl."

After about ten rolls back and forth, Doris felt a burning across her shoulders and a kink snagged her back. "This is too hard for me. Can I do something else?"

"You can choose a cookie cutter and cut the cookies after I've rolled them out," said Charlotte.

"Oh, good. I can do that. I've done that at home."

Fascinated, she stood by while Charlotte rolled the dough. One, two passes with the rolling pin, then she picked up the dough all in one sheet and flipped it around and rolled again. Sprinkled the flour over and rolled once more sideways.

"Okay, there. You cut and put them on the cookie sheet and I'll roll out the rest. What did you pick?"

Doris held up a gingerbread man. "I'm going to make Charlotte cookies. I'll decorate them to look like you."

"I don't think we have mousy-brown food colouring for the hair."

"Well, they'll be little bakers I can put a hat on them instead. And I'll put a sign by them to say it's you."

Immortalized in cookie dough. Maybe it was appropriate. Charlotte could save one, like the bricks of wedding cake people stashed in the back of their freezers for good luck. Ten years from now, when she dug through the Tupperware containers of chili and soup, she would come across the cookie bearing her likeness and become

173

nostalgic for the good old days at the bakery. Ten years from now, Doris may still be selling gingerbread men at Olafson's. Unimaginable? Probably not. But, at least she hoped for something more. It would make her work more bearable, to believe she was on her way to stardom. With hope comes happiness and bright, sunny thoughts for the future. Without hope, there is only fear and that can stop you dead in your tracks.

"The egg guy might come at lunch. You'll have to watch for him because I have to go try my dress on again." The Hobart churned behind them, kneading the stiff dough for the hundred loaves they would bake today. The sheets of cookies were filling up, ready for the oven.

"What?"

"The egg guy."

"Yeah, Thursday, right."

Graeme had been looming in Wade's head ever since last night. That tugging sensation pinched his heart. He'd been back in Norman for almost a year and he missed Graeme terribly. His mind had been such a quagmire when he left Winnipeg, he fled with the sole purpose of survival. Self-preservation. It didn't matter to him who got hurt. It was a panicked decision. He broke up with Laura in person and with Graeme over the phone.

"You're breaking up with me on the phone?" Graeme asked, in disbelief. "What kind of a coward are you?"

A bigger one than you'll ever know, Wade thought.

Once he got home, though he felt safety at a distance, the thought of what he had done gnarled his stomach. He was a coward. At least in breaking up with Laura he had been true to himself. He didn't want to be with her. But Graeme, sweet, gentle Graeme. How could he have let him go? What was he so afraid of that he couldn't allow himself the happiness of being in love?

He felt like Graeme was the only person who really knew him. Nobody would recognize him if they saw how he acted when he was with Graeme. He didn't like himself any other time. Pretending to be a tough guy, a manly man around everyone else. This was especially important in Norman, where he felt like the spoon stuck in the blender, disrupting people's efforts in maintaining a creamy smooth life. He did his best to keep things from getting lumpy and unappetizing.

The year in Norman had allowed him time to think and what he thought about most was getting back to Winnipeg to find Graeme and to start over. But, Norman, as much as it was harsh and judgmental, was also a shroud of security under which to hide. He knew how to act here. He knew what was expected and he knew all the lines and all the moves.

But like the secrets he had kept last year, the charade he now was performing was getting harder and harder to endure. It was like a muscle cramping up. He hated himself for doing it. It came down to self worth. What was a man worth who couldn't face himself? Who spent each day avoiding the very thoughts and emotions that shaped him?

As with the first time he walked into the bar, he circled a day on the calendar and determined on that day to pick up the phone and see if Graeme would talk to him. Maybe they could even get together. With his mom away for the weekend, maybe it would be a good time to invite Graeme up to Norman. They could hide out in Wade's apartment and not emerge until Sunday. The more he thought about it the better the idea sounded and by the time the pastry was rolled he had himself convinced to do it. Wade's mind whirred with these thoughts spinning and churning, creating an anxious clot in his middle which he knew now would not disappear until he got on the phone. He would call from his mom's after work. It would be perfect. Graeme would be at work and Wade could leave a message. That way if Graeme didn't want to talk, he didn't have to.

He spread the sheet of pastry lengthwise on the table and cut strips for the turnovers. The dough gave slightly with a touch of the knife. Like a body, stirred, deep in sleep.

* * * * *

The sign-up sheet had more names on it than it had on Monday. Charlotte scanned the list. Doris had put her name on the list and Charlotte wondered if she would bring her friends along; the ones who still went to school, but thought it was really cool that Doris had dropped out and now had a job. They came to the bakery at lunch-time and stood outside and waited for Doris to take a break. Then, they stood in a circle and smoked. There was one with pigtails and green braces, one who had streaks of purple in her hair and another one who looked thankful just to be a part of the group. Whenever they stood around outside the shop, Vi watched them and let them know it. Sometimes she shooed them away saying, "If you're not here to buy anything then take your business elsewhere."

Girls in groups like to be told off by adults. They shuffled two feet over and stood in front of the travel agency next door and spoke to Vi with sneers on their faces. "Is that better? Geez, the sidewalk's public property."

Charlotte watched the girls from behind the till. The thankful girl didn't smoke, but liked to light the cigarettes for the rest of them. Doris was out there now, having a cigarette before she came in. Talking with her friends and waving her cigarette around. Doris knew she led this pack. She was no older than any of them, but a steady income elevated her status. These were the girls who drove to the city on the weekend in somebody's parent's car and hung around in shopping malls and smoked there too, until somebody told them to get going. The young did not fear the old. Not anymore. They saw adults as a force to battle against, a barrier between them and their freedom. They were too young to know they would win anyway, fight or no. The adults can only dig in their heels and hold firm, try to prolong the time before they are overtaken. They are the ones who need to fight, but it's hard to fight when you're losing your grip. The future arrives one way or another.

Outside, Doris leaned up against the bakery wall and smoked with Stacey, Amber and Jennifer. It was just like being at school with them, when they used to huddle outside the gym doors and smoke and talk.

"Wade's cute, eh? What's he like?" Stacey wanted to know.

"Wade? Oh, he's great. I think he might like me," said Doris.

"My brother told me he's a homo." How could Jennifer know that?

"Ew. Do you think so?" Amber asked, her nose wrinkled in disgust.

"He can't be." Doris felt her stomach sink. Wade, gay? He seemed so normal. "How do you know?"

"My brother saw him at a bar for gays in Winnipeg."

"Well, what was your brother doing there?"

"Yeah, what was you brother doing there?" They all chimed in unison.

"I don't know. He just saw him that's all."

"I don't believe you. He's a good guy." Suddenly Doris wanted to defend Wade in front of her juvenile friends. What did they know about anything other than the dorky guys they drooled over in the hallways at school? They had no idea about anything but their stupid teen magazine fantasies. None of them ever had even kissed a boy. Unlike Doris who had come very close to actually having sex. She and Danny Fleck snuck up onto the auditorium stage and made out behind the heavy curtain. They were practically tearing the clothes off each other when from somewhere close by, through the darkness they heard a cough. They lay panting, suspended in utter silence until again, a deliberate cough was heard and they scrambled to their feet, buttoning up their clothes and returned to their friends and the dance. There, the exchange of envious glances from her friends more than made up for the fact that nothing had really happened behind the curtain.

The group broke apart and Doris came back inside. She must have seen Charlotte looking at the list because when she came in she said, "Thought I'd come to your party too. I figure I might as well see what it's all about, since in about a hundred years they'll be throwing one for me."

"I'm sure you'll find it suitably banal. I found out they're serving some kind of chicken mash. Are you bringing a friend?"

"Vi said Chicken Divan. It sounds so fancy. They wouldn't serve mash at your party, unless...since your heart."

Charlotte grinned. "I can still chew, as long as it's not too gristly. Gristle is hard on my heart, especially if I have to chew for more than a minute and a half. Things could get dicey. The doctor told me to be very careful of how much I chew."

"Really?" Doris puzzled over this a moment.

"I'm glad you're coming on Saturday, really. Who did you say you were bringing?"

"Oh, I thought I'd ask Wade if he was going. Maybe we'll come together." That would do it. Once she told her friends Wade was going on a date with her, there would be nothing else they could say.

"That's a good idea, Doris. I would honestly love it if you both were there." And Charlotte realized she *would* love to see both of them on Saturday. The rest of the people on the list meant nothing to her.

Doris popped a stick of gum into her mouth. "Thanks. I mean, you're welcome."

Charlotte hadn't really noticed, but maybe Doris did like Wade. It certainly would impress her friends for her to have a boyfriend, and one who wasn't still in high school but an adult. There never were any boys who came along with the girl group at noon. Surely if one of them had a boyfriend he would be dragged along to slouch and smoke outside the bakery. So, if Doris could get Wade, she would be the first. Maybe Doris was afraid of losing her school friends, now that she didn't see them all day long in class and didn't know what they were talking about when they derided teachers and discussed assignments. She needed something to help her hang on to them. She couldn't very well be friends with Charlotte and Vi. And that left Wade as the only person even close to her in age, though there had to be at least ten years between them. Charlotte, however, had her own theory as to where Wade stood when it came to women.

She watched Doris through the round window in the swinging door. Her slim hips wrapped in her apron. Her hair piled on her head with all kinds of barrettes and pins. She seemed happy enough and on the day she got her first paycheque her face lit up like a kid who has just discovered the tooth fairy. As though she couldn't believe all she had to do was show up for work and she would get money.

One day left, not counting today. When Charlotte was Doris' age she never would have imagined working at the bakery until now. She always considered it an interim, a stop along the way until she figured out what she wanted. But, events and circumstance had accelerated her past the points at which she was supposed to stop and change direction. A trace of Charlotte's life would appear flat, not like others, which had blips where things happened. Punctuation marks, which accented life: graduations, marriages, new houses, cars, trips, children. There may have been a small bump when her mother died, and then her father and then June moving home. But these were things that happened to them, not Charlotte. The signs did not appear to Charlotte and therefore the blips did not occur. She supposed this heart thing counted as a sign.

Beating out of control in response to some invisible force. Telling her, now you quit working. Now you rest, for the rest of your life, nothing else to do but watch for those wonky heartbeats and hope they don't get you.

Maybe Doris was just coming to the dinner to remind herself of what she didn't want. To shock herself into striving for more, getting the article in *People* magazine with the cheery pictures. Avoiding at all costs ending up with the first blip in your life being a regrettable dinner at the Driftwood followed by a black hole into which your life free-falls.

* * * * *

"Why do you like all that old geezer stuff?" Doris asked Wade while they were out back having a smoke. He had propped the window open and placed the radio on the sill so he could listen to Bill Evans. They weren't supposed to be on break at the same time, but Doris often stopped what she was doing to follow Wade outside. Today especially, she felt it important to keep on the lookout for signs.

"It's jazz," Wade said because the word was an explanation in itself and if Doris had to ask, then she would never understand anyway.

"How come you don't like talking to me? You talk to Charlotte all the time." She stood there, holding out her cigarette for him to light. His mind was full of Graeme and now Doris, with all her chatter buzzing about his ears, threatened to drive Graeme out of Wade's head. He lit her cigarette and continued to smoke his own. She slumped onto a chair and pretended to ignore him, twirling her hair onto her finger.

Girls like Doris made Wade nervous. She was the type of girl he was supposed to be attracted to in high school: skinny, skirt wearing, flirty girls who roamed the hallways in formation. Two to a row and the columns could number as many as four or five. Carrying their books and snapping gum, their laughter always directed at you, like those portraits whose eyes follow you around the room, these girls had the ability to make their caustic laughter follow you anywhere. He felt like he was in high school again and Doris was about to ask him to the dance.

"I was wondering if you were planning on going to Charlotte's dinner on Saturday?"

"I can't."

"Oh." Doris's face fell. He didn't say he didn't want to. He said he couldn't. That was a good sign. "Well I'm going. I just wanted someone to go with."

He didn't know what to say to Doris. How could he blurt out that he'd invited Graeme, his lover, for the weekend, who was expected on the five o'clock bus tomorrow afternoon from Winnipeg?

"Sorry, got plans." He took a long draught of his Dr. Pepper, hoping when he looked up she would be gone. He tried to imagine spending an evening with Doris, she smoking her menthol cigarettes sitting with her legs crossed, one swinging leg in constant motion, talking non-stop about her acting and some lame audition she had in Winnipeg with the daughter of some famous Hollywood producer. He'd have to pretend he was in a movie again, a black comedy.

"Charlotte," Wade said when he returned from his break. "Look, I'm really sorry I won't be at your party on Saturday. I made other plans before I realized."

Charlotte shrugged. "I don't think you'll be missing much. I wouldn't go either if I wasn't expected. I hope no one makes such a fuss when I'm dead. One retirement party is enough."

"Well, still. I'm sorry to miss it."

"It'll be in the paper next week. The lifestyle section. You can read all about it." She rolled her eyes at him but he didn't seem to notice.

chapter eighteen

T he house where Wade grew up stood on a street of white houses each with a different colour trim. They lined up in two rows with McLean Street running down the middle. They looked like plastic molded houses, as though you could pop off the roof and find them filled with candy. Grape in the purple trim house, lemon in the yellow one and his house, peppermint, not everybody's favourite. Or worse yet, spearmint.

The kitchen had been re-done last year. New cupboards, new table and chairs. He missed the old things. It didn't feel like the kitchen he grew up in anymore with all the light pine and white cupboards. He had the old kitchen set in his apartment and that didn't feel right either. Sitting at the same kitchen table where his mom used to give him his lunch, eating two packages of instant Chinese noodles out of a pot. The smell of the house was the same though. He noticed it more after he moved out. A silent welcome each time he came home. Some houses smelled like wet paint or diaper pails and laundry. For some reason he instantly disliked the diaper pail houses. They were usually damp and had plastic toys everywhere. His house smelled like stale sheets, like a bedroom that had been slept in all night with no window open.

There was a note from his mom on the table telling him to take the perogies in the fridge home for his supper. Wade picked up the pencil and scribbled a thanks and talk to you Sunday. He put it on top of the mail and stared at the phone. Not yet.

He wandered through the house carrying the cordless phone. His mom had turned his room into a sitting room. His toys, posters, comics and magazines had all been donated to the church rummage sale. His dresser and bed were now in his apartment and his mom now had a small television and writing table in there. And a love seat, which folded out into an uncomfortable bed for guests. He used to spend hours with Paul in his room, rigging up pulley systems out of string, which spanned from the window latch down to the leg of the dresser. They set up bunkers in piles of clothes and had commando fights with green plastic soldiers falling from the pulley into enemy territory, to their deaths in the folds of a flannel shirt. Once they were older they sat up there flipping through *Sports Illustrated* and listening to Meatloaf and Pink Floyd albums on Wade's dome record player. Paul left a *Playboy* magazine for Wade to look through. He showed Wade the centrefold. A woman with blonde wavy hair lay on her back in a haystack, a wheat stalk between her teeth, with her gingham blouse open, her shiny breasts beckoning and her naked legs in cowboy boots spread to show her glistening vagina. He said "Wouldn't you like to stick your pecker in her hole?" He was tugging at the front of his shorts, waiting for Wade to say something. "Come on man, she's hot. Doesn't she make you hard?"

"Yeah, I guess so." He didn't know what else to say. He didn't want to look at the picture anymore and closed the magazine. "I'll look at it later, if you know what I mean."

"Sure, man. I'll leave it here. I've got more at home, if you get sick of her."

Wade took the magazine out again when he was alone and studied the pictures. He knew all about sex. Paul told him and Wade put it all together when he looked at the woman in the haystack. He tried to imagine sex with that woman, suffocating while she pressed his face between her breasts, his prick being sucked into her, like a powerful vacuum and never being able to get it out again. He never wanted to get his prick so close to those dark pulpy folds. He thought it might sting.

He got out the *Sports Illustrated*, found an underwear ad and whacked off.

* * * * *

As soon as Wade hung up the phone, he panicked. He hoped he didn't sound too eager. He should have called from his own place. Then he could have had a cigarette while he talked. In his apartment, in the bedroom was a single bed with maroon and grey striped sheets on it from his mother. It was the same bed he slept in all his life. The one he had moved back and forth from Winnipeg. The reason he never had anyone over to his apartment there. How could he let Graeme come to his place for a weekend and sleep in such a pathetic bed? He got on the floor and did ten push-ups. Tomorrow was payday. He'd head right over to Beck's furniture and buy a bed. A double bed, extra pillows and new sheets. Something classy, maybe plain white ones. Hopefully, they could deliver it before tomorrow afternoon. He wouldn't even wait for Graeme to call. Of course he would come. Hadn't he said more than once how he'd like to see Norman, how Wade could show him the sights? They could go to dinner at the best restaurant in town, which Wade told Graeme was Al's café, where they could dine on greasy cheeseburgers and fries too hot to eat. Graeme had said he could hardly wait.

* * * * *

"Why hello Ms. Weiss, I wasn't expecting you until later, but you take the first dressing room on the left and I'll get your dress." Tiffany's tangerine suit had been replaced by a pale lime skirt and sweater set. Sweet in the summer, savory for winter. Charlotte wondered how Tiffany would look in rare roast beef. Tiffany disappeared and reappeared with Charlotte's bolt of *Oceana*.

"You're going to love this, I know it." She held the dress up for Charlotte to see. The fabric rested on Tiffany's forearm. Pins protruded from every seam.

"I hope I don't need a blood transfusion after this."

"I sewed it up with temporary stitches. After today, they'll be permanent. We don't have the luxury of a third fitting. I have to get it right the first time."

"Don't you always try to get it right the first time?"

Tiffany let Charlotte into a change room. Light pastels on the walls and the plush chair in ivory. What did the change rooms look like over at the tailor shop? They probably smelled of cigars and leather and other rugged things to make a man feel manly when he stands before himself in his shorts. Charlotte pulled her clothes off and stood in front of the mirror. Her white socks came to just above her ankles. From there her ill-defined legs, a mottled blue and purple hue, rose towards the folds in her knees. She first saw those wrinkles when she scrunched up her knees when she was about thirty-two. Later, the same wrinkles appeared at her elbows and loose flesh hung over the joints and served no purpose at all, except for her to pinch from time to time to see if it was even innervated. She wore large underwear. Large enough to cover the expanse her behind had become. Ninety-percent of women over the age of fifty suffer from incontinence. Ninety-percent. Charlotte supposed it was just a matter of time before she would join the legions of women who dribbled. At least her heart was something she never could control. It either functioned properly or it didn't. But her bladder:

all those agonizing childhood moments, all that training and heartache over peeing in the pot, gone, and her with no recollection how she learned to do it in the first place.

Her ratty, worn brassiere did little to support the weight of her breasts. She cupped each one in her hands and lifted them up until she created a significant cleavage. When she let them drop, they descended at least four inches. Remarkable. She pulled her underwear up and let her breasts hang down. Contact.

"How're we doing in there? Can I come in?"

"We're almost ready. Just a minute."

Tiffany had to help Charlotte on with the dress because of all the pins and loopy stitches.

"Oh, of course you won't be wearing those shoes, but God you look stunning!"

Charlotte looked down at her white sneakers and sweat socks while Tiffany tugged and re-pinned.

"You better try sitting down too. You're going to want to eat in it. What are they serving for your dinner?" What a cheery, happy, helpful girl. Did she keep this up all day? Maybe when the shop was empty and night fallen, Tiffany shed her pleasant self and skulked around the shop, fingering the fabric and cursing the customers she served. Maybe the sweater set was replaced by black leather, the spray teased out of her hair, before she headed for the biker bar to drink pitchers of beer and throw darts with fat, bearded dangerous looking bikers. She might even have a tattoo somewhere under her suit. Maybe a demonic rooster or a pistol shooting flames and smoke.

"Chicken Divan."

"Mmm, sounds fancy."

Then again, maybe not.

The dress took shape on Charlotte. Three-quarter length sleeves, a boat neck with a wide V at the back, no buttons yet and no belt. But a smart hem.

"I don't want it to look too bunchy up top."

"Oh no, I'll sew darts in to accent your figure. You might want to get a bra with a bit more support. One that gives a little lift and will fill out the dress."

"Oh, I've got one at home. Good idea. I don't like to be without support." Something caught in Charlotte's chest and her reflection wowed at the edges. Her body looked like it eclipsed a hidden sun behind her. Squinting her eyes made the rays squiggle.

"It looks fine," Charlotte said, catching her breath. She sat in one of the ivory chairs. Tiffany smiled with her Marigold lips, which complimented the lime sweater.

"Thought I'd practise sitting down, as you suggested." Charlotte wiped her sweating hands on her lap. A hiccup escaped from Tiffany's throat. She coughed to cover it up.

"Are you okay? Should I call a doctor?" Tiffany's cheeks had flushed. "I'll get you some water." She didn't want Charlotte to have a heart attack right in the middle of her fitting.

"I'll be fine, just a bit of nerves. These once in a lifetime experiences shake me up a little. The dress will be beautiful. Thank you." Charlotte rose and turned before she entered the change room. Drawing back the curtain, she looked at Tiffany and bowed deeply. "Thank you very much."

Tiffany gave a little half-bow back and said, "You're welcome, Ms. Weiss. Are you sure you don't need a doctor?"

So this was how it was going to be. Just when she had forgotten all about her defective heart, it kicked up with no warning, with no regard for where she was or with whom. It just did as it pleased. So there.

On her way out the door, Charlotte was nearly flattened by Wade who was running along the sidewalk. "Who's after you?"

"I'm going to buy a bed," he stopped and swept his hair off his face. How would he explain running to the store to buy a bed? Crazy. What was he blurting that out for anyway? He leaned his weight onto one leg and stuffed his hands into his pockets.

"What have you been sleeping on all this time?"

"Oh, I have a bed. But I've had that bed since I was eight. It's a boy's bed. I just thought it was time I got a grown-up bed. You know, a man's bed." And he laughed. Why was he telling this to Charlotte? What did she care if he had a new bed?

"You know, it never occurred to me to buy a new bed. I still sleep in the same bed I did when I was a girl. I suppose if I had married that would have been different. A new bed though. I'm sure you'll enjoy having a new feeling under you when you go to sleep. You'll have to tell me tomorrow how you slept. Maybe I'll buy myself a new bed too."

It had never crossed her mind to buy a new bed. It seemed like such a luxury. Maybe she would buy a double bed in which she could stretch her limbs in four directions and not feel the cold air grab her feet. To be able to roll over and not feel a draft at her back where the blankets didn't reach. The thought made her giddy. She would buy herself a retirement present, a new bed. Tomorrow she would go to Beck's after work and see what they had.

"Well, I won't keep you. Good luck."

"Yeah, see you tomorrow," and he sauntered the rest of the way.

* * * * *

The salesman at Beck's furniture knew Wade from high school. Bruce Laponte, the Norman Steers' toughest defensive tackle, the guy with the thickest neck. They were called the Norman Studs or Norman Thugs, depending whose side you were on. Still today, even though his football days were long passed, his neck still bulged from the collar of his shirt. Bruce had ended up like most of the Studs, married to his high school sweetheart, drinking beer on weekends and reminiscing about the glory days when they could screw each other's girls and still be friends. They took over their old football field once in a while and played a sloppy game. The jerseys still fit although now they filled them out with girth rather than equipment. Guys like this needed each other. A job right out of high school, a wedding a year or two later and presto, another family is created to fuel the Norman economy. They worked at the gas station, the hardware store, the furniture store, the bank and sold each other goods and services. Everybody relied on everybody else to stay in business and everybody knew who bought what from whom. There weren't many variations.

"If I buy a bed today, how soon can it be delivered?"

"We can have it delivered and set up by five o'clock. We'll send Todd out." Bruce winked at Wade. Todd, another of the football thug crowd. As if Wade wanted these guys in his apartment to set up his first double bed. In high school Wade steered clear of Bruce and his group of friends. They were the kind of guys who flexed their collective muscle any chance they got, especially when there was someone they could pick on and their girlfriends were watching. They chose people like Wade. Skinny, not very athletic and who blushed easily. Lightweights. Whenever he could, he avoided the entrance to the school where they hung out. Everybody did. At least Wade wasn't the only one they tormented. Those guys seemed to lurk around every corner. Highly trained commandos who always got their man.

"I'll just look around, thanks." Beck's showroom covered about as much floor space as Wade's apartment. Brown and gold upholstered chairs and sofas with highly polished wood accents. Clunky wood living room furniture all stained a dark brown. Coffee tables with inlaid glass. Colonial kitchen sets or whatever the style was called, with those knotty chairs. The bedroom section was a jumble of bunk beds and cribs and the captain's bed he always wanted as a boy, with the drawers underneath where he could put his toys. The only double bed had a pale green quilted satin headboard. Wade pushed down on the mattress a couple of times.

"You gotta lay on it." Bruce was back. "Try it out."

"Is this the only one?"

"You don't have to use the headboard, but it goes with the bed. It's the last one for now. Troy and Melinda are getting married this weekend and they came in and picked up the other one. You should have seen them. They had no problem trying it out. Go ahead, lay down."

There was another time, years ago, when Bruce had towered over Wade, his menacing face leering towards him. He had just fired a football at Wade, which had hit him in the gut and bent him in half. "Throw it back Pan-Scratch. What's the matter? You never learn how to catch a ball before?"

Wade figured by now the two of them should more or less be on equal ground. Bruce's muscle had turned to fat. What was Wade afraid of? If he turned his back, Bruce would have him in a full Nelson demanding his lunch money? None of his friends were here to encourage him. If he wanted to get Wade into an arm hold, who would be there to see? It would be worthless. They were fully-grown men. In his rational mind Wade knew he had nothing to fear, but he didn't turn his back on Bruce the whole time he stayed in the store and that same menacing feeling followed Wade while he browsed among the furniture.

Wade fingered the price tag, twelve hundred dollars. This was crazy, to be buying a bed on such short notice all because he invited a guy to town for the weekend. Just buying the bed would set tongues wagging, never mind Graeme and Wade making appearances all over town and was that who Wade had been in such a rush to buy a bed for?

Bruce was lying on the bed now with his hands behind his head letting out a series of long, exaggerated sighs and looking at Wade with a sly grin.

Wade sighed. "All right, I'll try it."

"Wait." Bruce jumped off the bed. "There. Now you try it. We don't want to give anyone the wrong idea, eh?" He jabbed Wade in the ribs harder than was funny.

* * * * *

Wade lay in the middle of the bed, his head on the pillow and stared up at the stuccoed, gold-flecked ceiling. The bed took up almost all of his room. He could roll from side to side and touch the wall from any corner of the bed. His dresser now stood in the hallway and all the clothes strewn across the floor ended up in a pile on the couch. The white sheets and pillows welcomed. It had taken the delivery guys about thirty minutes of jigging the bed back and forth before it fell into place. Did the whole football team work for Beck's? These guys were one of the main reasons he had left Norman, and now here they were helping him settle in, delivering a new bed.

"Where do you want her?" They asked him. Her, his new bed. The behemoth with the green satin headboard they wrestled up the stairs of the apartment building while Wade stood helplessly to the side. Everything they said reverberated through his head like the taunts of so long ago.

"It's a one bedroom."

His condescension would be lost on them, their thick skulls unable to absorb subtleties. That'd show them. Brains over brawn. That's what his mom told him to make him feel better. "You'll always be smarter than them." He wanted to be bigger than them. They didn't care what was in his head.

When he sat on the side of the bed, his knees grazed the wall. Only at the foot end was there any room to spare. It really wasn't much better than the sad, little bed which preceded it. He paid the delivery guys an extra twenty to put his old bed down in his storage locker.

His new bed didn't make him feel any better and now he was house-bound until Graeme called him back. If he bothered to call at all. Wade was beginning to regret having set the whole thing in motion. Buying a new bed probably would jinx everything. He should have just kept the old one and they could have squeezed in. They would have managed fine with the little bed. Wade rolled from one side of the bed to the other, over and over until he felt quite sick.

chapter nineteen

J une had spent most of the day lying on the couch with an ice bag over her eye, watching the television through the other. She had to get rid of the bruising before Saturday. Vi said the people from the newspaper might be there with cameras. The bruise on her cheek had turned from red to purple and, if by tomorrow she could get the green and yellow to come out, it might be gone by Saturday dinnertime.

June wandered from room to room muttering, "stupid, stupid, stupid woman." What kind of a person gets hit in the head with a baseball, especially when they see it coming straight for them? What made her think she could catch it? She had never been any good at sports. She wished the scene would stop running through her head. How many times did that ball have to hit her in the head before she could forget about it? If only, if only, if only. Sometimes she wished she could shut herself up. Of what use was an inner voice that made you feel stupid? Maybe that was her problem. She had to make that monologue droning through her head switch tracks, get a voice which fed her positive thoughts, rather than the drivel which repeated itself and berated and belittled her. It made her head pound.

At the piano, she pulled the bench out and plunked herself down. She hammered out a scale: G major, two octaves right hand, then the arpeggio, then the triads. Now the left hand. Her hands felt nimble on the keys today. Maybe that knock to the head had lubricated some clogged connections. There was choir practice coming up on Sunday before the service. She tried F major, hands together. It sounded a little ragged. Slow down, concentrate, try again. Better. And, the Clementi? Shall we have it? She played the first four bars. A little fast. Again. Keep it steady. And, she played it. Her Clementi sonata, all the way through. What a thrill she felt as she reached the middle section for the first time in decades. Don't think about it. Keep going, you're halfway there. Doing good, doing fine. Steady, steady. Then the familiar theme again and she strode to the end, her fingers found the keys as though they had rehearsed for months. She raised her hands before the final cord in a dramatic fermata...and clang, her hands crashed to the keyboard, releasing the final cord to ring through the house for hours. Except, it was interrupted by the sound of applause coming from the front door.

"What on earth?" She muttered as she made her way toward the sound of the clapping. Behind the screen stood Kuldip. "Oh, my. Kuldip. What brings you over?"

"Ah, Mrs. June, I come to see your terrible eye and bring you samosa." He held up a tin plate covered in foil. "I made for you."

June reached for the latch and opened the door. He handed her the plate. "Er, thank you, Kuldip. My eye is almost better."

"You sound like a professional. Piano, ta-ta-tum." He waved his hands horizontally through the air over an imaginary keyboard, mimicking the final chords he just heard.

June blushed. "Well, thank you again. I'm sure these will be delicious. What are they again?"

"Samosa. Vegetables inside. Mmm. Very good. You eat with Miss Charlotte."

"Oh yes. Thank you very much."

"Yes, very good. Bye bye." He skipped down the steps and walked toward the street. He was going to walk all the way around the block to get home.

"Kuldip, you can go through our back yard. It would be much quicker."

"Oh, yes. Thank you very much."

The tin plate was warm on the bottom and June carried it to the kitchen. She peeked under the foil to see what samosa was. Four pastry triangles lay on the plate with a small plastic container of a reddish-brown sauce. She dipped her finger in the sauce and touched it with the tip of her tongue. Her mouth puckered. Interesting. It tasted sweet and spicy at the same time. Unlike anything she had ever eaten. From the window, June watched Kuldip carefully unlatch and then latch the gate behind him. He waved and disappeared into his garage. Funny little man. He had moved into the house with his family way back when Charles was so ill. He lived in his house all alone now and she wondered how much he had suffered when he lost his wife. Well, not lost her, but she really wasn't much use anymore. Had to be fed through a tube. Ghastly. Getting old was bad enough, but becoming useless and crippled. How cruel life sometimes was. At least Kuldip hadn't shut down like her father had. He was still able to look after himself and even cook.

* * * * *

Charlotte came home and saw the samosas in the kitchen. "Where did these come from?"

"I wasn't sure what to do with them," said June. "Kuldip brought them over. I think he wanted to look at my black eye."

"Let's have one."

"Oh, I'm not sure I'll like that spicy stuff. He didn't say what was in it."

Charlotte had already bitten a wedge and dunked the rest into the sauce.

"Oh my, these are good. Mmm. I'm going over right now to thank him."

"Over to Kuldip's house? I already thanked him."

"Why not? We're neighbours aren't we?"

Kuldip was in his back garden on his hands and knees picking beans into an ice cream pail.

"Oh, hello Miss Charlotte. For tomato-bean salad. Fresh vegetables. The best. You come for dinner with Mrs. June? I make chicken curry for you. Very special. Please come. Very nice."

"Well, I certainly will. I don't know about June though. She's not feeling very well."

* * * * *

Kuldip's head was visible above the open kitchen window and from inside Charlotte could hear the clatter of pots and the hiss from the stove. The sidewalk to the back door was flanked by rows of tomato plants. The smell of growing tomatoes and the aroma of sweet curry from the kitchen mingled in the air. Heavenly, just as Charlotte experienced those nights she dressed for work, only more intense and somehow being so close to what had once drifted her way by chance, made it more surreal.

Kuldip met her at the back door wringing his hands around a checkered tea towel.

"I'm afraid June can't make it. Is it all right if it's only me?"

"Oh," he made a tut, tut sound. "Yes, her eye still very bad. You come in."

The counter was strewn end to end with vegetable tops and onion-skins. His spices were kept in little clay pots along the top of the stove with ceramic spoons in each one. Kuldip knew exactly how much of each one he needed without even tasting. A row of elephants, tiny ones made from heavy iron, circled the sugar bowl on the little kitchen table. A wide-eyed bronze Buddha looked down onto the four stove elements, which generated a heat typical of a summer day on the prairies. His feet were bare in flat sandals and looked dusty, as though he had just walked through the desert. He wore a little round cap on his head, a long cotton shirt and his baggy pants rolled up at the ankle. Charlotte thought she had arrived in Katmandu.

Kuldip led her to the dining room where an old maple table had been set with white plates and napkins and heavy silverware. A pitcher of iced tea stood in the centre of the table with water pooling around it. He offered her a chair and poured a glass of tea and left her there while he returned to the kitchen.

Charlotte sat and listened to Kuldip humming in his high-pitched voice, melodies she would never comprehend. Tuneless, at least to her ear, the phrases and note groupings were unfamiliar. A foreign musical landscape being patterned onto her brain. Charlotte sat back and waited while the clatter from the kitchen intensified. A sagging couch with a dented pillow and cotton sheet was angled in the corner so the late afternoon sun shone directly on it. Where Kuldip slept, in the afternoon because he could not sleep at night, his body warmed by the sun and his cat by his feet. He had a television on a wire stand and a pair of pliers sticking out where the channel changer had broken off. A stack of newspapers and flyers, not yet yellow, lay under the coffee table. Charlotte could see Kuldip had made himself quite comfortable in Norman.

"Ta, da. Dinner for Miss Charlotte."

Kuldip made three trips to the kitchen and set the dishes in front of Charlotte. A plate of yellow rice, red-orange chicken and vegetables steaming in a creamy, fragrant sauce, some flat bread and several little dishes with preserves. He stood over the table and pointed at each dish.

"Basmati rice, chicken curry, vegetable korma, nan and chutney, mint chutney and mango." He then served Charlotte a spoonful of each over the fragrant rice. Never had she smelled or seen food so lush, so exotic. He hummed a little song and put food on his plate. What a wonderful feeling, to be hummed to and served a warm meal. He sat down and they ate. The taste in Charlotte's mouth awoke a emotion within her which had not surfaced in a long while, a longing, a yearning. For something which would not come clear, a sensation or an image with loose associations to thoughts which her conscious mind could not grab onto. A beach, white buildings, hot sun, lamps at odd angles in cramped rooms with brick walls, fabrics from a time gone by. Strange images, visions of a place and time she knew only in her mind. How did it do that? Come up with things she had never seen or experienced? The food tasted marvelous, she savoured each mouthful, chewing slowly, trying to dissect each taste and then put it together again.

Kuldip was chattering at her between bites. His wife had taught him to cook. Taught his daughters too. Pamela and her husband had a busy restaurant in Toronto. Sarah worked at the CBC in Winnipeg. A good job, television. They were good girls; called him every Sunday, so he could tell his wife each Monday at lunch what each of them was doing. He was glad they came to Canada. His daughters had a much better life here than they would have otherwise. It had worked out well. Except his wife was sick, but that could have happened in India also. And the hospitals and nursing homes were much more modern in Canada. He thought she received better care here, by far.

Sure, it had been hard for him. For a man to admit he cannot provide for his family at home and accept charity from a foreign land. Who chooses to uproot his family and take them to a place where not even their God is welcome, where his daughters will learn of customs antagonistic to their genes, and adopt them as their own? Where he, the head of a family of four, is left alone to care for his ailing wife who can no longer speak his name nor inhale the smell of his flesh.

Norman was not what he imagined Canada would be, he admitted to Charlotte. He had seen pictures of the Rocky Mountains and had been disappointed not to be able to see them from his doorstep.

Their plates were empty. Kuldip looked at Charlotte. "Some more?"

"Please."

He served each of them another plateful. "Miss Charlotte, you have a husband? Before?"

The question took her by surprise. Part of life in a small town included nobody ever asking you such a question because they knew your whole life already. Nobody had ever asked her that before.

"No, no. Never married." It was not the most comfortable thing to say aloud.

"And Mrs. June? She married, yes?"

"Well, no. Almost, but no."

"No?" His eyes grew large. "Two sisters, nobody marry? In India, impossible. Two sisters, two husbands."

Charlotte leaned forward. "Maybe we should have looked in India for husbands."

"Hee, hee, hee. Oh, yes. In India you find for sure."

Were she and June really such an odd pair? Two old sisters living together in their childhood home? She could see how it might strike some as peculiar. Marriage was never something she searched for or yearned for the way June had. Charlotte never felt any need for a man in her life. Even Ray, she never imagined marrying him, just having fun with him.

Looking after her father so long, she couldn't imagine marrying and doing the same thing all over again for someone else. And, as for June, her disastrous affair with Lionel showed clearly how much pain love can bring into your life. Charlotte had to go to Winnipeg for two weeks to stay with June after Lionel abandoned her. That was after the D and C the doctor said was necessary to scrape the last bits of fetal tissue from her uterus. June almost refused the procedure thinking maybe parts of her baby would live on inside her. By the time Charlotte got there June was a complete wreck. Not sleeping, not eating, crying all the time in front of the television. Her friend Estelle came over and convinced June to see her doctor again who prescribed a mild sedative. Once she started sleeping better she gradually perked up. By the time Charlotte left, she was ready to go to work again and had stopped replacing the photo of Lionel on the mantel each time Charlotte put it away in a drawer.

How did that line go again? Better to have lost in love than never to have loved at all. Love wasn't something Charlotte ever prepared to seek out or put a lot of effort into finding. If it found her, she thought she would deal with it when the time came. But, until then, she would enjoy her own company and find pleasure in the things at hand. Actually, she thought her life quite fine.

"I've had a good life. Even with no husband," she said finally, though she wasn't sure Kuldip would understand.

"Yes. Very, very sad when one go away. Too sad. Better alone always, than suddenly alone." His eyes scanned the array of photos on the wall, photos which made him feel terribly sad and alone.

All these years Kuldip had lived here and now over the course of a dinner, she would catch up on thirty years. She may not have spoken much with him, but she had watched him age. While all these things were happening, the ones he described, Charlotte had seen him through her window or briefly in the back lane on garbage day. She saw him age before her, without knowing how his time was passing.

Was his life unfolding as he'd hoped while he struggled to keep the garbage bag from bursting?

Charlotte cleared the dishes into the kitchen. "Thank you Kuldip. Thank you very much. Very good food."

He packed her a bag to take to June. Each dish was in a separate yogurt container. A piece of the nan in wax paper. This must be what his lunch looked like when he visited his wife.

Back home, June set the four containers in front of her and peeled back the lids. She jabbed at each one with a fork and gingerly raised it to her mouth. Over and over until the food was all gone.

"June, you know that line? It's better to have lost in love than never to have loved at all?"

"Mmm." June raised her eyes and nodded.

"Is it true?"

"No," June said. "It's better never to have loved at all."

"That's what I thought." Even with the exotic aroma of Kuldip's cooking, the house smelled very plain to Charlotte at that moment.

* * * * *

Charlotte flipped through the pile of LP's in the cabinet. Most of them had been her father's and some she had bought herself. In the study, she and her father sat and listened to recordings of Lester Young, Lennie Tristano and Bud Powell. There were hundreds of LP records in the cabinet. Charles would slide the glass doors and reach in and pick a record. Whatever he pulled out, that's what he played.

"What luck, ladies and gentlemen, we have with us this evening the grand duke of jazz, Mr. Ellington himself." He would announce this if his hand happened to claim *Mood Indigo* from the stacks of records, his favourite.

"Let's give him a warm welcome." Applause from Charlotte as the needle dropped and Charles sank into his chair with a grin he couldn't help, escaping his mouth.

Sometimes it was *Mood Indigo Night* and Charles would play several different versions by three or four performers and had Charlotte tell him which was her favourite. Some of the arrangements were so far removed from the original, she had to check the record sleeve to make sure her father wasn't trying to trick her. For Charlotte nothing came close to the sound of Nina Simone and her raucous piano and wailing, mournful voice. Raw emotion. To listen to Nina Simone was to experience the divine.

After he got sick he couldn't tell her what he wanted to listen to and Charlotte had to choose. He didn't really care anymore what Charlotte put on for him. At least that's how it seemed. She tried to play it up, like he used to. Announcing the music for him as though he was there to see a live act, but he just stared blankly in whichever direction he was pointed and waited until the music stopped and Charlotte or June came and led him to another room.

* * * * *

In Norman, imagination was as essential to survival as the highway out of town. Sometimes when Charlotte played her bass, she imagined herself living in another time, in a more exciting place. When jazz was emerging as the life force, the underground pulse of Chicago and New York. And musicians had names like Eubie and Kid or Fats and Jelly Roll. In her small room, alone with her bass and the piano, Charlotte would play a record, Charlie Parker or Dizzy Gillespie, at high volume, pick up the bass and play along. Looking over at the piano, she imagined the Count sitting there, sweating out a tune in a room full of smoke and revelry. A true rent party. What a thrill they must have been.

Whole tenement houses would fill up, with people spilling into the stairwells and onto the street. The walls vibrated with the beat of the party and at the core you would find Duke Ellington or Scott Joplin in a tiny room pouring sweat over the keyboard of an old upright, playing stride at the piano. The smoke swirling throughout the room could be coming from their fingers on the keyboard or the sweet marijuana cigarettes, passed from hand to hand through the crowd. Or flasks of forbidden whiskey, in the days when drinking added to the excitement of the adventure. Oh how Charlotte would have loved to experience such a thing. The music took her there.

Tonight, the highway out of Norman led to New York City. The Cotton Club. The lamps on the tables shot beams of soft light up into the faces of the patrons. The place was packed tonight. Beautiful, dark women wearing white dresses with fringes and tassels and their tough looking boyfriends in their hats and suits, ready to kill for them in an instant; pull a knife from their boot or a gun from their pants. Honour prevailed and no one threatened anybody's honour in this place and got away with it. People hung together, bound by love and duty. You didn't come to the Cotton Club without an entourage of the people prepared to fight for you. Living on the edge, these places exuded a sense of ethereal impermanence, a danger hung in the air like a vapour which in an instant could spark an inferno. That was the ambiance. Finding yourself in the middle of a revolution. A fight could break out. The place could be raided by police. Someone could be killed. And through all that you drank and danced and laughed and flirted. The evening was filled with the most sensual, intense music, as though the waves of sound could keep the demons at bay, keep things from getting out of hand, keep the switchblades in their handles. The loose piano riffs, the coronet player twirling in and out and the rhythm section providing the energy to propel the music. They played as though they would never stop. The music had no end until one of the players committed them all. No one wanted to be responsible for stopping the music.

Charlotte picked up her bow and sawed out the lowest version of *Nobody Knows the Trouble I've Seen* possible on the bass. Charlotte found the power in the bass to be in those thick strings, vibrating just about as slow as anything can and still make a sound. She pulled the bow across the strings and watched them vibrate. A stash of cigarettes lay hidden in the drawer of the writing table. Every so often, after spending an evening accompanying Nina Simone, she would pour herself a scotch and light a cigarette and listen to her favourite recording of *Mood Indigo* until the party died down in her head. When she spent an evening like this, it made Charlotte feel like she had been somewhere no one else in this town ever would go.

But, tonight, in between songs, the sound of the television bled through the walls. Charlotte didn't like to watch television with June. The shows were of no interest to her, melodramatic stories of love gone wrong. The tissue box, always ready for the first sign of heartbreak and by the end of an evening there could be ten or more crumpled up on the table beside June. Every night June sat there. Starting with the news and the horrific sensational reporting and then the game shows with frenzied contestants, vying for prizes they couldn't live without. June was there for every victory, every kiss on the host's tanned cheek. How she could watch night after night, was beyond Charlotte's comprehension. Had she lived this way in Winnipeg? Sat in her little apartment with a whole vibrant city all around her and watched television?

Oh, and her figure skating. Every televised competition kept June riveted to the screen, ready to judge the skaters and malign the judges. The German ones were always the toughest, not a sentimental lot. They sure didn't give any points away. She leaned towards the screen the way she never leaned toward the minister in church. Intent upon capturing every emotion her skaters went through as they looped the loop along the ice, their fluttery sleeves fibrillating with excitement, she sat at attention in her seat, guiding her heroes across the ice. She knew all. Who had injuries, who had a new coach, who fell in competition last year. With held breath, chewed lips, hunched shoulders, for hours at a time, with the TV table beside her loaded with a teapot, cup and a plate of cheese, pickles and crackers, June sat and lost herself in the drama.

Charlotte listened to the television for a moment before she turned the record player off and joined June. They sat in silence, June on the couch with her tea cooling on the table beside her and Charlotte in the easy chair, watching the television send a beam of silence into the room. From her vantage point in the chair, Charlotte could see June's eyes following the drama on the screen. As soon as an ad came on, June moved towards her tea. "There's more in the kitchen."

"Do you think we'll manage all right, June?"

"What do you mean?" she asked, blowing on her tea.

"Well, come next week, we'll both be here all the time. I won't have to get up for work. I'll stay up later in the evening. Do you think we'll fall over each other all day long?"

"I suppose things will work themselves out. I have my things to do you know. My week's pretty much booked."

"So, you're not worried about it?"

"What's to worry about? This isn't the first time we've lived here together. Remember?" June directed her gaze back to the television. The program had started again and Charlotte sank into the chair. Maybe there was nothing to worry about. She could grow beans and tomatoes like Kuldip. Perhaps the abilities of a baker and those of a gardener were not too far apart. She could get up each morning and work in the cool soil and feel the sun's intensity increase on her back as it rose from the horizon to the sky. Sweat would form on her brow, but it would be from a heat within her, not the heat from the ovens. The heat would energize her rather than leave her limp. She could nap in the afternoon and not worry about lying awake for hours when she went to bed. Her eyes would open in the morning and the sun would be up. She would get just enough sleep every night, her body waking her when it was time. Maybe the heavy feeling in her arms and legs would disappear. She would no longer feel like she had to carry her limbs around. They would support her.

Dread had clung to her all week, making her feel like a wet dog. She needed to shake it off, smarten up and realize it wasn't impossible to enjoy life, it just required some effort, some faith in the world and in herself. After all, she wasn't the type to shrivel and moan. She was stronger than that. Maybe her heart had started quivering to signal time for a change but also to let her know it beat within her regardless of age, duty and routine. It would beat for her, keep her going through her last week at work, through the party at the Driftwood and through whatever was to follow. Change was coming. It might do her some good.

"How did you feel when you moved home? Left the salon?" There was another commercial on the television. "Was it all right for you?"

"Well, I suppose I did feel a bit out of sorts. A little sad, but you know. I worked there with Estelle for almost thirty years. The girls she hired got younger and younger. They came with new ideas and resumes. The young clients all went to them. Had I been starting over in this day and age, I would never have been hired. Where do these kids get all their qualifications?"

"It's a lot of nonsense, most of it. You're right, though. The world has outgrown us. We're no longer qualified. So, we retire. Hopefully with some grace."

June took a moment to stare at her sister. "I suppose. It's important to recognize when to go. I'm sure if I hadn't quit, I would have arrived at work one day with no clients waiting for me and none on the books. Those thieves gave me an excuse to leave at the right time. The last thing we need in our old age is to embarrass ourselves in front of young people."

Was this the answer? Once you reached a certain age, you directed your energy towards the singular goal of not embarrassing yourself? Was this why all of June's friends were older? So they would embarrass themselves first? They could view her as the youngster. The up and comer on the bowling team. The only one who didn't wear a hearing aid or need a cane. Why would she surround herself with people who joked about how often they had to pee at night? How depressing.

"Well, I'm not old."

"Yes, you are Charlotte. Just like me, hard as that may be for you to accept."

"I accept it, I just don't feel it yet."

"Well, you better get used to it. You can't fight it."

"I don't feel as though I have to fight anything. I feel fine."

"You have a heart condition."

"There are three-year-olds with heart conditions, June. Are they on a list at The Pines?"

"Don't be ridiculous, Charlotte. That's completely different."

"How is that so different?"

"They're young and you are old. That's the difference."

They sat in silence a moment. It was almost eight and Charlotte had to get up one last time for work.

"Well, I'm going to put these old bones to bed."

"That a girl."

Even with the television on, the house felt unnaturally still as Charlotte gripped the banister and went upstairs to bed. She stared at the black of the ceiling for a long time before she fell asleep. In her dream, June was lying on a hospital bed, fighting off a nurse who was trying to stick electrodes to her chest. Charlotte stood beside her and tried to calm her, but June had herself twisted in the sheets and her skin dripped with perspiration so the electrodes wouldn't stick. There was little Charlotte could do to get a grip on June who thrashed about the bed like a toddler with a temper. A needle jabbed violently into June's arm and the panting and writhing stopped. A look of amused benevolence came over the nurse's face. "That's more like it," the nurse said.

chapter twenty

B ehind the bakery, Wade sat on the edge of his chair and wagged a breakfast sausage through a gap in the fence. "Come on boy, it's real good." Wade held the sausage closer and the dog growled. "Don't be such a suck, come on over here. Come on."

The dog usually ate when nobody was around, but lately he'd been lurking about, staying close to the bakery. Never close enough for Wade to touch him, but if Wade talked to him he seemed to listen from a comfortable distance. Wade sat back and took a bite of the sausage himself and held the remaining part out to the dog. This time, the dog, who had been staring at the bit of sausage with pained indecision, crawled forward through the fence toward Wade's outstretched hand.

"Come on boy. That a boy." Wade held his breath and sat still. The dog crept closer, sniffing intently. Then Wade saw he was swaying a bit, favouring one side. The legs on his left side seemed to want to collapse beneath him. The dog managed to lunge at the sausage and snatched it from Wade.

"Shit," he said. The dog had bitten Wade's finger and broken the skin. Wade sucked on his knuckle. Tears pooled at the corners of his eyes. The dog hacked and coughed up the sausage. For some reason he couldn't swallow it. What was wrong with the dog today?

Wade lit a cigarette and inhaled until he felt the smoke hit his brain. Damn dog bit him. That was his last chance.

Wade puffed. Trying to tame a dog he couldn't catch. Trying to get a guy he couldn't have. Couldn't even get the stupid dog to pay attention to him, even with a sausage. White man, white pants, white shirt, white apron, white cigarette, white blonde hair, white flour all over everything. A baker, a shitty lousy baker. What kind of guy bakes for a living? He blew smoke into the air and watched it curdle. That set him apart. Smoking. Sure, smoking made him cool. It was okay to be a baker as long as you were a cool baker. And it was okay to live in this stupid town as long as you were cool. Except Vi didn't want the customers knowing her baker smoked. They might start to complain their bread tasted like smoke. He couldn't even come out as a smoker in this town. Everybody thought he was some nice guy, who came home to look out for his mom and work in the local bakery, gave up life in the city to come back to his roots. What a guy, what a fucking, great guy. The people of Norman could be proud.

"So how'd you sleep?" It was Charlotte, coming up the back sidewalk. "Oh, he's letting you watch him eat. Looks like you've made some progress."

Wade was studying his hand and blinking the tears from his eyes. The bleeding had stopped but the skin was raw and swollen. "Yeah, little bugger got a piece of me this morning, though. Thought I'd finally tamed him and he snagged the sausage along with a piece of my finger."

He let Charlotte hold his hand to look at it.

"Let's get some ice on it. At least he didn't chomp off the whole thing." It really wasn't much of a bite, but Wade looked so upset about it, biting his lip, she thought she'd better do something about it.

"I think something might be wrong with him."

"Really?"

"He's limping and he can't eat. He choked on the sausage."

The dog snarled at Charlotte when she tried to touch him. Usually he would have run off by now. But it was clear he couldn't move easily. In between growls a whimper sounded from his throat.

"Do you think it has rabies?" Wade asked.

"Oh, I doubt it. Go inside and call the vet. Tell them we're coming with the dog. And tell Doris we need to borrow her car."

Charlotte took a deep breath, bent over and picked up the dog. It growled but didn't bite. She gently placed the dog in the back seat of Doris's car. By the time they reached the clinic the dog had grown limp and his pink tongue hung from his mouth. She lay the dog on the stainless steel table and stood back with Wade while the doctor examined him.

"Is this either of your dog?"

Both she and Wade shook their heads. "He's just a stray. Been around for years."

"He's probably had a stroke. Recovery from something like this is unlikely." The vet stroked the dog's snout. His eyes were closed now and the panting had stopped. "You don't have to stay. I'll make sure he doesn't suffer."

That did it. Wade gave in to the mounting tears. He looked at the doctor, then the dog, and then at Charlotte. The dam crumbled and the tears gushed forth. All morning he had been miserable, thinking about the horrible night he spent in his new bed. Graeme had called after Wade had fallen asleep to tell him he wouldn't be able to make it for the weekend. Something in his tone, the hour at which he called and just the way he said it. "Wade, man. Got your message. Listen, great idea but I just can't, buddy."

Buddy. Did Graeme think Wade was some fifteen-year-old kid? A little brother? As soon as he heard that, Wade knew he had made a huge mistake. Graeme had probably laughed his head off when he heard Wade's message.

Time allows your memory to embellish. It creates gaps and lets you fill them with any detail you desire. It takes a phone call like that to make you realize most of what you had in your mind was created by your imagination alone. And it makes you want to puke, because you had no idea what the build-up of false notions felt like until they were spewing into your system like the poison from a burst appendix. The poison of a shattered dream can make you just as sick. Make you feel like you are going to die, but does you no such favour.

Wade knew Graeme was calling from the club. The noise in the background, the giddiness rising from Graeme's throat, almost giggling as he spoke. Drunk. Probably surrounded by his friends who had heard all about Wade's invitation. They all had a good laugh. As if Graeme would consider going all the way to Norman to get laid. Wade could just picture them all standing at the bar, watching Graeme at the pay phone, signalling his friends when the phone was ringing, raising his eyebrows when Wade answered. Speaking with exaggerated expressions so his friends could tell at which point he told Wade no. The scene looped through Wade's head unceasingly. It bored through him and gouged a pit where his heart was.

Maybe it served him right. He had been a prick. To Laura. To Graeme. What did he expect the outcome to be? Would they all move in together and live happily ever after? With him in the middle getting to choose every night where he wanted to stoke his rod? He was lucky they didn't leave him first. How soon before his cover would have been blown? Shit, he didn't even have a cover. Just dumb luck.

All night he lay in that wide bed and kicked himself for being so thick, so stupid. It was only for sex. Graeme never once gave any indication of wanting anything more and now Wade had gone and humiliated himself. He even bought that stupid bed. That goddamn, stupid, fucking satin bed where he was having such a great sleep before the phone rang. Thank God Graeme didn't know about the bed. Thank God he didn't show up here and laugh at his bed.

Suddenly he felt Charlotte's arm encircle his shoulders. "Wade, you know this is the best way this could have happened. He's a stray dog. He could have died anywhere, but he decided on our company instead. We should feel honoured."

Wade's body shook as he tried to control his crying. Charlotte led him away from the clinic and they drove back to the bakery. The fresh air cleared his head. The lump in his throat settled down and his tears stopped running into his mouth.

"So, tell me about your bed, your new bed. How did you sleep?"

"Ah, I don't think I'm going to need it. I mean, I feel better in my old bed, I think."

"Really. You looked so excited yesterday when I saw you. You don't want it now?

"It's too big. There's too much space in the bed and not enough in my room. You can have it if you still want a new bed."

"You got me thinking yesterday. I'm going to go to Beck's after work to see what they have."

"I bought the last one. You can buy mine from me. I'll give you a deal."

Charlotte frowned. "I'd have to try it. You're supposed to lie in a bed before you buy it. I am kind of set on the idea. Would you mind?"

"You would actually be doing me a favour. Honestly." At least if she liked it, he would be rid of the bed, sissy headboard and all. Back at the bakery, Wade let Charlotte hold an ice bag on his hand. "Thanks, Charlotte. Yeah, we'll go. If you like the bed, I'm sure the guy from Beck's will bring it over for you."

* * * * *

Was it the bed that made Wade so upset? His voice still hadn't recovered quite from his crying at the vet. He seemed pretty anxious to be rid of it now. It couldn't just be that dog. Charlotte had been feeding it long before Wade came along.

She'd be happy to take the bed off his hands if that's what he wanted. But, what was with his crying? He seemed unable to stop. Even now, as he filled the meat pies, his face was red and streaked, and with every breath he snuffled his nose.

Something else had his attention today. Maybe later Charlotte would have a chance to ask him, but for now he would be better distracted by his work. What a lot of commotion on her last day. They worked together quietly until the store opened and they heard Doris rattling around in the front. She stuck her head through the door.

"Hey guys. I hope you're giving Charlotte a bit of a rest today, Wade. She has to meet her public later on you know. Free Charlotte cookies for everyone."

Wade looked like he might cry again so Charlotte stepped through the door to the front. In honour of Charlotte's last day of work, Doris was wearing black pants and a black turtleneck. She had dark lines painted under her eyes and her nails were a deep burgundy. A sticky name-tag on her apron said: *Hello My Name is Doris* and then she had drawn a happy face with an upside down smile and a tear dropping from one eye.

"What's the sad occasion?" Charlotte asked.

"It's a sad day for us, I always try to dress the way I feel."

"If I've died and gone to heaven, I want a refund because I'll be damned if I'm going to spend eternity here."

"Oh Charlotte, you're so funny." Doris laughed and gave Charlotte a light slap on the arm. "I'm going to miss you like crazy around here."

"I am the crazy one here."

First she signed up for the dinner and now here was Doris, in mourning for Charlotte. Was Charlotte this sentimental as a teenager? She had seen many staff come and go and as far as she remembered they all got the same treatment: balloons, streamers, free cookies for the customers. One day Doris would quit and she'd get here on her last day and see the same thing. Well, she was still early in her working life. Forty years from now, she would react with resigned indifference when her colleagues moved on to better jobs and opportunities and left her behind to the routine of the day.

"It's not because you're dead, it's because we are all so sad today is your last day."

"At the bakery, not on earth."

"Do you like the decorations? I stayed late putting them up."

Charlotte nodded. "They're very festive. If it weren't for your sombre attire this morning I would think you were happy to be rid of me."

"My what? Oh, come on Charlotte."

A banner had been strung across the ceiling: *Good-bye Charlotte.* Streamers hung from corner to corner and balloons bobbed at the ceiling. Free cookies and punch to all the customers. Free cake as long as it lasted. Wade had made the cake this morning. No inscription, thankfully, just the blue icing. People came for free cake and to gawk one last time at Charlotte. Vi had arranged everything and Doris had done all the work. The dinner was sold out, seventy-two tickets. Charlotte sat up on a stool by the cash register and smiled at everyone. Her cheeks ached. Vi told Doris to keep the punch and cookies filled up and to make sure nobody took more than one. Vi worked the till today. It would be a high volume day and she didn't want Doris handling all that money herself.

Though she recognized everyone who came in to see her and eat a cookie, Charlotte found it impossible to relax. Vi wanted Charlotte 'front and centre' between ten and noon, the time the free cookies had been promised. Charlotte's head was swimming, her mouth dry. Who did she really know here? Why were they being so kind, saying lovely things about her? The air filled with voices, like intermission at the theatre. All the voices blended together into a uniform hum and then if she paid attention she could make out individual sounds and the most unusual voice among them was her own. After she noticed it, she became distracted and could pay attention to nothing but the sound of her own voice droning out of her head, "Thank you for coming; yes, it will be wonderful, thank you; oh, yes, well, I'll see you there then." She hadn't any idea where that insipid sounding voice came from, she just wished she could shut it up.

At noon, Vi took the sign about the free cookies down and had Doris clear away the plates and punch.

"Well, Charlotte, I guess this is it," Vi said. "You might as well go a little early. Everything is done."

Doris started to cry. It had been a heady morning, one of those mornings when the adrenaline courses through your veins and doesn't stop when the party is over.

"I'll help Wade clean up and then I'll go. I'm not ready just yet."

The kitchen had its usual clutter, but today it was all Wade's mess, the way it would be from now on. He stood by the sink spraying off the pans before they went through the dishwasher.

"Ready to go?" he asked.

"Sure," Charlotte shrugged. "It's been quite a morning. How are you holding up back here?"

"Oh," said Wade. "I'm calming down. Thanks for getting Doris out of here. I don't know what's wrong with me today."

"We are all allowed days like this, Wade. They're normal. When you're a woman you can blame your hormones."

"I think that's exactly what's wrong with me. I'm hormonal. Bitchy, you know." He laughed. "Whatever."

Charlotte rinsed her hands under the tap and hung her apron behind the door. They could retire her apron the way they did hockey jerseys. Hang it from the heat ducts for all eternity. Wade was already outside lighting a cigarette and waiting for her. No need to linger. It was time to go try out his bed. They walked in the midday light. Both of them in whThe rapping at the door woke June, who was lying on the couch in her dressing gown. She had woken with a pounding headache and had taken some aspirin to help it settle. When she jumped up, her head instantly throbbed with such force she feared she was going blind. She stumbled to the door, sliding her feet into her slippers and tied the sash around her waist. How long had she been asleep? It better not be Kuldip again. She didn't want him getting into a habit of dropping by whenever the mood struck. But it was Vi she saw through the window, looking at her watch and then peering through the window in the door. As always, perfectly put together down to the neat shoes and matching purse. June opened the door.

"Um, if I'm here too soon, I can come back. Are you not well today June?"

"Oh my, I lost track of the time. No, no. Come right in."

"Are you sure?"

Ever since June had left the Anglican Church and went over to the United Church, Vi had been a little wary of her. People didn't just up and switch churches unless there was a good reason.

The incident in question, which drove her from the Anglican Church had something to do with the alto section of the choir. There were too many altos and they overpowered the entire choir. So either people had to practise and train their voices to sing tenor or soprano, or trade off every other week for, the beauty of the Lord's music would be lost if all people could hear was the alto line. When June took a turn and sat out one Sunday, she noticed nobody else had. When she brought it up at practice, she was ignored, snubbed. Nobody thanked her, nobody had offered to take a turn the next Sunday, so June left and vowed never to return, stating it had been a conspiracy to get her to quit the choir. Those back-stabbing women never liked her, so she gave them what they wanted and stomped across to the United Church and joined their choir practice. The United Church never had enough altos. Most of their members wanted to sing the melody line, so they were happy to have someone volunteer to sing alto. That hardly ever happened.

June blinked at Vi. "Oh, I'll survive. I'm just a little under the weather. The stress of the week is getting to me, I think. Tomorrow it'll all be over." June sighed. "Come in, I'll make some tea."

June felt her way across the hall to the kitchen. There were swirling patterns everywhere she looked. The floor veered away from her, causing her to lean heavily into the doorframe.

"You sit June. I'll make the tea. We'll make it short so you can rest up before tomorrow. What on earth happened to your eye?" Vi had just noticed the yellowish, green bruise on June's cheek.

"Oh, just a little accident. Do you believe the things that happen to me? Some days I feel like I've been put on this earth for others to look at and say, 'at least we're not her'."

The spinning in her head worsened and she half fell onto the table and sank into a chair. What had her life become in the last week? The week had been a blur of activity with Charlotte's dinner, the dress fittings, the planning for the hall, and then Charlotte stupidly agreeing to go to Kuldip's for dinner in the middle of the busiest week of her life. And Charlotte had no concern for her heart, throwing herself into all this. She was so careless about it, still walking to work, even working at all. She should have quit right away. Why hadn't Vi forced her to quit when she got the news? And, she'd been playing that bass all week, nearly every night, and fast pieces too. Visions of Charlotte grey-haired and hunched over her bass, back in a band after her retirement reared through June's head. It wouldn't surprise her. She best keep that notion to herself, or Charlotte would likely to start a band herself.

"Drink this, June dear. You've gone all spacey." The teacup sat in front of June, steam rising. The sun fell across the counter towards the fridge meaning it was close to noon already. June couldn't remember when she last felt so miserable. She remembered sometimes feeling this way after a birthday party, when she was young. When the excitement was over, the giddiness didn't last for days in her head, rather a melancholy draped over her, because the event never measured up to the thrill she anticipated. After any party, June dawdled home in a daze, wondering what to do with her left-over energy. She would get so worked up beforehand there was always this energy to spare afterwards. Hopefully she wouldn't feel that way after Charlotte's party. She wanted the evening to be perfect for both of them.

chapter twenty-one

Wade led Charlotte up the dark linoleum stairs, the kind that were hard cement with sharp edges and slippery on washing day. Charlotte tightened her grip on the railing.

The apartment was gloomy and had a stale smell. Charlotte half expected to peer into the darkness and see a shrivelled old figure wrapped in layers of knit blankets scowling at them. Once Wade opened the drapes, the light poured in and turned everything white. A blanched room. An overstuffed, tweedy couch and chair, a pressboard coffee table and a television were the only things in the living room. The carpet had a grey tint, though Charlotte suspected it was originally white. A calendar from the bank hung on the wall, along with a poster from some movie about men with guns. Old flyers, newspapers, *National Geographic* magazines and tattered paperbacks lay strewn across every surface. So this was how single men lived. This apartment could belong to an eighteen- or an eighty-year-old. She could imagine Wade in this little apartment until he was a wee old man. It would always suit him, always be good enough for him. A place where he could come home, keep his shoes on, lie on the couch and watch television in his underwear. Drink coffee from the same cup all week and his scotch too, for that matter. She could see why he wanted his old bed back. A new bed broke the comfort. Now he had to either get everything new, or put his old bed back. A new bed just didn't fit.

"Come on in, it's in here." Wade called her from the bedroom. The bed took up most of the space in the room. "Well, go ahead, lie on it, jump on it, do whatever you need to do."

Charlotte sidled along between the wall and the bed and sat on the edge, lifting her legs up and over. She lowered herself onto the pillow and stretched out on the bed. It was wonderfully spacious.

"You know, I have no idea how a bed is supposed to feel. It's so hard. I'd have to get used to it." She burst out laughing. "I'm sorry. I can't help it."

He managed a weak smile.

"Just look at us here, Wade. I have invited myself into your bedroom on the pretense of trying out your bed and here I lie, with you looking on. If this was a movie, we'd be well into things by now, but then I suppose neither of us really fits the part."

Wade blushed, then sat down on the edge of the mattress.

"It's got good springs." She bounced up and down on the bed on her behind. Seeing Wade bouncing on the other end of the bed made her laugh even harder. "Oh God. I guess I'm a little giddy today. I'll take it. I'll buy the bed."

Charlotte leaned against the pillows to catch her breath. "So, who was he?" she asked after a moment.

"Who?" asked Wade, biting his thumb.

"The guy you went out and bought this big bed for?"

Wade gaped at Charlotte. Then, like a tap being turned on after a long winter, he started to sputter and cry. He had been holding it together all day, holding it in since last night. The outburst at the vet had only been a prelude to what came over him now. A toxic virulent swell of anger, disappointment, loathing, regret, and every other noxious emotion he thought he had squashed now spewed from inside him. All the questions he never bothered to answer, the feelings he had never acknowledged, the roads he stubbornly had taken in an effort to sustain himself now threatened to reduce him to a quivering shell. Not even quivering. Nothing.

Charlotte leaned forward. "Oh, shit, Wade, I didn't mean to. I just thought, you know. I mean I've known this about you forever. Not like I heard it on the street, but I just had a feeling you were that way. I thought it was kind of understood between us. I thought you knew I knew."

She rested her hand on his knee. Tears fell onto his pants. Big, splashing, sobbing drops of rage and hatred. Charlotte put her arm around him and he sobbed into her shoulder. He felt so hot, his body under her, breathing wet hot air onto her shoulder. They sat this way and she held him and rocked them both back and forth until Wade's body stopped shaking.

"It must be awfully hard for you here."

"I thought I could have Graeme up here, but it's really impossible." He sounded like he had a rope around his neck. The words lurched from his throat and he started sobbing again. He looked at Charlotte. His whole face was wet. "I'm getting so sick of lying to everyone. You wouldn't believe what I've done, the people I've hurt. I make myself sick."

They sat on the edge of the bed, his hand clasped in hers. He talked at the wall and the floor and into his lap: about his time in school when he first realized he liked boys and hated sports; his mom never suspecting a thing, until the day he came home almost crying, sixteen-years-old and crying because his best friend Paul had a girlfriend; his lack of connection with Laura; Graeme and how he stupidly fell in love and felt so great for the first time in his life.

His heart had been stretched, filled to bursting and now hung weakly under his ribs, deflated and aching, beating so limply he felt at any moment it may stop and he would have to go through life without a heart. He hated himself for getting to this point, for stumbling along with his feelings, letting them trip him up. He hated that he listened to his heart. Stupid, dumb fuck.

When Charlotte held him, he hugged her tight for a while and Charlotte hung on too.

Finally Charlotte got up. Wade stood in the doorway holding a tissue to his nose and blinking his eyes. She smiled gently. "Don't be a stranger. We can talk about this any time. You can come to tea next week. It'll be tight but I'll make some time for you."

He nodded and sniffled and waved her down the hall. The beer in his fridge, cold and sharp, made him feel a little better, but he knew he wasn't done yet. He could still feel the sick in his stomach. That familiar tight clamp, which blocked emotion, stopped it from getting to his brain. The smartest thing he had done all week was buying a case of twelve at the beer store.

Coming home again to Norman made him feel like that East Indian family must have felt when they moved here. The only coloured people in the white sea of Norman. He felt like them. Having just spent the weekend among his own people, his own kind and then coming home to straight-shooting, God-pleasing Normans. It distracted him, how different he was. If they knew what walked among them, what fear he could instill, the terror people would feel just to have to look at him. He was used to feeling that way now. Made an art of being inconspicuous. Plain, old ordinary Wade. Look, there he goes.

Everything looked so small, too. Homes too close together, people too friendly. It was like an overly sentimental television show he'd rather not watch; the kind where people do the right, selfless thing every time. And with a smile, a knowing smile. Like the people in line at the bakery. Wade watched them through the window in the door and when their attention strayed the smile turned to perplexity or sometimes, just blank, an empty head. But the smile always returned. Go with what you know. The vague, tight-lipped smile of people who can't find fault with their life and yet know something is missing. What he hated most was he had become one of them. The happy on the outside, nothing wrong on the inside people. Nothing on the inside. Everyone watching is outside.

* * * * *

Charlotte made her way down the stairs back into the brightness of the afternoon. Poor Wade. It didn't matter to her who or what he was. Norman would kill him though, of that she was sure. There was that time Andy got pummeled by those farm kids after their show. Charlotte and Ray took him to the hospital. He was swearing and crying and punching the walls. *Next time we'll kill you, fucking faggot.* Vicious. Pure hatred. Charlotte and Ray heard them shrieking, almost hysterical, as they tore away. The threat was real. Those guys would and could kill him if they felt like it.

People who knew what really happened behind the bar, didn't look Andy in the eye when they passed him on the street. His face was a mess, purple rings under his eyes and his nose the size of a turnip. It was harder not to look, to pretend not to notice. To them he was a walking reminder of how the protective coat they thought was there, sometimes wore away in spots. It was all so false, the shelter and sense of ease. Seeing Andy in the diner or at the bank, reminded them to step back in line, blend in and smile. Don't show any interest in what happened to Andy. Go along with the story about how he walked into a door. One sign of compassion could spell the end. You'd be lumped together with Andy, the queer, the homo, the guy who finally left town on a bus, so everyone could finally stop ignoring him and start talking about him. Charlotte and Ray saw him off. All he took with him was a knapsack with his clothes and a box of books. What choice did he have? Nobody talked about it, nobody complained to the hospital. They were glad to see him go, but of course nobody said so. They weren't that cruel.

It wasn't long before some other bit of gossip occupied everyone's attention and they forgot all about Andy. As though he never lived here, grown up here, gone to school and graduated. Andy who?

* * * * *

The day stretched before her. The sky, sunny and blue, looked like it would stay that way forever. She loved the prairie sky. Clear and bright, during the hottest summer day or the arctic cold of January. That unending sky soothed the senses when the temperatures became unbearable. Charlotte stooped down and pulled on her new gardening gloves. There was a spot in the back yard where the sun shone most of the day. She picked up the little spade and poked it through the earth. A clump of grass overturned to reveal dark wet soil and some black bugs, a worm and a nail. She dug out a circle, shook the mud loose from the grass and then worked the soil with her new rake.

In the window of the hardware store a display of garden tools had been erected on green indoor-outdoor carpet. Miniature spades and rakes and trowels nestled on simulated lawn. Terra cotta pots sprouting shiny green plants. Charlotte had never been interested in gardening. Always too exhausted at the end of the day to change her clothes and launch into another physical activity, she usually came home, made a pot of tea and read the paper. The tools looked strong and durable. Steel tools with rubber handles. Charlotte wanted to know what it felt like to hold them. Then, she discovered the seed rack. She wanted to buy all of them. The pictures on the packets promised strong, vital plants. Flowers with perfect, symmetrical blooms and blue ribbon vegetables grew from each and every seed. She eventually settled on a packet of daisies and one of carrots. That would do to start.

The sun beat on her back and reminded her of summer holidays at Grand Beach. When she got out of the water and lay dripping in the sun and didn't bother to use her towel, just let the sun dry her off, then, after she was dry, she would start to heat up until she couldn't take it and ran back into the water.

In the middle of the mud she made two circular trenches and dropped in the daisy seeds. Gently, she replaced the earth and patted it down. Around that she dug one more circle and planted the carrots. She filled the watering can, so pleased with her new things. While she tended her garden, Kuldip's head popped over the fence.

"July, too late for planting your garden."

"Well, I'm just practising for next year." His stuttering laugh made Charlotte grin.

"Hee, hee, hee. Very good. You practise. No more work. Now you garden. More hard work."

Charlotte walked over to the fence. His face brightened. "Thank you so much for dinner yesterday," she said. "Everything tasted wonderful."

"Not too much spicy?"

"Oh no, perfect. You're an excellent cook." Charlotte saw Kuldip was standing on a cinder block on the other side of the fence in order to talk to her. "How is your wife?"

"Oh, my wife. Not so good. Same, same. Every day the same. For ten years, nothing change. Better she die, but God wants her to live."

"It's so sad. You are very good to her. Did you visit today?"

"Oh, yes. Everyday. I visit everyday. She no know, but I know." He shook his head. The tears had run dry years ago. All that remained was routine, a routine which connected him to his wife when nothing else did. It was all he could do to preserve the life they had shared. If he didn't do something now, take it upon himself to keep his beloved wife in his life, to make her a part of his day, they might as well never have met. If he turned his back now, it all would be rendered worthless.

Charlotte invited him to the Driftwood dinner and he accepted. Bowed his courteous little bow and said, "Oh yes. Thank you Miss Charlotte. It will be a great honour to come. Tomorrow night. Yes, yes."

* * * * *

"What?" Charlotte was back in the house and June sat with a magazine in the living room. "Kuldip? Why?"

"Because I want him there. He's a nice man."

"There aren't any tickets left."

"The guest of honour can't invite a guest?"

"I'm your guest."

"I don't remember inviting you."

June flipped the magazine open on her lap and resumed reading. "I made hair appointments for us tomorrow morning. I could do yours, but we might as well both go. You would not believe the day I've had."

Charlotte scraped the mud from under her nails. Did other people go overboard like this for their retirement? Getting dresses made and hairdos? Dinner in rented halls and sign-up sheets at work? How did they prepare for their farewell parties? As hard as she tried, Charlotte could not get excited about it. It was depressing, making all these preparations. It was hard enough to recognize she could no longer work, harder still to have people celebrating the fact and expecting her to join in. Such bizarre traditions.

Poor Kuldip would have to get his nose pretty close to his plate if he wanted to figure out what he was eating. It would probably remind him of the stuff his wife got through her tube. Dr. Wilson would be there to make sure the meal was heart-smart and to watch how much butter Charlotte spread on her roll. She couldn't imagine who else would be there. Seventy-two tickets sold and Charlotte could only think of five people who had told her they were coming: Vi, June, Doris, Kuldip and Dr. Wilson.

She hoped none of them had prepared a speech. Dr. Wilson could say how sorry he was to have found her heart to be defective. Vi would start off by talking about Charlotte and then switch into a motivational speech about women in business. June could pretend she knew something about Charlotte. Doris would be the best prepared, but would no doubt get overly sentimental and start crying, or acting. And through all that Charlotte would sit and try to be gracious. Smack her lips over the meal, smile through the efforts of the Driftwood staff, who had given up their Saturday night to work and serve plate after plate of food they had served a hundred times before and still couldn't believe people paid for it. She would shake hands elegantly with all guests, striking a confident pose and demure countenance. At least she would be entertained.

chapter twenty-two

The big day started with the delivery of her bed. A good omen, thought Charlotte, and a good thing, too. The old mattress lay in the yard next to Charlotte's new garden. A grapefruit-sized hole in the stuffing had launched hundreds of moths into Charlotte's bedroom when the movers overturned the mattress. They fluttered past her and plastered themselves against the window, making the room remarkably dark, for a blanket of bugs.

"I can see why you're wanting a new bed, Miss Weiss."

At least they worked quickly and didn't seem to mind June's mounting hysteria as the new bed was installed and the time for the hair appointments drew near. Before the truck even pulled up and blocked the driveway, June had been standing at the front door waiting for Charlotte.

"Oh good they're here," said Charlotte. "I was hoping they'd come before we left."

"Who?"

"My old bed has had it. I had to buy a new one."

"What on earth!" June watched the men lower the mattress out of the truck. "You ordered a new bed?"

"A retirement present. Remember? I'm supposed to rest."

"You bought a bed? We have to be at the hairdresser's by ten."

Charlotte was beginning to regret agreeing to the hair. It was all getting a bit much. Everything would have been fine had yesterday simply been her last day of work. She was anxious now to get her new bed set up and go fuss over her garden. Launch into her relaxing, maybe treat herself to a gardening magazine, go over to Kuldip's and ask him some questions. She had more important things to do today than get prettied up for a party.

"This'll take two minutes. I'll meet you there. Tell the girls to take you first."

The men from Beck's brought the bed in the front door and up the stairs.

"It's gigantic. Like a life raft. What do you need a gigantic bed like that for?"

With the white sheets and the sun glinting off the satin headboard, her new bed was an inviting site. It transformed the whole room, which before looked small and dingy. Somehow it looked a lot less cramped with the bed there. She had them place it under the window. Her old bed had been stuck in the corner, only one side free. She wanted to try having both sides free and the outside air within reach. Yes, a new bed.

* * * * *

Saturdays were busy at the salon, but June had insisted they go the same day as the party. "You can't get your hair done and then sleep on it."

This was the final concession, the hairdo. Charlotte had agreed to the new dress after an evening spent in front of the mirror with June on the bed, beside her a heap of dresses, which she had emptied out of her closet. Over the years Charlotte's wardrobe had shrunk to include only what she needed for the bakery and home and that did not amount to much.

"Where do I ever go that I need a choice of outfits? One dress for any funeral I may attend, including my own, otherwise I work and come home. I don't need a lot of clothes for that."

But after trying on all of June's dresses: the floral, the plaid, the paisley, the argyle, the plain, scoop neck, v-neck, mock turtle neck, real turtle neck, zipper up the back, zipper down the side, buttons, hooks, even velcro, Charlotte thought any dress, even a new one, would be better than showing up for her party in one of June's.

The salon was hot and smelled like burning hair and melting plastic. Three women sat all in a row under the domes of the dryers, reading magazines like the ones in the doctor's office. It was understandable to have fashion and beauty information available at the salon. Maybe you will come out looking like a Parisian *Vogue* model. But when retched with fever or covered in itchy hives which have just started to weep, what one wants is relief, not to have one's self-esteem undermined by looking at the nymph-like, glowing-with-health and sexual satisfaction creatures in *Glamour.*

She and June sat in the waiting area on hard-backed chairs.

"You know, the techniques really haven't changed much, just the chemicals. They still have to put the rollers in one at a time, just like I did." June sat raptly at attention, watching the girls in the salon at work.

"Who are we getting?"

"Well, I've booked in with Tanya and I told them to give you whoever was available."

"What if all that's left is the girl sweeping the hair out the back door?"

"Oh for Pete's sake, Charlotte. They're not going to let her cut your hair. You'll get one of the regular girls. I didn't think it mattered to you."

Charlotte watched as women all around her agonized over their reflections. Why did they subject themselves to these modern day rituals with such frequency and then call it a treat, a luxury? It wasn't comfortable to wrench your neck while somebody else scrubbed your hair with their armpit in your nose. Then to have to sit for an hour and look at yourself in the mirror and see other people in the waiting area looking at you. It was very unnerving.

In the end, Charlotte got a French twist. June's stylist had insisted on covering the yellowing bruise and had swept June's bangs from behind her ear and onto her face, as though they covered some devastating deformity.

"You look fine. People will have expected you to get your hair done. Nobody will know." They still had to pick up Charlotte's dress and Charlotte was having some difficulty getting June away from the mirror in the salon. "If you keep playing with it like that, you'll have to come back for a touch up. Just leave it. We can always get them to dim the lights for the evening."

They left the salon, the pungent odour of hair product wafting all around them. The dress was supposed to be ready by noon and so June and Charlotte got into the car and drove one block over to Rosa's. Tiffany greeted them with her usual exuberance. She jogged to the rack at the back and filed through the row of dresses to get to Charlotte's. "I think you're going to love it Miss Weiss. It's absolutely gorgeous."

It was hard to make out the dress under the thin sheath of plastic. Charlotte was most impressed by the belt. A hand crafted belt. Of her own design.

"Are you going to try it on once more, just to be sure?" Tiffany's outfit today had been made from bright lime-green fuzzy material Charlotte feared might set off a reaction in anyone prone to allergies.

"I wish you had shown me that material when I first came in. I may have considered it. People would have an easier time seeing me tonight. Mine looks kind of dark now," June complained.

"Oh, no Miss Weiss. You chose a lovely colour. I think this colour would be too playful for you."

"You don't think I suit playful?"

Tiffany turned to Charlotte. "You better try it. Besides, I want to admire my work."

"I'm sure it will fit," Charlotte said in feeble protest. She wanted to get home and rest and she wanted to make sure she ate something before the dinner, since she still wasn't quite sure what Chicken Divan was.

Their double-team tactic worked and Charlotte took the dress to the fitting room and hung it on the brass hook. With her hair freshly done, she had to be careful not to have the whole French twist unravel as she pulled the dress over her head. Once she had the dress in position over her hair, she discovered she hadn't undone the zipper enough and couldn't maneuver her arms into the sleeves. She stood a moment looking at herself in the mirror, her *Oceana* dress hanging from her neck and the empty arms limp at her sides. From the speakers came the sounds of some awful music, but Charlotte picked out the beat and turned her shoulders back and forth until the arms were in full swing on their own, wrapping themselves around the dress. They somehow got entangled in the zipper in the back and stopped flopping about. The effect was like a straight jacket. Charlotte pressed her nose up against the mirror and crossed her eyes. "So, I'm crazy. What are you going to do about it?" She hissed at her reflection and made the mirror fog over.

She stepped back and saw her head sticking out of the dress with one empty sleeve hanging beside her and the other twisted around behind like a rung out rag and stuck in the zipper. The bulk of the dress sat bunched on her hips, her French twist perfectly intact.

"Everything okay in there?" Tiffany's voice sang through the door.

"Sure, sure, that's a nice song you're playing." The dress muffled Charlotte's voice a bit as she wrestled it back over her head.

"Do you need any help?"

"Oh no, I'm just strategizing."

"It's probably easier to step into it rather than try to get it over your head."

"That is an excellent suggestion. I was just about to do that."

When Charlotte emerged from the fitting room, Tiffany and June stood side by side, watching the door. Tiffany squealed with delight when she saw Charlotte.

"You – are – stunning!" she said, emphasizing every word and shaking her head. "Absolutely stunning. Blue becomes you."

Not to miss a chance to tug on the fabric one last time, Tiffany flitted about Charlotte's hem and caused the same anxiety in Charlotte as she had the first time her hands came so close to Charlotte's thighs. "There, that's just about perfect. You can take it off and I'll wrap it back up for you."

"I think I'll just wear it until tonight."

"Oh no." Tiffany gasped. "You can't."

"Why not? I'm not going to do any gardening in it. Dinner is in about five hours anyway. I'm ready early, that's all. I'll sit quietly on the couch and promise not to eat any chocolate."

Back in the car June said "I think you've caused that girl an awful lot of worry, wearing the dress home."

"That girl takes her job far too seriously."

Tiffany looked like a disapproving teacher as she rung up the bill. Furrowed brow and pursed lips. "I'd really rather you not wear the dress home, but I guess I can't stop you." She handed over the bill. "It's a final sale." Like a teacher or mothers looked until you came to your senses and did things their way. Like that look alone makes them right and you wrong. Charlotte laughed out loud.

"She's old before her time."

"I'm going to send her a thank you note."

"You do that."

* * * * *

They pulled up to the house. In a few hours things would be underway. Charlotte could hardly wait to have the party over with. She was looking forward to it for that reason alone. A grey mist filled her head. She lay down on the couch, on her side to preserve the intricate knot at the back of her head and carefully smoothed her dress out beneath her. Her eyes fixed on the window and she watched the tree outside bend and sway with such grace. The sun filtered through the leaves creating a speckled golden pattern on the floor. She shifted her gaze between the floor and tree, the pattern dancing on the floor and the tree dancing in the yard, a reflection of original beauty. Could a reflection appear more beautiful than the object transmitting the reflection? Or a different type of beauty, something inherent in the tree you can't see when looking directly at it? A byproduct, like the fruit which grows on the branches. One cannot appreciate the sweetness by looking at the tree, one has to eat the fruit.

She remembered that Charles sat for many hours in this room, staring out the window much like Charlotte was right now. The easy chair in the corner offered a slightly different view, a new perspective on the tree and the street outside. Did he tire of this? Being led every day to the same chair and covered in layers of blankets and left to stare out the window or at the television. Would she lie here come Monday, with no apparent reason to move? What did June do all day? Would they both be vying for a spot on the couch? Or would they both pretend to have so much to do, they never needed or wanted to rest?

She didn't want to think of that now. Filling her days would be something she would have to take as it came. For now, she would just think about tonight. This party which seemed most important to June and Vi and those people on the list who wanted to come. What was it that compelled people to attend such functions? Some unfounded, deeply ingrained sense of obligation stemming from years of attending birthday parties of unpopular kids in school just because the invitation was extended? Would the people there tonight feel fulfilled once they returned to their cars? Feel like they had done a good deed for their community, for her? People did things for external reasons; wanted to ensure their standing in the community rather than because they wanted to or loved Charlotte. She could just imagine their conversations Monday morning. "Did you see who wasn't at Charlotte's dinner?" or "It was marvelous. You should have been there. Where were you anyway?"

These kind of events had a way of bringing a community together, more than honouring Charlotte, it gave people something to do, a place to get together. Whether it was Charlotte's retirement or Suzie Thompson's wedding or Mr. and Mrs. Porter's fiftieth wedding anniversary party. People attended to get caught up with each other's lives. In a small community in order to get along, you had to be up on other people's lives. Who had grandchildren, whose kid moved to Winnipeg, whose property was vandalized over the weekend. By the time the *Norman Herald* came out every Wednesday, if you didn't already know what would be on the front page, you felt out of touch. She already knew Sherry Douglas would be there, ready to take notes and photos. *"The Chicken Divan was divine."*

The town mayor, Bill Wozylyshyn had been contacted and invited and according to Vi had accepted. He would sit at the head table with his vapid wife and make a speech after dinner. As the week wore on, Charlotte had become more horrified with the magnitude of the celebration Vi and June thought necessary. Who would remember any of this Sunday morning? Charlotte already was beginning to wish it away.

"I have to head over to the hall for a while. I told Vi I'd meet her there to make sure everything is ready." June stood at the door with her coat on.

"Don't they have staff who prepare everything?"

"Well, they said if we wanted any decorations we had to do it ourselves."

"We don't need decorations. Why don't you rest?"

"Vi needs help blowing up the balloons."

Charlotte rolled her eyes.

"Don't look like that. This is all for you." With one hand on the doorknob and one clutching her purse, June threw one last look at Charlotte and was gone. From her spot on the couch Charlotte watched June back tentatively to the edge of the drive, check three times in each direction and then coax the car out of the driveway and to the stop sign on the corner.

Now that June was out of the house for awhile, Charlotte got off the couch and went to the hall mirror to take a look at herself. From the foot of the stairs, she turned and walked towards the mirror, the way Doris had showed her, each foot in front of the other and her hands on her hips.

Charlotte had to admit her approach to the mirror looked formidable, confidence oozing with each stride. She reached the mirror and pivoted on her foot to turn and walked back to the stairs, throwing herself an over the shoulder look, she tossed her head back and smiled a super-model smile. Everything would be fine tonight. It didn't matter if the mayor and his wife sat beside her or if Sherry Douglas ran her mini tape recorder all night. The night belonged to her and she resolved to enjoy every inane moment. Maybe she should have taken some acting classes from Doris too because she did feel a bit the impostor and hoped nobody would notice her lack of enthusiasm.

Wearing her dress all afternoon would help her get into character. An haute couture-wearing, gracious, dignified retiring baker. How did they act?

In the dining room, she got a crystal wineglass from the cabinet and practised a toast. "To Charlotte, whose bread was fluffier than most."

She would be dignified, regal even. Astonishing all who were present. Shaking hands, smiling thoughtfully at what people said, sipping her wine with a demure manner. Remembering to hold the glass by the stem for the toast until the ting of the crystal reverberated through the air and brought the crowd to their feet, holding their glasses and clinking each other until the room sounded like a bell choir with intonation difficulties.

Suddenly, she felt a little faint. She wasn't used to being the centre of attention. All eyes would be on her tonight. All along she had thought of tonight as Vi and June's party. She was going along with it for them but of course their perception was tonight was for her. They would bask in her glory, sure, but the attention would be on Charlotte. It was impossible to change her mind now. She sat and caught her breath in the kitchen. Okay, she had to get through it somehow. Surely she could sit through an evening at the Driftwood. She used to perform there. Stand on a stage in front of a roomful of people and sing. It took guts to sing out loud for an audience, to open one's mouth and sing. You lay your soul bare when you sing aloud. Leave yourself vulnerable, naked for whomever listens. You stand there and sing naked and let the people gawk. That takes nerve.

Tonight people would be gawking too. Let them, she resolved. Let them look, because I'll be fabulous.

chapter twenty-three

The day ended, finally, with the party. June returned, to make sure Charlotte hadn't left town. Then Charlotte and June drove with Kuldip in the back seat. He had his hair smoothed over with some pommade and wore a brown suit and newly polished shoes. In his hands he held a vase with water and a bouquet of daisies and sweetpeas for the head table. For Charlotte and June, he had picked each of them a gardenia for their dresses.

Vi met them at the door. Golden-gowned and crowing.

"Charlotte, dear. Don't you look wonderful. Absolutely gorgeous, dear." She stopped short when she saw Kuldip get out of the car. "Oh, and who's this?"

"This is our neighbour, Kuldip."

"I didn't know you had a neighbour, Charlotte." And to Kuldip, "So very pleased to meet you."

"Very pleased," he replied and bowed. This made Vi titter.

The room was filling up. Vi and June apparently had only enough breath for about ten balloons, which had been taped along the head table. A few streamers hung along side the balloons. Ten round tables had been set up with white linen tablecloths. Vi stood between the banquet room and the kitchen, holding the door open the way she did at the bakery. An ear and an eye in every corner of her bakery and now in every corner of her rented hall. From where she sat Charlotte could see the cooks in their white coats, their movements quick and precise. Kind of how she imagined she looked while working at the bakery. They came in each day and prepared the same things. How many times had they served Chicken Divan? How many loaves of rye bread had she made? They could do their jobs by rote, like machines. Maybe that's what retirement was for: to relieve you of the pressure of consistency and reliability. You spend your working life with others counting on you to be predictable. When you retire, you are absolved of that responsibility. Free from predictability. It sounded good to her, for the first time.

The ceiling fans swung lazily in their orbits, looking like each revolution would be their last. They seemed to be blocking out the yellowish light behind them. A little stage in the corner had been set up with a table and stereo system and big speakers stared from each corner of the room. She couldn't imagine being up there now, playing to this crowd. She used to. They got gigs playing parties like this. From the stage they could see everything. Charlotte and Ray used to try to guess who would go home with whom and then place their bets between sets. Because one of the reasons people came to functions like this was for the free flowing liquor and what that promised at the end of the night. It was funny then, watching middle-aged, fully-grown men and women embarrass themselves at a community event. Paired off after performing a few pathetic overtures. She was certain those things still happened and was thankful she no longer was there to witness it. If she were still standing on that stage watching those dramas unfold, the pathos of the situation would find her in utter despair. She was not up for utter despair.

The music hadn't started yet, but Vi thought some dancing after dinner would keep the party festive. A music man came with the room rental, so why not? All it took was for a few people to get things started and then everybody would be on their feet. Who in this crowd would want to dance, Charlotte wondered? Maybe Doris and Wade would start things off.

Charlotte spotted them at the doorway from her seat at the front table. Seeing them there saved the evening for her. They grinned at her from their table. Doris grinning because she probably thought she had convinced Wade to abandon his plans and come with her and Wade just grinning. He looked at Doris then looked back at Charlotte, winked and laughed aloud. Charlotte raised her eyebrows back at him and shook her head a little. So here he was, after all that yesterday, here he was with Doris at Charlotte's party. He must be feeling better. Instantly her stomach let go and her breathing became light. Until she had seen Doris and Wade, her stomach had tethered itself way down inside her and clamped up. This was just like having all the bakery customers in the store at one time. Just she, Doris, Wade and Vi and then everybody else. Everything would be fine tonight.

Until Charlotte saw Reverend Bowen come through the doors. "Did you invite your minister?" she asked June.

"He bought a ticket like everyone else. He wanted to come."

The minister stood, like a beacon in the middle of the room while people from every corner of the hall hoisted their sails and floated towards him. A flotilla, honing in. Beside him, stood his ever-present wife in a perfectly pressed blouse, ambiguous length skirt and non-committal hair. Smiling her weak smile, probably resentful of her secondary role, but resigned to it as better than not. As good as she could expect, and everyone was always so nice.

Charlotte watched June surge through the crowd and elbow past three people in her effort to reach the minister, grab his arm with both hands and whisper something in his ear. To which he nodded several times, which got his wife nodding and June too. Whatever were they nodding about? As quickly as she left, June returned and announced triumphantly, "He's agreed to say grace."

"Grace? Don't these people ever take a day off?" Charlotte could think of nothing less appropriate, considering she was already starving and never had even met the good reverend. "He better not try to recruit me."

"He's not recruiting. It's his job to say grace. To some people it's important to have their food blessed before they eat."

"Well, some people are more gullible than others. Let him feel important and say grace, as long as it doesn't go on too long. I don't want to lose my appetite."

Who else had come? A light bulb flashed over by the minister's flock and Charlotte knew Sharon from the *Herald* had arrived. Sure enough, Vi left her post at the kitchen and headed toward the light. It wasn't so bad sitting at the head table. Charlotte could see everything from here, especially if they tried to spring anything on her. Here they came, Vi, Sharon and the photographer, as promised.

"Charlotte, Sharon is here. Let's get a couple of shots before dinner."

"Well, all right then," said Charlotte, who took the cue to finally pour herself a glass of wine. "Cheers."

"Oh, that's perfect. Get a shot of her with the wine like that, Glenn. That's funny."

They were about to set up and take the picture when Mayor Wozylyshyn and his wife entered and Sharon squealed, "Oh, the mayor. Quick. The mayor." It was the only time Charlotte ever felt so distinctly affected by a dignitary's entrance. She watched, relieved as Sharon and her photographer scuttled through the crowd. "Excuse me, press. Excuse me, *Norman Herald*. Thank you."

With the minister and the mayor there, Charlotte wondered if anyone knew she neither went to church nor voted.

The picture they ended up printing in the *Herald* was of Charlotte, June, Vi, Reverend Bowen and the mayor. All squished behind the head table before the plates had been cleared away. Framing the picture on the right was the sleeve of Kuldip's suit and on the left, the hand of Mayor Wozylyshyn's wife holding her husband's cigarette. And the accompanying interview glorified Charlotte to the heavens and wished her a wonderful time on her cruise.

By ten to seven the room was full and Vi took to the stage where a small podium and microphone had been set up. She stood behind it and got everyone's attention by tapping her finger on the microphone. People filed to their seats and waited for Vi to give further instruction.

When the time came for the grace, Reverend Bowen took his place behind the microphone and unfolded a sheet of paper. "For what we are about to receive may the Lord make us thankful. We thank Thee O Lord for Charlotte and all her good work over the years and her service to the community. May she find rest and comfort in the days ahead which she so very much deserves." She was horrified to hear her name mentioned. She didn't like to be so closely associated with God. Her heart sped up, waiting for Reverend Bowen to accuse her of heresy or ask God for her salvation. Why didn't he just bless the food and get on with it?

"And thank you Lord for all these people who came tonight to honour Charlotte." It was like being at her own funeral, where the eulogy was being spoken by someone she had never met, someone put up to it. Like at her father's funeral, when he had been in the nursing home only six days. Some of the staff hadn't even met him. Charles had never met the minister who conducted his memorial service. The minister read the obituary from the paper with feeling, as though he had written it himself. Very believable and heart-felt. You couldn't tell he was acting. It made her cry.

She felt more like heckling now. Would this ever end? Beside her, June had her hands clasped tight and her eyes shut. What could she be thinking? What kind of image went through her head when somebody said grace? A benevolent God, smiling upon her, happy to provide her with yet another tasty meal? He'd watch her eat it, too. Did He start frowning and begrudge you your food, if you didn't say grace? Who knew?

With everything duly blessed the room crescendoed into a symphony of silverware on china and the humming of voices. Servers in white and black carried steaming trays from the kitchen. Everybody dug in as soon as a plate was put in front of them. June sat between Kuldip and Reverend Bowen, for whom space had to be made at the head table after he agreed to say grace. This displaced Vi to another table and the reverend's wife squeezed in at the end of the table by the leg. The mayor's wife sat at the other end, nibbling on a roll.

Kuldip reached for the white wine and poured some into Charlotte's glass.

"This will make you happy," he said and giggled.

"Thanks. I'm parched." Charlotte took a swallow. Sweet, reasonably cold – although not as cold as the red. The evening stretched before her and seemed not as dreadful as it had. Even the food tasted okay. A bit overcooked but she could see what they were getting at.

Sitting back in her chair, her stomach full and her head light, Charlotte felt a contentedness unknown to her before. The effort of living lifted. All she heard around her was the sound of cheery conversation. Maybe people really did like these parties. In a way she felt somewhat responsible they have a good time. They were all here because of her, after all. Most of the people in the room she recognized. Seventy people wasn't all that many. She would never have guessed she knew seventy people. And never would it have occurred to her that seventy people

244

thought so highly of her they would attend a dinner in her honour. It truly did astound her. Made her feel a little sheepish knowing she probably wouldn't do the same for them.

A large gift-wrapped box was produced from somewhere and, with the appearance of the gift, came a warping of time and space. From the moment Vi stood at the podium and motioned for Charlotte to come forward, the evening became a soft blur, as seen through a Vaseline covered lens. It did not panic her, the box or the microphone. Her brain simply switched gears. There was no way to prevent it. It protected her from the experience. One time zone removed from the event at hand. Kind of the way your body temperature drops if you fall into a cold lake. Your systems slow down to their base rate, pumping out only what is necessary to get you through the ordeal intact.

Her memory didn't fail. She remembered everything. The box contained a CD player. Charlotte even spoke into the microphone without it shrieking back at her. Whatever she said was met with loud applause and she returned to her seat.

After that the music started and the staff moved some of the tables aside for the dancing. Charlotte glanced around the room and spotted Wade tapping his foot under the table. He saw that Charlotte had noticed the music and gave her a little wave. Doris rummaged through her purse for her cigarettes and Charlotte watched Wade light it for her. Such a gentleman. This could well be the best night of Doris's life. Things settled into a comfortable atmosphere and Charlotte forgot for a moment that this all was taking place at the dismal Driftwood. How had Doris convinced Wade to come tonight? Maybe she paid for his ticket, fifteen dollars. That wasn't cheap, for her. Sweet though, how they came together.

And left together too. Both of them drank steadily throughout the evening. They hadn't actually come together. In the parking lot, Doris had parked next to Wade. He pulled up just as she was getting out of the car with her mother. With Graeme festering at the bottom of his gut and the weekend stretching before him, Wade decided at the last minute to come to Charlotte's dinner. At least there would be cheap booze. The way Doris's face lit up when she saw Wade get out of his car both pleased and depressed him.

"Hi Wade. You came." Why the hell was she always so happy to see him? Not even officially out of school yet, age-wise anyway. What was she, seventeen?

"Yeah." His head hurt. The glare of the sun filtered through his sunglasses. "I'm going to have a smoke out here before I go in."

"Me too."

So this was how it was going to be. He would spend the evening with Doris, the way she had wanted all along. Might as well make the best of it.

"Here, have one of mine." He held the package out for her.

"Thanks," she said. A little nervously, he thought.

This was his second time at the Driftwood today. His head humming with a hangover, he drove straight to the beer store at the back of the hotel at ten-thirty this morning. All day he had spent on his couch, watching American football, of all things, drinking beer and chain smoking. Like a man. Like Bruce from Beck's and all his buddies. Football and beer. What men are made of. He joined the thousands of men across the continent in their Saturday afternoon recreation. He cheered for whatever team had the ball and wondered what anyone saw in cheerleaders. During the commercials he stumbled around between the bathroom, kitchen and living room. At six o'clock he had a shower and then drove to the Driftwood.

What the hell, it was Saturday night. At least he could stay drunk.

He ended up flirting with Doris all night long. It wasn't hard. He stayed drunk and brought her drinks without asking. She had been flirting with him since the parking lot.

"Wade, how do you think I look tonight? I bought this skirt in Winnipeg."

"You look like a juicy plum."

"Juicy enough for you to sink you teeth into?" God, it didn't get worse than that, did it? Did she really want this to go anywhere, or was she just practising? He already could picture the two of them at work on Monday morning. Dancing around each other, pretending nothing happened, everything normal. He groaned out loud when he thought about her gaggle of friends, staring at him through the window as he backed through the swinging door with the bread cart. There was no way he was going to let anything happen. It bothered him just to have to tell himself that. Maybe he should stop drinking. But, it was too late for that. Doris's swinging leg brushed his with each pass. Her arm rested on the back of his chair and every so often her fingers grazed the back of his neck.

They sat together at a table in the middle of the room, among people they didn't really know and drank watery beer and smoked their cigarettes and laughed at everything. For most of the evening, Doris had her hand somewhere on Wade: his shoulder, his arm, her knee against his. He didn't stop her. In his heartbroken, weakened state, even Doris's touch felt soothing. She wasn't turning him on the way she thought she was, but her touch made him yearn for more. It had been a long time since anyone had touched him with any kind of affection, other than Charlotte on that wretched day. He leaned in closer to Doris and soon her arm was around him and his head on her shoulder. There was no chance that they were reading this situation the same way and Wade knew before the evening was over he would have to contend with Doris and what she was after. But for now, he was happy to be close to her and feel the warmth of her embrace, his head lolling drunkenly on her shoulder as she laughed and tightened her arm around him.

When it was time to go, when most of the people had left and Charlotte and her sister were looking so tired and saying goodnight, Doris took him by the arm and said, "Let's go." She led him to the parking lot and they got into his car.

"Where to, my lady?"

"Your place. I want to make sure you get in the door without hurting yourself."

"How gallant." He turned the key in the ignition and wondered what he could do to get rid of her before they got to his place. Her hand rested on his thigh. This was not over yet. He concentrated on the road and not her hand. At his place, he turned to Doris before he turned the car off and asked, "How are you getting home?"

"I'll walk. First I am walking you home."

"I am already here. I'll make it the rest of the way."

"The way you were stumbling in the parking lot, I'm not so sure you will."

The flirtatiousness was gone from her voice. Maybe they were sobering up. She reached over and pulled the key out of the ignition. "Come on. I'll put you to bed."

Weirder and weirder. Doris was going to put him to bed? What was she now, his mother? He liked it better when they were flirting. Now she was making him feel stupid.

"Bed? Why don't you come up for a drink?"

"Well, I'll come up, but I don't think I need another drink."

This was unbelievable. Now she didn't want him? No wonder he never went for women. They could turn on a dime. But, then again, so could men. Wade trudged up the stairs with Doris behind him. She had to be checking out his ass.

"Are you checking out my ass?"

"No, I am making sure your feet hit the steps."

"Yeah, right."

"Whatever."

Inside his apartment Wade fell onto the couch. Doris stood in the doorway under the harsh light. "Wow, it's nicer in here than I thought. Flowers and everything."

Wade had forgotten about that. The place was still all spiffed up for Graeme. He had candles on the dining room table and some fresh-cut flowers in a vase over by the window. He had tidied like a mad man yesterday and even his day on the couch hadn't disturbed things too much.

Doris shook her head. "Well, I guess I'll be going. You're okay now and not about to hurt yourself."

"I don't feel right about you walking home. Let's have some coffee and in half an hour I'll drive you." He couldn't believe she was just going to go. What had she been up to all night? Doris didn't move from the doorway.

"C'mon Doris, aren't you going to kiss me good-night?"

"You're drunk."

"I'm no drunker than you. Come on. All night you've been all over me and now you're just going to leave?"

"You don't really want me to kiss you, do you?"

What? If Doris was onto him, then that whole gaggle of friends of hers would be and if they all knew then everyone knew. That was it. He was going to have to leave town before sunrise. Was he really such an obvious flamer that even Doris could figure it out? And here he was still trying to fool her and fool everyone. How long was he planning on doing this? Was he really prepared to make out with this kid just to show the world who he wasn't? His stomach roiled and lurched. He leapt from the couch and threw himself into the bathroom and knelt in front of the toilet. Puking and retching, he didn't know for how long. He heard the water running in the sink and saw Doris's platform shoes beside him.

"See, I knew you didn't want to kiss me."

What made her so damn mature all of a sudden? Shit. She dabbed his face with a cool cloth. "It's okay Wade. I know I'm not old enough for you. I wish I was sometimes. You're a great guy and everything, but I know it would never work out between us."

Don't say anything, Wade commanded himself. He bit hard down on his tongue and simply nodded. Saved again. By what divine being he had no clue. Whether it was the puking or Doris's brief revelation, Wade was feeling much stronger.

"You know, I think I can drive you home after all. I'm feeling much better."

"Yeah, since I got you off the hook. You're going to have to learn that for yourself one day, Mister." She paused. "Sorry, I don't know why I just said that. It sounded like something my mother would say. Yuck."

They traipsed back down to the car. Wade opened the car door for her. "Thanks," she said and patted him on the arm. Things were already clearing up. They didn't say much in the car. Wade's mind was far away and Doris was feeling very proud of herself and mature.

"See you Monday," she said from the curb.

"Yeah, see you later."

He eased the car back onto the road. He drove down Main Street, awake now and restless. All was quiet in this small town. The storefronts were dark and the streets deserted. His was the lone car on the road. The headlights cast a beam all the way down Main Street and far into the night. Wade kept driving, letting the shafts of light guide him towards the outskirts of town. The glow from town faded quickly as the car streaked onto the highway, creating a black hole between himself and Norman. It was eleven forty-five on Saturday night and Monday was miles away.

* * * * *

June, Charlotte and Kuldip made their way through the remaining guests to the back of the room where the doors led out of the hall. Charlotte was stopped several times by people wanting one last glimpse of her before she disappeared into the night. Eventually they escaped and made their way down the thinly carpeted hallway, the bald light glaring overhead. Strains of music reached them from the bar. At first Charlotte thought she was hearing things. Her whole head was abuzz from all the commotion of the evening. But then she heard it. Quite distinctly. A woman's voice singing: *Imagination, it's funny. It makes a cloudy day sunny. Makes a bee think of honey, Just as I think of you.*

She couldn't believe her ears. Angels had descended upon the Driftwood the night of her retirement, and they were covering Jimmy Scott. She walked towards the doors. Bass, drums, piano, a female singer. It was all there, just like forty years ago. She closed her eyes and listened. *Imagination, it's crazy. Your whole perspective gets hazy. Starts you asking a daisy, what to do. What to do.*

"Umm, it's four dollars," the pimply kid watching the door said.

"What?" The voice startled Charlotte.

"Four dollars if you want to go in. But, I'll let you all in for ten, if you want. It's kind of empty and they told me to try to fill it up."

Charlotte's eyes met June's and then Kuldip's. He was shifting the CD player from one arm to the other. The bruise on June's cheek was starting to show through her make-up. They were exhausted.

"One night only," the door person said.

251

"Oh, hell," said Charlotte. "I want to stay. You two go ahead if you're tired. I'll take a taxi home later."

There are times when the people you know best astonish the hell out of you, Charlotte thought later. June even paid. "Well, none of us has to get up in the morning. Church isn't until eleven. Consider it your retirement gift from me. It might be nice to unwind a bit before we go home."

They found a table near the back and sat down. The waitress came over and they ordered drinks and ate pretzels. There weren't many people there. Norman had still not developed a taste for jazz. There were other nightclubs in town now where the young people went when the Driftwood's offering was too sedate.

The darkened room was relaxing after being in the spotlight all night. It was a relief to pay attention to the band and not feel all the eyes in the room upon her. Kuldip lightly tapped his hand on the edge of the table and grinned at Charlotte, at June, at the band. He grinned in every direction. The music was too loud to talk. The Driftwood had acquired a high decibel sound system. June would mention that for sure in the car on the way home. But for now, Charlotte was enjoying the best part of her evening. She watched the bass player, the drummer. She watched them all. The music was tight, the sound clear. The band was delivering a good set to the small crowd. There were no hecklers in the room. Everybody knew to clap after a solo. Charlotte even whooped after their rendition of *Don't Get Around Much Anymore*. It was the perfect end to a difficult week.

Before she left, Charlotte went over to the bar where the drummer was drinking a beer. She tapped him on the shoulder and said, "Excellent set. I enjoyed every minute. You have a great band."

Sweat still dripped from his brow and Charlotte remembered how Ray used to sweat when he played. The drummer wiped his forehead with the back of his hand, still holding his beer. A most gracious smile crossed his face and he said, "Thank you very much. You have an excellent ear."

* * * * *

The car crawled through the streets of Norman. In the back seat, Kuldip watched out the window and hummed quietly, his arm resting on the box with the CD player, while Charlotte and June rode in silence in the front. Charlotte could still feel the bass drumming inside her. They turned onto Elm Street and into the driveway.

"Here we are," June announced. "Kuldip, you can cut through the yard."

The night was over. Charlotte felt as though she had just been pulled from the sea after spending hours bobbing with the ebb and flow. Her head felt light and there was a giddiness in her heart. She had to adjust to terra firma when her feet hit the pavement. The first few steps towards the house jarred her whole body.

"I will see you in your garden tomorrow, Miss Charlotte?"

"Oh, I'm quite sure you will." Her garden. Yes, she would work in her garden tomorrow. Kuldip smiled broadly and bid her and June goodnight before he walked around the side of the house and into the back yard.

Once inside, Charlotte flopped into the easy chair. She picked up the card from Doris. The signature was well-rehearsed, a big loopy 'D' and the swan-like 'S'. Three big sunflowers on the front and inside: *Three Cheers for You!* Doris had added something herself. *Dear Charlotte, I will miss you at the bakery a lot. You are someone I always look up to and admire and you were fun to work with. I'll be sure to invite you to my retirement party. Ha Ha! Hopefully I will be in the big time by then. Doris Richards.*

Looked up to and admired. What more could a person ask? Maybe Doris would one day surprise them all and make her dreams come true. Charlotte set the card on the table under the lamp so the light shone onto the sunflowers. "Who knows?" she murmured. "Maybe it will be worth something one day."

Charlotte sat back in the chair and smiled at the ceiling. What a night. She kicked her slippers onto the floor and wiggled her toes. June padded by and leaned on the doorframe, looking in.

"Well, I'm going to bed. I've had it."

"Goodnight, June. Thank you for the evening."

"It was nice, wasn't it?"

"Better than I expected."

"Are you glad it's over?"

"It is a bit of a relief, yes."

Charlotte listened to June's footsteps on the stairs, for once going to bed before her. After tonight, nothing would ever be the same. Finally.